Also by Benjamin Anastas

*An Underachiever's Diary*

*The Faithful Narrative*

*of a*

*Pastor's Disappearance*

# The Faithful Narrative

# of a

# Pastor's Disappearance

## Benjamin Anastas

Farrar, Straus and Giroux

New York

Farrar, Straus and Giroux
19 Union Square West, New York 10003

Copyright © 2001 by Benjamin Anastas
All rights reserved
Distributed in Canada by Douglas & McIntyre Ltd.
Printed in the United States of America
First edition, 2001

Library of Congress Cataloging-in-Publication Data
Anastas, Benjamin.
    The faithful narrative of a pastor's disappearance / Benjamin Anastas.— 1st ed.
        p.   cm.
    ISBN 0-374-15214-4 (alk. paper)
    1. Afro-American clergy—Fiction. 2. Missing persons—Fiction.
3. Massachusetts—Fiction. I. Title.

PS3551.N257 F3 2001
813'.54—dc21

                                                                00-045609


Designed by Jonathan D. Lippincott

There is nothing that the devil seems to make so great a handle of, as a melancholy humor; unless it be a real corruption of the heart.

—Jonathan Edwards

First Part

 The founding member of the Monday Reflection Group noticed first, arriving at the church to find the pastor's driveway empty and the curtains in the parsonage still drawn, but she knew nothing of his sudden and astonishing disappearance, not yet, only that the Reverend Thomas Mosher, well-liked minister of the Pilgrims' Congregational Church ("An Historic Church with a Modern Message" they included below their name in all the literature) in W———, Massachusetts, spiritual mentor to his well-heeled but undeniably eccentric congregants, author of competent—if sometimes esoteric—Sunday sermons heavy on the Book of Psalms, culminating in his very last one, "The Shapes of Love," which had veered away from the usual Easter Cycle to explore the possibility that God is an "infinite sphere," an idea that had bored some members of the church *dumb* and had seemed to others inappropriate for a Trinitarian; eligible bachelor rumored to have carried on an affair with a married woman in the church, Bethany Caruso (née Coleman), the mother of a preteen son and pious daughter widely considered *angelic*, if, at times, unusually frank when speaking to adults,

3

and prone to disruptive behavior during Sunday school, the product, many believed, of Bethany's frequent separations from her husband (not a regular churchgoer), making her, already envied for her smoldering good looks and close relationship with the pastor, the object of persistent disapproval, despite the fact that an adulterous tryst between the two had never been confirmed, and the Reverend Mosher, according to the local women who openly pursued him—Sadie Maxwell, flashy owner of the town's leather boutique; twice-divorced Alessandra Palacios y Rio, self-styled socialite and beneficiary of a Hollywood divorce settlement—showed no interest in matters of the flesh, possessing, as he did, an awkward bearing in the world of men and women, little sense for the subtleties of flirtation and its deeper second step, seduction; truth be told, the Reverend Mosher seemed comfortable only at the pulpit, draped in his black Geneva gown and elevated *slightly* above his audience, able to communicate with an ease that usually escaped him, projecting authority with his lovely voice (they all agreed that, with their eyes closed during the morning prayers, his intonation could often be *transporting*), while in life he was acutely absentminded, a chronic mumbler, famous for calling members of the church by the wrong name, as well as accident-prone (how many times had he driven his car, the unfortunately named Ford Probe, off the road? The product of relentless dreaming), known for his inept pitching in church league softball, and sloppy housekeeping, according to the Thursday Housekeepers, who grew so tired of scrubbing down the parsonage they pooled their resources and hired a cleaning woman; no, the Reverend Mosher was not like the dull and energetic middle managers who had lately moved to town for a short commute and joined the congregation out of some *imagined duty*, who talked too loud among themselves and, but for a few opening minutes, paid little attention to his painstak-

4

ingly prepared sermons, although there were notable excep-
tions, troubled men who had no choice but to display their
depth, like high-strung Carlo Wagner, a physicist with a wide
repertoire of nervous tics (clearing his throat, touching his
glasses, pinching the end of his nose, scratching his ear with an
index finger, and twitching, all in no particular order), or Ed
Brooks, a school administrator who was obviously manic-
depressive, but refused his wife's attempts to have him seek
counseling and—this was her ardent hope, expressed in weekly
talks with the Reverend Mosher—a prescription for antidepres-
sants, no longer a stigma in the community, or even a topic of
gossip and/or debate, quite the opposite: Paxil and Zoloft had
long since entered the local vocabulary, and stood, now, for
happiness and hope, as if a tablet could ever contain these
illusory states of being, reinventing the founding principles of
W———, Massachusetts, as well as of every other place in the
New World chosen by displaced men and women for settlement: a belief in the value of work, the importance of family,
the dominion of God over all things personal and political . . .
The pastor was a complicated man and seemed to live across
some subtle divide from *life*, certainly from *happiness*, and
often from the members of his congregation, still he was an
admired figure on the pulpit (already mentioned) and in the
church office, the scene of so many helpful—if halting—conversations, and, as the black leader of a traditionally white church
(although this, too, was changing), the object of some pride, as
if his position were irrefutable evidence of their forward-
thinking politics and enlightened Christianity; but no one in
the church—not one worshipper out of a scant few hundred
souls—could have predicted the events that began to unfold on
the fine spring morning in question, when the Monday Reflection Group, such as it was, convened at the appointed time,
and the Reverend Thomas Mosher was missing.

The spring of the pastor's disappearance had been remarkable, everyone agreed, from the arrival of the first red-winged blackbirds in late February with snow still on the ground (the Old Farmer's Almanac had been reliable once again, predicting heavy snowfall followed by an early thaw) to the return of the orange-breasted robin just a few weeks later, scouring the dormant lawns and irregular backyards still sloped, stumped, and littered with immovable stones—the landscape that so burdened the Puritans—for worms, to the skunk cabbage pushing through the sodden earth at the base of old stone walls in the deciduous woods, through the sand alongside fresh concrete foundations in the new development communities (the Walden Estates, Hawthorne Terrace, the Minuteman Apartments) fed by dripping eaves and rain gutters overfilled, to crocuses and snowdrops and daffodils in neglected flower gardens, littered with the broken ends of planting stakes and the faded plastic tabs, flattened and scattered now, identifying last year's batch of annuals, to painted trillium and trumpets in the roadside

7

swamps and daylilies along the winding New England roads, modest only in habitat and in the brief duration of their bloom, followed by true forget-me-nots, and on the ancient-looking tree on the church grounds, crab apple blossoms, exploding with the wild promise of inedible fruit by late summer.

Margaret Howard, matriarch of Howard Homes, the thriving real estate business she had built from the ground up, without the help of her husband, who was a burden to her, was the first member of the Reflection Group to arrive on Monday morning. In the realtor's trade she was known for her sweet maternal smile, competitive spirit, iron will, and free use of profanity. She had loaded the trunk of her bronze Cadillac with the apparatus of her gardening obsession, planning to follow up her reflections on John with an hour or two of triage in the congregation's flower beds. Artemesia Angelis, her closest ally on the Grounds Committee, and not one to reflect—or do anything else, for that matter—before eleven, would show up when she could manage. When Margaret saw the pastor's empty parking space a grateful spirit rose in her chest and she guided her floating Cadillac into this cherished spot; she had a twenty-five-pound bag of manure to worry about, after all, persistent bursitis in her right shoulder, a possibly infected gallbladder, and an internist who had warned her about the ill effects of heavy lifting. The car reminded her with the gentle ringing of an electronic bell to pull her keys from the ignition, and she did, stepping out of her chariot-on-tires with some pride of ownership. She slammed the door behind her, pressed a button on her key ring to automatically lock the car with a *chirp*, and set out across the lawn in her high heels.

The pastor was not on Margaret's mind that morning. Her son Bradley, a ne'er-do-well just like his father, had sleazed his way up to the real estate office on Saturday asking for a handout. And on his motorcycle! Bradley was a college dropout, a constant source of worry and embarrassment who somehow felt entitled to every penny she had ever earned against odds that he would never *fathom*, a devious loser who dreamed of spending her legacy on motorcycle parts and elaborate bongs. She had done the right thing, as difficult as it had been, kicking him out of the office and ordering him to Easy Ride his chopper off the property. What if a potential client had picked that moment to drive up? The nerve it took to walk into her place of business with his hair all hanging down and *probably unwashed*, dressed from head to toe in black leather—she knew what those biker getups cost—and then to smirk about it, parading in his knee-length boots past all the employees, who just loved to gossip about her family life and looked at her, after another one of Bradley's visits, with pity in their eyes, *Pity!*, for the woman who signed their paychecks every month, imagine the idea! It seemed like Bradley had spent an hour revving his engine in the parking lot before he finally peeled out into traffic. Since then, Margaret had been able to think about nothing else.

She arrived at the back door of the church in a state, stopping, for a moment, to frown at the flower beds, which would need a thorough going-over before she could even think about planting seedlings. With one hand on the railing she cleaned her heels with a tissue, cursing, under her breath, all mud, sloth, tardiness, and her ungrateful child, who might as well have been *adopted*, as little as he reminded Margaret of herself. The Reflection Group had been her brainchild fifteen years earlier, her first period of "crisis" as a parent, when Howard Homes was finally taking off and Bradley's adolescence—a Holy War that she would rather forget—had driven her to a closer study of the Scripture; participation was purely voluntary, and since the Group convened on Monday morning, the slowest day at the church (in the afterglow of Sunday, most everyone felt *prepared* to accept God's grace for another week), Margaret was often disappointed by the turnout. The pastor had disappointed her further by delegating authority over the Group to Jane Groom, the assistant minister, a humorless woman who wore men's clothing and obviously cut her own hair, and she, in turn, had given the Group over to the laity, making monthly appearances in blue jeans to cloud their reflections with lesbian propaganda, or so Margaret believed. She finished cleaning off her shoes and let herself inside the church, turning on the lights in the stairwell leading down to the Sunday School Room in the basement, which flooded at every rainstorm and smelled unpleasantly of standing water. Had she come early? The children's desks had been stacked in an orderly fashion against the wall, and Margaret could just make out the words HOLY SPIRIT on the chalkboard—erased poorly, she thought. She set up a chair for herself in the middle of the room, sat down, and opened her Study Bible to the bookmarked passage in John (13:33, "My children, I am to be with you for a little longer; then you will look for me, and, as I told the Jews, I tell you now: where I am going you cannot come") and read quietly, moving her lips without making a sound; soon she was aware of the empty room with its poor fluorescent lighting, the buckling linoleum floor, a smell of chalk which reminded her of schoolchildren, and she was stricken with her greatest fear, that she would die alone, unloved by her family and mourned by no one, and her shoulder, which had been quieted by a new prescription, gave a sudden throb as if it had been listening to her heart, a sympathetic torment to distract her from a deeper problem, so she winced in pain, closed her Bible, and stood up, wild, for a moment, with her discomfort, before her practical genius returned, sending her into the corner for another folding chair—a simple remedy, in an empty classroom, for loneliness. She opened the seat with her good arm and placed it beside her own. Then she sat back down and resumed her reading as if nothing had happened at all.

Artemesia Angelis found her working on the flower beds an hour later, draped in a denim smock and wearing aerating sandals over her Stride-Rites. Margaret had left the stinking basement short of an hour and changed into her gardening clothes. She was quite a sight, a prim and heavyset New England lady in spikes, stomping violently on the ground.

"Need any help?" Artemesia asked, watching her friend with a little awe. Her mind was still buzzing with the pastor's "sphere" sermon from the day before, and it was all she could do, beneath the windows of the parsonage, to put one leg in front of the other.

"You can carry all my junk over here," Margaret answered. "My shoulder's been acting up again, and the doctor says no lifting." She believed Artemesia to be slow on the uptake and, in religious matters, something of a heretic, but her worship of Margaret's self confidence, obvious to everyone who saw them together, more than made up for these shortcomings. Artemesia was a loyal friend, overly generous in her opinions, and kind to everyone in the church regardless of their beliefs or social standing. Margaret directed her toward the gardening equipment and started in on a monologue. "Guess how many in the Reflection Group today? Is the suspense killing you? Solamente uno, Margaret Howard, who reflected like crazy in that *shit-hole* of a basement all by her lonesome. Things are really changing around here, dear, and not for the better if you ask me. And I don't have to keep my voice down because the pastor isn't even here! He could be out tomcatting in the a.m. for all we know . . ."

Artemesia had a moment of uncertainty when faced with the Cadillac's open trunk, but she rallied, and picked out Margaret's spade, her English Hand Fork, and her favorite trowel, all from the Smith & Hawken catalogue, and started back across the lawn.

"What about Jane Groom?"

"Oh, she's probably home writing love poetry," Margaret said, trying to approximate, roughly, on her circuit around the flower bed, the re-icing pattern of a Zamboni. Why couldn't Bradley have stuck with playing hockey? That's when the trouble had started: crying fits outside the rink, cutting practice after school, trading his expensive skates with that pot smoker for a skateboard, the creep, the little monster. "I can't say I care too much for this Liberation Theology, or whatever she calls it. Are you dragging my spade?"

Artemesia arrived at the flower bed and dug the spade into the ground so it would stand up on its own. "No, Margaret."

"That's stainless steel, you know."

"You're just suffering from homophobia."

"I'm not homo-anything, thank you."

"Of course not. There's nothing *ever* wrong with you."

"Well, I sell houses to them, don't I? And I don't mind saying, the gay couples really *do* seem to have a way with property. They're not afraid to sink some *capital* into an older home."

Artemesia asked her in genuine shock, "Are you wearing *stockings*?"

"I'm needed at the office later, dear."

"Margaret, you're the last of a dying breed."

She stopped aerating for long enough to catch her breath. "Did you forget that bag of cow manure?"

When Artemesia came back with the manure she complained, "Sometimes I feel like it's my lot in life to carry other people's S-H-I-T around. Do you want it here?"

"Just drop it there is fine." Margaret had finished stomping in the garden and she was sitting on her stool, unstrapping her sandals with an athlete's calm. "There's nobility in simple work. Sometimes at the office I look outside the window and see Jerry, pruning the shrubs by hand, branch by branch, or mowing the lawn on his beloved tractor, and I think to myself, *Now who has the better job?*" Jerry was her husband. After he had been "downsized" (or so he liked to claim) from a part-time sales position at the Home Depot, Margaret had hired him to keep the grounds around Howard Homes. "And I tell you one more thing, he's not out the window wishing he was in my office, answering phone calls."

"I was more complaining about the smell," Artemesia said.

"You could be the IRS," Margaret added, "now there's some dirty work." Artemesia's husband owned a lumberyard that earned him a small fortune, mostly through graft and unfair hiring practices, and his reputation in the community—the whispers, the snobbish contempt—made Margaret feel protective of Artemesia, who, it was plain to everyone, was a trusting soul. Though Margaret believed in honesty when dealing with the government, she had sympathy for Angelis's tax problems, having grown up in the fierce Yankee culture of New Hampshire, home, until recently—the crime!—to the most militant state motto in the country, LIVE FREE OR DIE. She knew something, too, about whispers and shiftless husbands. "There's an extra pair of kneepads in the trunk, or you could shovel."

Artemesia considered the spade beside her and the bag of manure on the ground, feeling overwhelmed, all of a sudden, by a sense of responsibility, and a little nauseated by the prospect of handling that stuff with a shovel, but she wanted, for Margaret, to appear strong. Her house was a mess and under permanent construction, her eight-year-old, after failing a series of tests, had just been transferred to remedial classes, and there had been talk, just the night before, of frozen bank accounts, not to mention her blood sugar following the yield of her high-risk money market account. Whatever happened to Governor Dukakis and the centerpiece of his failed presidential campaign, the Massachusetts Miracle? If only that man hadn't climbed into a *tank* to prove he had the goods to be Commander-in-Chief! If only miracles, *divine* miracles, would return to Massachusetts in the form of an infinite sphere and spread the blessing of His love from Boston to Brewster!

"Hello!"

"Sorry . . ."

"Kneepads or—"

Artemesia pulled the spade from the ground, raised it, and split the white plastic bag open with a single stroke. She would shovel cow manure for Margaret because it was lowly work, each spadeful would sicken her, and she would be *profoundly humbled*—perhaps her hands would blister—and the stinging pain would bring her closer, so much closer, to the everlasting love of God.

"You can pile it over here first," Margaret told her, setting up her stool nearby.

But she was horrified by the substance of her burden! All the richness of the earth chewed by animals bred for use or slaughter, passed through an intricate digestive system and some hopeful agricultural process to rid the cow manure of that which made it natural, leaving useful nutrients intact, of course, man's ingenuity and God's will, in a terrible combination, spilling from a plastic bag and vaguely stinking at the end of her shovel! It was all too much, simply too disturbing, and Artemesia dropped her spade, stumbled a few paces away, and sat down in the grass, about to faint.

"Take a deep breath," she reminded herself.

"Artemesia, dear," Margaret asked, "are you all right?"

"I'll feel better in a second."

"You're so pale!"

"I think I need to speak to the pastor," Artemesia said.

"Well, that might be hard right now, seeing as he's not in the parsonage. What that man does with himself in his free time I'll never know, Monday after the sermon or not . . ."

"You're wrong about him," Artemesia replied, newly serene. How could a man of such holiness be capable of adultery? And even if he was, did it really matter? Compared to all the wounded grace that fairly emanated from his heart?

Margaret went back to her gardening with the same blind dedication that had brought her to the pinnacle of the local realtor's trade, despite the naysayers and a fiercely competitive market, that had won her the respect of the Chamber of Commerce and an influential term as chairperson of the Local Redevelopment Corporation, that had intimidated her husband for thirty years and finally, through brute force, reduced him to a hopeless state, that had belittled her only son and driven him into a profound and continuous rebellion. She dug with a Hand Fork and shoveled with a spade and pulled her stool to another spot and did the same all over again. All the while, Artemesia sat behind her in the grass, looking peaceful and a little dazed. Margaret watched her every now and then with a growing anger that she would later regret. Finally she tossed her Hand Fork to the ground and asked, "Just how long do you propose to wait?"

 Did the Reverend Thomas Mosher see a final sunrise through the old distorted glass of his bedroom window, or was he already gone by morning? Did he wake up on his back, cold, as always, despite a great piling of covers and the space heater humming by his side, casting its orange glow, and wonder in the chilly half-light, *Why am I alone?* Did the quiet of his bedroom high in the eaves of the parsonage, and the shabby bachelor's order (he stacked his books along the wall and on his desk beside neat piles of papers and notes; he owned two identical pairs of dress shoes and lined them up each night inside the closet; he kept the throw rug, which he had never cleaned or vacuumed, in the perfect center of the room) offer little comfort, in fact, did his circumstances fill him with a *crippling doubt* and seem to speak openly of his *estrangement from the world*? After he was gone, and the members of the church began to wrestle with his sudden disappearance, a consensus formed that the Reverend Mosher had been suffering before their very eyes, but from what affliction no one knew—they

had never thought to ask what troubled *him*, despite the sadness that had bathed him, they remembered now, like a mantle, or the fact that his smile had seemed to require so much effort, and his touch, as they filed out of the church each Sunday morning, had left them strangely cold. Thomas had fooled them with the language of faith and optimism! Was his final Sunday sermon, baffling to so many with its references to an anonymous text in Latin, *a dead language*, he kept emphasizing, an instruction manual for reading the events to come? Was he aware, as he delivered his text with a monotonous low fervor, that hardly anyone was listening? That even fewer would remember his parting words? Or was he speaking to God alone—the same God who, in His omnipotence, would recognize and understand, as they couldn't, the temptations of his boundless sorrow?

*Bethany*, her husband thought when he woke up alone that fateful morning, three days into his latest banishment from the marital bedroom, lying on a leaky yard-sale water bed that he had purchased to fulfill a teenage fantasy (sex, beer, and floating, as if on a dirty cloud) and had set up in the apartment over the garage, with a confusion of hoses and some gravitational difficulty, only to have his wife announce, "I will never fuck you on that thing." So the water bed had leaked away in isolation all that winter, soaking the indoor/outdoor carpeting he had installed himself (even his son had refused to help him with the job), until, with springtime surging through his veins and granting an uncanny intelligence to his scrotum, Bethany had decreed for the third time in as many years that she needed "space to think" and he was reunited with his grand unfinished project to ensure the future of their marriage, a "fornicatorium" separate from the house, no telephone, no E-mail account, no demanding kids, just the water bed, a set of Velcro straps he had bought from a high-class catalogue, and a bathroom cabinet filled with tubes of lubricating jelly. It was Bobby Caruso's special torment to sleep in his dream house of unlimited orgasm by himself.

He loved sex! and thought about it constantly, he loved the nervous moments before the act and the guiltless nuzzling afterward, the way that sex could interrupt, like nothing else, the passage of the hours, he loved the difficulty of insertion, the strange position of our sex organs on the body, he loved the *thump* and *slap* that made him think of dolphins, and the little squirting sounds, but most of all he loved having sex with Bethany, his beautiful wife, while she treated lovemaking (with him, anyway) like a necessary chore. He was faithful to Bethany even in his fantasy life, where she ruled him tenderly, usually wearing something leather, holding, more often than not, a steaming muffin tin straight from the oven (he also loved muffins) and suggesting pornographic scenarios the real Bethany would never have abided; in the rare event that they did have sex his wife kept very quiet, worried openly about the kids, heard phantom noises in the basement, and had been known to check her watch, but lately her desire for him, iffy in the first place, had all but absented itself from her body, that beautiful, unbelievable body, such a gift whenever he was allowed access, so soft, so hard, so flat, so round that even he believed she must have come directly from the hand of God.

It took some effort for Bobby Caruso to roll himself out of the water bed, stained a greasy "walnut" by the previous owner, and plant his feet on the soggy carpet. Marriage to Bethany, as he saw it, had been a verified miracle followed by a series of rude awakenings—the first came on their honeymoon in Sicily, when she had refused, despite the cost of the hotel suite, to *swallow*, not a catastrophic loss, he had decided in the end, and they had thoroughly enjoyed their remaining weeks in the ancient sun, giddy newlyweds in a foreign land, eating their weight in seafood and cannoli, slipping from their clothing at the slightest provocation (okay, so maybe Bobby had been reduced, once or twice, to masturbating guiltily beside her while she slept off a bottle of the "local" wine). Once they had returned home and established a regular pattern he calculated a significant reduction in blow jobs, but so what? He still enjoyed the rest of her body—that is, until the unexpected arrived, EARLY PREGNANCY, a spirit-breaking wallop from which he would never, ever recover. Sure, he loved his son madly, but what kind of trade was this? His sex life for a baby boy? Six years later came a daughter with terrible colic, fraying Bethany's already tender nerves and bringing to an end the last habitual intimacy of their marriage, the occasional back rub, while the latest rude awakening, he figured generously, was Bethany's rejection of his winter's masterwork, the fornicatorium. He wanted his wife more than ever, and didn't have the heart to speculate about what else, in his sexless conundrum, could go wrong.

Bobby crossed the driveway in his pajamas and bedroom slippers, disturbed by the singing of the birds, which sounded, that morning, like nature's special taunt for the separated husband. Inside, his wife would just be finished with her shower, directing the morning activities in her royal-blue terry-cloth robe, hair wet, perhaps a towel draped around her shoulders, in a foul mood that made her even sexier, to his mind; in the early days of their marriage she used to slice his muffin in half, smear it lightly with butter, and put it in the toaster oven, a selfless act, considering she was also in a rush, but he could no longer look forward to that bit of morning erotica. Now he was lucky if the children left an extra Eggo waffle for him thawing on the countertop. Bobby rang the doorbell and waited for an answer, trying not to think about how many neighbors might be watching from their windows.

"Who is it?" his six-year-old daughter, Jessica, yelled behind the door, loud enough to startle him.

"It's Daddy, cough-drop. Can you open the door?" The girl was such a tyrant that she chose her own pet names, employing them on a rotation that he could never quite figure out.

"Who's cough-drop?"

"Open the door for Daddy, please."

"Who's *cough-drop*?"

"Open the door, Jessica."

She began to laugh hysterically, cut short by her older brother, Devon, who finally opened the door for Bobby. The boy was awfully introspective for twelve and so nervous that he bit his fingernails down to stubs—although the latest development, thanks to the older kids at his school, had been his interest in rap, right down to the baggy jogging suit he was wearing now.

"Devon!" Jessica yelled, because her voice knew only one volume. "You ruined everything!"

"Morning, Dad," the boy said, heading back upstairs in his artfully untied low-tops. He told his sister, "Shut up."

Bobby dreaded reentering the family melodrama, the yelling, the tears, the constant need for discipline, the testing of his will to punish—but never without love—and during Bethany's "trial periods," when she made him sleep above the garage, his authority, with the children, was noticeably undermined. The marital bedroom, as it turned out, was the seat of all power. And his children (especially the girl) had been born with an expertise in manipulating power structures; at the very worst she might end up a union boss, at best a presidential biographer. (Jessica lacked the charisma, he thought, to run for President herself.) Children demanded everything you had, and in return they offered you report cards for signature. They shared nothing! On his last birthday Jessica had presented him with an atrocious drawing, which would have been fine had it been of something sweet, like a butterfly, or a ladybug, or a pretty flower, but she had given him a huge *self-portrait* in Magic Marker. Her mother had taken dictation for the caption, "Jessie takes a walk in the woods." *And gets lost*, he had thought to himself, beaming with his best version of the father's proud/touched smile. Bethany had suggested that he hang the picture in his office, so he dropped it off at the frame shop and promptly forgot about it. When the shopkeeper called the house a month later he paid dearly for the oversight! And all for the sake of this child who was shameless, greedy, inscrutable, loud, and had made it her personal project, from the time of her colic, to see that Bobby would never have sex again for the rest of his life. Jessica followed him into the kitchen with an annoying attachment, dragging her favorite handbag, a gift from Bethany's mother, who was suffering from the late stages of Alzheimer's and lived—such as her life was nowadays—in a nursing home over by the Danvers shopping mall. Bethany hadn't been to visit her since February (at least) and he had chalked up her recent mood to *guilt*, and her abiding sense that she had failed her mother.

"Mommy's upstairs," Jessie reported, "combing her lovely hair."

"Is she taking you to school today?"

"I *think* so."

"Did you sleep well?" Bobby asked because he felt like he

should, pulling a coffee mug down from the kitchen cabinet.

"Yes," she answered, sitting down at the table to resume a messy bout of cereal eating. "I got scared and slept in Mommy's bed."

"You don't say."

"I have a purse!" she yelled.

"I can see that, Jessica."

"We're out of muffins!"

Bobby poured his coffee and considered the merits of earplugs, although there might not be a substance, he figured, natural or synthetic, that could muffle the sound of his daughter's voice.

He spoke to Bethany once that morning, without incident, on his way upstairs to use the shower. She had already dressed for work in the tight-fitting beige suit she saved for springtime, and it took all of his willpower not to thank her for so thoroughly sexualizing the drabbest of all shades of color. Instead he met her at the bottom of the stairs and compared notes with her on the day to come, who needed to be where and for how long, what to have for dinner, something about a meeting running long and her car beginning to sputter, and once they had reached an agreement, on terms that confused him, they parted ways. How could she be so, well, *functional* when they hadn't slept together in six months? The bathroom was still humid with her steam and he soaked up all he could, standing in a puddle of her rinsing water; with the shower running and his eyes closed he imagined that Bethany's hands, and not a tiny fraction of the municipal water supply, were gliding over him, touching his shoulders and the middle of his back, working slowly down his chest to the lower regions of his body, warming him with sensual love. Every knucklehead in his office envied him after seeing her wedding picture on his desk, making the standard joke about wife swapping; his friends at the tennis club were forever dropping hints about mixed doubles; his little brother Sam, the dateless wonder, worshipped him for his good luck—but all the admiration in the world meant nothing if Bethany didn't want to fuck him anymore.

"Bye, Daddy!" his daughter yelled downstairs, disrupting his thoughts. If he made a recording of her "Bye, Daddy," and sold it to the military, they could use it to drive dictators underground . . .

"See ya," he called back, meant only for her mother. Just a word would have cured his morning frustration, anything at all: a curse, a snide remark, some meaningless formality; he waited for Bethany's answer while the water heater lost its muscle and his shower turned lukewarm. Bobby heard the door to the mudroom slam shut downstairs and opened his eyes to the ghastly salmon-colored bathroom, emptied, suddenly, of all sexual potential. He felt a telltale release in the area of his scrotum as his wife entered the attached garage. *Too late.* The shower went completely cold.

Bethany felt crazy when she didn't take her Zoloft, and on the morning of the pastor's disappearance she had gone thirty-six hours without dosing, a deliberate oversight: the side effects of her 200 mg-a-day prescription had been bothering her for a while now (sweaty palms, dizzy spells, nausea), and she was trying, in spite of the best medical advice, to detoxify. As a result she had lost her appetite, not that she ate regularly to begin with, misplaced her car keys until Jessie, her little savior, found them by fishing through the bowl of junk mail on the kitchen table, and forgot to wear her wristwatch, an anniversary present from Bobby—but which anniversary?—that had never seemed all that sentimentally important before *right then*, the moment when she touched her wrist in the darkness of the garage and found that it was gone. Somehow the morning's imperative propelled her forward, and she reached over a three-month pile of recycling to engage the automatic garage door opener. Jessie waited patiently in the front seat of the car, safety belt already fastened, singing "Part of Your World" from *The Little Mermaid*, the VHS tape which Bethany had used too early and perhaps too often as a mind-and-body pacifier for her daughter. Jessie's hunger for the familiar seemed to have no bottom. Ariel, the mermaid who longs to be human, had been Jessie's first obsession in life, and over the course of the last two years she had filled her room with every relic of the animated movie on the market—most she had come by honestly on holidays, the rest were a direct result of bad-faith negotiating at Toys "R" Us. Jessie's public tantrums arrived swiftly and were furious in force. Once she had wanted a replacement magic wand *so badly* that she had fallen into a trance on the aisle floor, convulsing in front of a stranger's shopping cart, a performance that had shaken her timid father and sent Bethany, once they had carried her, still twitching, across the vast parking lot and driven her home in silence, straight to her secret store of dope, a vice she had picked up, actually, from a therapist, although she rarely indulged in more than a few hits, and had stopped seeing that particular quack when he dropped to the floor at the end of an afternoon session and started sucking on her ankle. Compared to *that* little episode, Jessie's fascination with an animated mermaid seemed downright healthy. How she loved her daughter for the way she got just what she wanted, for her uncompromising will and fierce devotion to her toys! Bethany mistrusted the Disney Corporation for their treacly product that had so entranced her children, for their cynicism, greed, fake feminism, and multicultural hocus-pocus, but she had to admit, few things made her happier than listening to Jessie sing her favorite hymn from *The Little Mermaid* with its selfish-spiritual refrain about wanting more and more.

And now she couldn't risk the trip upstairs to get her wrist-watch, not with Bobby mooning around the bedroom, ready, she knew, to launch into an impassioned defense of their marriage, and, when he had finished, remove his pants or open up his bathrobe in the hope that she might be feeling merciful that morning. The thought of one more conversation following this model left her heartbroken. But her wrist felt weird without her watch and she could see it on her bedside table, a place where Bobby, scanning the room for clues about her inner life, would find it and accuse her, after the family dinner (an awkward charade for the children), of being not only insensitive but ungrateful. Yes, in his case she was often both. Or had she left the anniversary watch in the bathroom? If so, the crystal would fog up, compelling Bobby to deliver his "water-resistant vs. waterproof" lecture, certain grounds for a divorce . . .

Without realizing it Bethany had climbed into the minivan, and she found herself already in the driver's seat, clutching the steering wheel. The garage door had retracted to reveal a beautiful spring morning. Jessie sat beside her, fishing through her handbag. Time ruled Bethany when she didn't take her yellow pills.

"Aren't we going to school?" Jessie asked, lifting her head from her task.

"Right," Bethany repeated, "school."

After a short time her daughter said, "Get moving!"

Bethany obeyed and jerked the car out into sunlight. She worried more about her driving when she felt unstable than she did about screwing up at work, a nowhere job in Human

Resources that Bobby had found her through "his people"—maintaining files, basically, on the thousands of jerks who worked for Bobby's company, a high-tech subsidiary of a conglomerate that made everything from refrigerators to microchips to missiles. Bethany managed her corner of the office, oversaw performance reviews, checked the odd reference when necessary, and specialized in performing exit interviews, asking questions from a script—written, it seemed, by a clueless Grand Inquisitor—and filling in the answers on a standardized response form. ("Did you feel your contributions were appreciated by your supervisor and others?" *Mostly, yes.* "Did you have the appropriate equipment and resources necessary to perform your job?" *I'd say so. That's a fair assessment.*) What finally became of this all-important survey data, who knew? The office park where she worked was just off Route 128, two exits north of the office park where Bobby's division was housed, a landscape of parking lots and bright green grass and gleaming silver office towers rising from the woods.

"Devon!" Jessie yelled when they passed her brother's bus stop around the corner, excited to see a familiar face in the outside world. But Devon ignored them, having adopted, once he reached the end of the driveway, an aggressive hangdog posture he had learned from watching music videos. His warm-up pants hung noticeably lower than they had in the kitchen a few minutes earlier, and he was wearing, despite the weather, a black knit ski cap pulled down to just above eye level.

"Why doesn't he look?" Jessie asked.

"Because he's your older brother," Bethany answered, "and he's a boy. Boys do strange things, if you haven't noticed."

"I don't like boys," she announced with great authority. "Not if they won't wave 'hello' to me."

The statement moved Bethany to wave at her daughter.

"You can't *wave*," Jessie protested, "you're taking me to school!"

"Who says I can't?"

A thoughtful look crossed Jessie's face and she asked, "Mommy, are you losing it again?"

"I don't think so," she answered, not being entirely truthful. "I'm just adjusting my medication, that's all."

"Like aspirin, you mean?"

"Yes," she explained, "like aspirin, only stronger for adults."

"What's it called?"

"Zoloft."

"*Zoloft!*" her daughter repeated, laughing maniacally.

"It is a funny name, I guess."

Jessie rolled down her window and yelled outside the car, "Zoloft!"

Bethany took a detour on the way to Jessica's Montessori School and passed the Pilgrims' Church, the spireless centerpiece of "historic Old Town," *firstly* because she couldn't bear another minute without thinking of the pastor, and the church, in her mind, was so thoroughly his; *secondly* she remembered wandering in one Sunday morning looking for a consolation that would stick, and somehow she had not discovered Him, but *him*, the only man that she had ever loved unselfishly; *thirdly* wasn't happiness within their reach? Her marriage was a failure, and though she loved her children down to their little bones, Motherhood alone was not enough (she didn't have the strength for the female martyrdom routine), and the pastor was unmarried, repeat, a single man; *fourthly* she had repeated the church Covenant in good faith, but she had her doubts about this God-in-Christ business, while Thomas Mosher was a true believer and still trembled when they held each other, listened to her every word and knew her machinations better than her husband; *fifthly* their love seemed an impossibility and still it persisted, even though, from the first acknowledgment of their shared condition, they had known only the sweetest agony and lived a secret life of phone calls, long drives in the countryside and after-hours meetings in the parsonage; *sixthly* love made Bethany a minor-league stalker, and she drove by the church as often as she could.

In front of Jessie's school, watching as her daughter adjusted the strap of her oversized handbag, Bethany's eyes welled suddenly with tears and she swore to herself, and not for the first time recently, that she would go and visit her mother at the nursing home.

"Get a grip!" Jessie cried when she saw her mother's tears, jumping out of the car without asking for a goodbye kiss. Such a small girl, trying so hard to know everything—would she remember her mother as a fragile being who broke her home in two? Would she remember her childhood as *tragic*? Or maybe it was just the lack of serotonin reuptake inhibitors in Bethany's system that gave everything that morning a gauzy, After-School-Special quality.

"Who's picking you up today?"

"Ulla!" Jessie answered, already running toward her independence. "I'm not stupid!" Security was tight at the Montessori School, and Bethany waited in the idling minivan while her daughter rang the children's buzzer. Sandra, the most annoying of all her teachers, answered the door and let Jessica inside, giving a quick and unfriendly wave to Bethany. Such a harsh judge of working mothers! And this from a woman who wore baggy sleeveless dresses to flaunt her wealth of armpit hair, who owned the most expensive clogs they sold at Sonny's Shoes and lived, rumor had it, with her boyfriend in a Volkswagen camper! Those tufts of armpit hair had been Jessie's favorite

29

topic of conversation for a solid *month*, they had even given her nightmares, and somehow Bethany was irresponsible? One day she would have to tell Sandra about the confusion she had engendered in Jessie, the Scotch-tape-and-cat-fur episode, the way she had stood up on her chair one morning at breakfast and announced, "I'm growing a beard, Mommy!"

A familiar dread visited Bethany on the highway as her minivan joined the stop-and-go traffic, and she turned on her radio, set permanently to NPR, which she found soothing, especially on her morning commute. But the news anchors annoyed her with their constant prattling on—the oh-so-smooth delivery, their faintly disapproving tone—and the emptiness of her commute, suddenly, seemed overwhelming: so many cars of so many different makes and models filling four lanes in both directions, how could she not wonder who these people were, absently picking their noses, talking sweetly into their mobile phones, sipping coffee from bulbous travel mugs that adhered, somehow, to their dashboards; every now and then she caught sight of a distinctive car or a familiar face, but most were strange to her, and while the traffic slowed before the next blind curve on snakelike 128, she catalogued her neighbors: that executive in his Mercedes with a fistful of rings, the MD applying lipstick in her mirror, that car pool full of grim white faces . . . Why this daily exodus to the Great American Workplace? To office buildings with unnatural lighting and no ventilation? She understood the problem of the mortgage payments and the credit rating, the new appliances and improved home electronics systems, and the children, of course, who needed the right "tools" for their education and clothes that would not humiliate them in the schoolyard; she understood the rudiments of the market economy and did her very best to participate, spending slightly more each year than her annual salary, hoarding her scant vacation days, and she even went the extra mile by voting in obscure primaries and midterm elections barely covered in the press, but somehow, in aggregate, *it was all so depressing*, and the fact that her family had everything they needed was not a comfort but a threat, and she felt it on the highway, trying to cross two lanes to reach her exit, and she felt it in the parking lot outside her office, gliding into her neat diagonal space, and she felt it passing by the grid of cubicles on the way to her perimeter office with its laminated "wooden" door, and only the Reverend Thomas Mosher, who cared nothing for the things that money bought, could take this empty feeling from her soul.

She called him for the first time at 10:05 and got the answering machine in the parsonage, hanging up before the beep. Anita, her secretary, had decided at nine o'clock to take another personal day, so Bethany had requested, and received two hours later, a temp to handle the phones. Her name was Pam, "from Danvers," the woman offered, a classic townie with feathered hair and a spiderweb tattoo on the fleshy part of her left hand. Bethany gave her a tour of the supply room ("You got lots of Wite-Out," Pam remarked), pointed out the bathrooms, which Pam would visit with an alarming frequency during their time together, and brought her to the vending ma chines—the scene, later that afternoon, of a "scene": Bethany had gone in search of a Diet Coke and happened to stumble onto Pam in front of the snack dispenser, on her knees, one arm thrust inside, trying to steal some candy.

"Any luck?" Bethany asked, standing in the doorway. Pam, if that was her real name, had gone to the trouble of taking off her burgundy leather jacket and spreading it out beneath her.

"It took my fuckin' change," she said, and smiled faintly. Bethany ended up buying her a package of Reese's Pieces, signed her time card for a full afternoon, and sent her back to the North Shore. She called the pastor again and left a message, something discreet about needing some understanding, and she spent the rest of the day rewriting a memorandum on the Family and Medical Leave Act (FMLA) that was destined only for recycling bins, the thought of which—families in distress, stray paper—made her miss the pastor all the more.

On her way home from work Bethany stopped at the parsonage and rang the doorbell. She left her car running in the driveway, the voices of "All Things Considered" leaking from her open door. When Thomas didn't answer she went back to the car and rummaged through her glove compartment for a pen, writing him a dirty, blasphemous note,

Dear Rev. Mosher,

I am in a dilemma. Coming to your church makes me very horny. I have tried the route of self-pleasure in the pew but found it disappointing. After the sermon this Sunday, will you fuck me?

knowing better than to sign it with a name, but he would know, he would know. She folded the note carefully and wedged it in a conspicuous place beside the door latch, pleased to feel the blood rush to her face. All the way home she thought of Thomas reading the note in the parsonage, and this imaginary congress helped her face the prospect of seeing her husband, a man who, of all things mysterious and supernatural, had come to believe in the clairvoyant powers of his groin.

Thanks to Ulla, their Swedish nanny, the Caruso household was humming perfectly that night. The table had already been set for one of Ulla's heavy meals; the dishwasher had been run and emptied; the children's laundry had been washed, folded neatly, and deposited in their respective hampers at the bottom of the staircase. How the nanny maintained such order, Bethany would never know. Three days a week Ulla spent the afternoon watching the children, and the rest of the time she was a graduate student in geology at Harvard. They had found her through their neighbors the Swensons, an honest, hardworking family who still chopped their own wood in the backyard and attended the Pilgrims' Church every Sunday—and who struggled, in a jaded time, to convince the neighborhood that the ideal surface of their family life hid nothing shady. Bethany envied Ulla's youth and effortless androgyny: she was tall and lithe, shaved her thick black hair close to her elegant head, and had the biggest blue eyes Bethany had ever seen. She wore T-shirts and ripped jeans exclusively, and didn't walk so much as glide like an insect light enough to balance on the water's surface. Jessie loved her fiercely. Her cooking, however, was another story, and Bethany's nausea returned at the dinner table when Ulla lifted the tinfoil off the baking dish and revealed to the gathered family her rendition of finnan haddie. Bobby sat at the foot of the table with a stupid cheerful grin, one hand on his after-work Samuel Adams. Thankfully Devon had retired his ski cap for the evening, and since he loved Ulla in a different way, he stared quietly at his plate, ready to blush when she addressed him. He had left the headphones for his Discman around his neck, cord dangling below the table. And Jessie, restless girl, knelt on her chair blessing everything with her magic wand. Ulla sat beside her filling the plates and sending them around. The head of the family table was a lonely place, Bethany thought, chin resting on her hands, watching Ulla charm and feed everyone.

"*Tack så mycket!*" Jessie yelled, having learned a little Swedish to impress her beloved nanny. "Everyone say *tack!*"

"*Tack*," Devon answered first, and blushed a deep, reassuring red. Bobby followed with an obsequious "*tack*" of his own, still smiling, maybe it was something in the watercooler at his office, or this beer was his eleventh—

"Say *tack*, Mommy!"

Bethany obliged her to get it over with. "Please don't take this personally, Ulla, but my appetite might not be up to finnan haddie tonight."

"Are you sick?" Ulla asked, already digging in. She ate like a horse and it never showed! Come to think of it, Bethany had never seen an overweight Swede in her life. Is it possible that being earnest burned calories?

"My stomach does feel a little shaky."

"I love it!" Jessie pronounced, cream sauce dribbling down her chin. For good measure she blessed Bethany's plate with her wand.

"It's really good, Mom," Devon added, trying to ingratiate himself with Ulla.

"I'm just warning you," Bethany told them, "at some point I might have to lie down." She stuck it out for a while, ignoring Bobby's plaintive stare from across the table, and listening to Jessie describe for her captive audience a lunchtime dispute between two of her classmates, mediated with great skill, apparently, by Sandra the judgmental hippie. Bethany ate three green beans and a new potato until, without thinking, she took a mouthful of the creamy haddock. Low tide! The dairy cow's gone fishing! Bethany excused herself and rushed upstairs to brush the rank taste of finnan haddie from her mouth, using, by default, Jessie's bubble-gum-flavored toothpaste, filled with sparkles, which only enhanced her suffering in the short run. Once again she was reminded that children's products had a way of traveling beyond their rightful boundaries, like, well, children themselves.

Now the pastor would not leave Bethany's mind, and she took to her four-poster bed from Ethan Allen and fell into a *nonplus*, worrying not about his whereabouts (not yet) but about their love and its predicament, how she, a married woman with two young children, could ever free herself to love him openly, and he, a minister of the church, could ever free himself from public opinion and accept her, never mind the different colors of their skin, still a problem in Massachusetts even though it was no longer supposed to be (in private the pastor spoke about the subject of *race* with some bitterness), and her children, innocent bystanders to it all, were quickly catching on that maybe something wasn't right between their parents, soon they would turn dark, start acting out at school and requiring sessions of Kiddie Therapy where they would scream their lungs out during role-playing exercises and beat inflatable "parental figures" silly—enough, she thought, I can't take it, and sandwiched her head between two buckwheat pillows.

Ulla stopped in before she left and gave Bethany, still lying down but no longer smothering herself, a progress report on the children. Both of them had eaten well, enjoyed their nightly TV fix—no graphic violence, one hour of PlayStation maximum—and had gone off to bed without whining too much. Their father (the beast) had already kissed them both on the forehead, and had recently retired, with briefcase, to his apartment-in-exile. Now it was time for mother's nightly blessing! Bethany apologized for escaping early from the dinner table and thanked Ulla for her patience; she tried to give the nanny some extra money for her trouble, but Ulla refused the offer quite briskly. How were graduate students, who could afford it least, capable of such altruism? Downstairs Bethany locked the front door and activated the alarm system, downed a glass of white wine in two quick gulps, turned out all the lights, and headed up to Devon's room. A few months earlier they had let Devon install a lock on his door for privacy, another wise idea of Bobby's, and since then she hadn't been able to set foot inside. Adolescence, or the behavioral part of it anyway, had started visiting the boy in preparation for the final showdown.

At the first knock Devon answered, "Yeah?"

"I came to say good night," she told him through the door.

"So say it, then."

"I just did, Devon."

"Then we're done, right?"

Bethany tried the door for the hell of it and he immediately started rustling around inside. She wondered if Bobby's pornography collection had become, between the two of them, a point of bonding. "What's going on in there?"

"Nothing, Mom," he promised.

"Sleep well, then," she answered, giving up the fight for her son, which lately had begun to seem hopeless. She worried that Devon was changing before her eyes into a suburban monster, the kind of unkempt boy who "tagged" mailboxes and set stray animals on fire with lighter fluid. Devon answered with a sullen, "Night, yo."

One down, she crossed the hallway diagonally and found Jessie in her nightgown, eyes wide in excitement, having just dumped the contents of her handbag on the floor of her room. Bethany swooped in and bundled her daughter in her arms to friendly squeals, lifting her over to the bed, where she deposited her among a petting zoo of stuffed animals, each with his or her own name, psychological profile, and genealogy. She turned off the overhead light while Jessie chattered with a group of her animals.

"I'm glad I don't have to sleep in the garage," Jessie said as her mother tucked her in.

"Well, your father's not actually *in* the garage."

"He's in the water bed!"

"That's right."

"I hope he floats away," she said, and giggled.

"Be careful what you wish for," Bethany instructed.

"I was only joking!"

She had the sweetest little yawn! Bethany felt her maternal fascination rising, mixed pleasantly with cheap white wine, and lunged to kiss the nearest part of Jessie's body, her left ear. After a short giggling session they had a conversation about where Ulla lived, and with whom, and why, the upshot being that Jessie wanted her to move in with them.

"She can sleep in the garage," Jessie suggested.

"Then where will Daddy sleep?"

"With you!" Bethany had forgotten that within the heart of every child lurks not a libertine but a family-values Republican, and she fell silent. "Mommy?"

"Yes, Jessie."

"Isn't Ariel the prettiest?"

Bethany carried another glass of wine to bed and stayed up for a while flipping channels on the television, disappointed, as usual, by her lack of options. Here a "verité" detective show, there a teenage sex soap, across the way a newsmagazine that had planted explosives in pickup trucks to make a story more dramatic, all to be followed up, later, by the accident-filled local news and garish talk show comedy. At least the wine tasted good and she was near the phone in case the pastor called, not that he would—ministering to the congregation kept him busy at all hours, and she hadn't been able to tell him, yet, about her latest trial separation from Bobby. She was angry (1) at herself for being miserable, (2) at the Networks for putting so much crap on television, (3) at Ulla for the finnan haddie debacle,

(4) at her husband because he was her favorite scapegoat when her medication wasn't working right. She was also (a) tired, (b) nauseated, and (c) depressed. Probably she was (d) premenstrual. She missed the pastor terribly, and wanted, if nothing else, just to hear his voice . . . Suddenly, with this last thought, it dawned on her that maybe, just maybe, weaning herself from the Zoloft had nothing at all to do with her volatile mood (although it couldn't help matters); it had been years, of course, since she had known anything to compare her desperation to, but wasn't she in love? With a man she couldn't spend her nights with? And wasn't love, above all else, *painful*? She turned off the television and closed her eyes, letting the images of disaster and celebrity fade from her mind, until she was alone with her desire, and his absence, a miraculous discomfort that made her feel like a saint or something, at the very least a Holy sufferer.

O *Thomas*, she thought, *where are you?*

**4** On the morning of his final Sunday sermon the Reverend Thomas Mosher was preoccupied with a nimbostratus cloud that seemed to have formed in the sky above the church grounds, threatening a rainy Sabbath for his congregation. He kept checking the cloud's progress in the window while he wrestled with his temperamental notebook computer, some fly-by-night IBM clone that the Council, in their infinite stinginess, had purchased on the cheap from a local dealer in reconditioned office machines. First the hinge on the screen had broken, and the pastor, to keep the top of his computer upright, had been forced to stack his dictionary and thesaurus behind the thing and lean the screen against it, an arrangement that worked fine as long as he didn't need his reference books, which he often did, meaning he had to close the screen and remove the dictionary, say, from its anchor position, triggering some kind of automatic shutoff system and consigning whatever work he had just been struggling with to binary oblivion. His printer was another story, just as maddening, a donated LaserJet something-or-other that required him to hover overhead and pull each

sheet of typescript out as it rolled through the manual feeder; left to its own devices, the machine doubled as a surprisingly efficient document shredder. How many pages had he lost to its hungry innards? How many paper jams had he been loath to clear? That morning all the pastor needed was to give the text of his sermon the final once-over, and in record time—twenty minutes—he had managed to print all twelve pages of the revised version. Since he was on a roll he thought he might try and check his E-mail, but his external modem, when he plugged it in, was not responding to the usual commands. The nimbostratus cloud had been growing darker in the sky, suspending the appearance of the morning, and Thomas stepped outside to rescue his Sunday *Globe* from the rain that would surely follow. He scanned the paper over breakfast, "Mostly Sunny," the meteorologists had predicted. They were so often wrong, why didn't they just admit their ignorance? The weather was a minor passion of his, and he often tuned in to the late local newscasts to watch the Doppler radar make its clockhand sweep over all the firmament, identifying patches of precipitation, biomorphic rain shapes, and tracking their movement in the lower atmosphere. The weather's ever-changing face seemed to him an utter mystery. Even if the meteorologist, with his tailored suit and mindless patter, pretended to have it mastered—the brightly colored radar screen, after all, merely told them what was already happening, and an honest extended forecast in New England would have gone something like:

| | |
|---|---|
| Monday: | Can't tell |
| Tuesday: | Who can say? |
| Wednesday: | Won't venture a guess |
| Thursday: | Out of range |
| Friday: | Hubris! This is Heaven's business, and not for the likes of men |

He picked through the front-hall closet looking for an umbrella and came out with a vintage pair of galoshes, in ten more years they would be "antique," just one artifact, out of many, that filled the hidden corners of the parsonage, and reminded him, as if he needed it, that he was tenant in the home he lived in, the latest in a long succession, going back two hundred years, of men (and recently women) who had ministered here, and lived with their families, for half of that time, under the same patched roof, full of phantom leaks, that he did. Had the galoshes belonged to Samuel Puryear, pastor of the Pilgrims' Church for thirty years, who had stepped down from the pulpit tearfully, against his will, in 1963? Or to Harrison "Hal" Chambers, who followed him and, much to the alarm of the conservative members of the congregation, became a leader in Boston's antiwar movement?

The pastor liked to open up the church himself and let the Sunday air in first, before the energetic choirmaster, Mike Flynn, alcoholic-in-recovery and leader of the Tuesday night AA meeting, cranked up the pipe organ and led the uneven choir through their paces at nine-thirty; before the head usher, Stephen Silva, shuffled in with his undertaker's air and Dostoevskian beard (in contrast to his appearance Silva owned a family seafood restaurant, a Go Kart franchise, and a cozy bed-and-breakfast on the outer Cape) to prepare the coffee urn for the after-sermon social hour, arrange the cookie platter, and polish the pewter offertory plates with perhaps too much reverence; before Jane Groom arrived in her Toyota pickup with her dog on an extend-a-leash, coming early to coach the morning's lay reader on his or her technique; before the elder widows of the congregation either hobbled down the aisle or were wheeled by professional attendants, eager to gossip in the rear pews, to compare notes on the latest change in medication or experimental treatment, and to share with the pastor, once he came over to pay his respects, their outrage, finely calibrated, at the latest unforgivable transgression committed by a child, church member, roommate at the nursing home, or career politician. They spoke in the elegant cadences of a bygone age, and though there may have been, on the surface, much to separate the pastor from them, the elder widows, in their own oblivious way, had *accepted him* from the moment he was called to lead their church. They were women who had married young and lost their husbands, but for a few, very early; raised large families on their own to revere tradition, just to watch them all disperse to places like Irvine, California, and Seattle, Washington; they had seen the certainties of their childhood fade slowly and then disappear; fought loneliness and broken hips, cancer and emphysema, and survived it all, faith in God and family intact and *hearts wide open*. The children squirming in their seats throughout the morning prayer may have been the future of the Pilgrims' Church, but the elder widows, with a sparkle in their hooded eyes and love in their arthritic fingers, were evidence of the Congregational faith's great promise: that Christ the Mediator spreads His Fountain of Grace among the children of a living God.

No rain yet, the pastor found when he opened up the front entrance and stepped outside for a minute, and by force of wind the ominous cloud seemed, at last, to be drifting east, toward Grace Church and the conservative Episcopalians, Tories in the past and now, under the energetic rector Skip Waterbury, crusaders against Anglican Modernism, although Skip, after watching his attendance drop steadily, had recently begun co-opting the methods of his ideological opponents by sponsoring Tuesday night writing workshops and inviting Christian folksingers to perform with his choir of perfectionists. And they were sore winners on the softball field—at least the Catholics had creamed them (18–2? St. Mary's third baseman coached Varsity at Holy Cross and they platooned at every position), a fate the Pilgrims' Church had avoided only by failing to reach the seven-player minimum. St. Mary's had offered their *children* (three players between the ages of six and seventeen) but the pastor had refused their "charitable donation" out of principle. Out came the beer coolers for a forfeit celebration! Perhaps the nimbostratus cloud would take a right turn after soaking Grace and pelt St. Mary's ten-foot-high statue of the Virgin.

Back inside the pastor took his customary seat in the last row of pews and granted himself a moment of reflection. He had been told all his life, first by his mother, brought up Baptist in Virginia (she had come North to attend a women's college, married young, and assimilated into New England's first religion), and then by a series of Sunday school teachers and ministers, that a church was never empty, that the Holy Spirit filled the air and underwrote the creaking planks and settling timbers. He had seen truth in the idea until, as an ordained minister himself, he started every Sunday morning with a moment just like this, and it seemed to him, after gaining some experience in the matter, that he was *perfectly, profoundly alone.* There, underneath the stained-glass windows of the Puritan saints, the pastor felt as if he were *lost in a great wilderness,* a sensation familiar to the Elder William Brewster, layman of the First Church of Plymouth, standing before the famous Rock in the highest window, flanked by Governors John Carver and William Bradford, and the Deacon Samuel Fuller; and to John Winthrop in the pane just below, arriving in Salem Harbor aboard the good ship *Arbella*; and to the minister John Harvard (lending his Grace to the balcony), who left that feeling on his early deathbed; and to Thomas Hooker, on the western wall, driving the Evil One from the Connecticut River valley; and to the good Anne Bradstreet, poised at her writing desk; and to the heretic Anne Hutchinson, tried as a Jezebel and jailed in her Eden for instigating the Antinomian Controversy. One stained-glass window stood out most of all, however, and each time, on Sunday morning, the pastor's eyes caught sight of it, he lit with a sense of the *familiar*: The window portrayed John Eliot, missionary to the Roxbury savages, standing beneath a shade tree and offering, with a look of charity, his Indian Bible to a sun-drenched Native, pictured in face paint and loincloth, who weighed the Puritan's gesture with a faint hostility. The pastor recognized himself in both halves of the picture—Eliot on his father's side, founders of the New England faith, the Native on his mother's, descended from Africans and West Indians kidnapped into slavery—and as a child of two opposing worlds, all things being equal, he could find a home in neither. But this quandary was only a beginning:

What if the historical roles had switched and he, part savage, had been elected by the children of the missionary class to lead them out of darkness, of savagery, and into the Divine and Spiritual light of the Creator? What if he had failed them? What message—above all—should he deliver to the inheritors of this spoiled Eden? Of all the variable shapes that God had taken in the minds and languages of men, was there a single understanding great enough to enclose the pastor's *soul-sickness*, to *empty him*?

> *Deus est sphaera infinita cuius centrum*
> *est ubique, circumferentia nusquam*

Or, roughly translated for the purposes of his sermon that morning, God is an infinite sphere whose center is everywhere, the circumference nowhere. He expected a disquisition on the subject to strike some members of the church as being hopeless, but Thomas no longer cared to appease his critics with spiritual sound bites and easy inspiration. Let them roll their eyes and grumble in their seats, cough throughout and punish him at the offertory plate; let them whisper behind his back at Fellowship, stuff the suggestions box with anonymous complaints, and threaten to raise issue with his leadership at the next church meeting . . .

So where was his sudden revelation? The Scripture's voice answering his loneliness with the Son's offer, *Come to me, all who are weary and whose load is heavy; I will give you rest?* Silence? Too late to constitute an answer to his prayer, the rain cloud finished passing overhead and the missionary Eliot's window filled, from top to bottom, with a gentle light, refining the colors, and the outlines, of the pastor's melancholy. He heard a sound, then—the choirmaster, whistling a pop song on his way up the steps, and calling his name from the entryway, "Thomas?"

"I'm here, Mike."

"Do you reckon we missed the rain?"


When the house alarm woke Bethany early Tuesday morning from a deep sleep she had a premonition about the pastor, that he no longer loved her, and that she would never see him again, this while she shot from her bed out of reflex and rushed to the hallway, the better part of her awareness slow to follow. "It's just me," Bobby called out over the nerve-grating alarm, and turned on a light in the front hallway. "Since when did we change the code?" By this time the children had come to their respective doors and looked out with worried faces. "It's just your father," she told them, and sent the children back to bed. For some reason, probably the "emergency situation," they took her directions obediently. Bethany had started to wake up now and her heart, tender muscle, was still pounding as she descended the stairs. Bobby squinted at the alarm's keypad in his pajamas, looking, as usual, swollen and foolish. The phone rang before they had time to disable the alarm, and Bobby went into the kitchen to apologize to the police. The security system had come with the house, a five-year-old contemporary Colonial, and over that time they had averaged a full-fledged false alarm every six months. Two more alarms in their basement, for Carbon Monoxide and Radon, cleared the house intermittently, although testing had never showed unhealthy levels of either toxin.

"This is ridiculous," Bobby complained after he had finished with the police department. Bethany had already disabled the alarm and restored an uncomfortable silence. In his hand Bobby carried the reason for their trouble, a small stack of Oreos. "Why should I have to break into *my own house* for cookies?"

"It's not the time," Bethany told him, trying to keep her voice down, "and I'm not the one who set the alarm off, am I?"

"Don't get testy with me, Beth."

She ignored his desperate use of the diminutive. "A minute ago I was fast asleep and now I'm standing in the front hallway."

"So I'm sorry."

"I can't do this right now," she told him, heading back upstairs.

"What's the alarm code anyway?"

"Jessie's birthday for the eleventh time."

"You know I'm not good with dates, Beth."

"Then comb your fucking memory . . ."

Devon seemed to have gone back to sleep already, either that or he ignored his mother's knock, but Jessie, slightly traumatized by the alarm, called out from her bedroom, "Mommy?" She wanted to sleep with Bethany again, and wouldn't take "No" for an answer. Bethany relented, carrying her down the hall, and they climbed underneath the thick comforter together. First Jessie wanted to share one pillow. Then she wanted to talk, and Bethany, trying to appease her, made the mistake of mentioning Bobby's Oreo run. From that point on, only the threat of being returned to her own bedroom would quiet the girl down. Bethany knew there was no way she would sleep that morning, not with Thomas on her mind, and she was happy to have Jessie's little furnace of a body beside her. As a baby she had smelled unaccountably like lemons, and now that she was older, Jessie's fragrance was more akin to a strawberry patch. Could it be her children's shampoo? Or was she eating so many jelly sandwiches that she *shined* the stuff? Bethany stroked her child's hair until her breathing changed, and then she watched her sleeping off another stressful day of childhood, this brave and tender girl, part of herself yet something entirely other. *She is mine,* Bethany thought, knowing full well that this was an untruth, *she is not mine* being the necessary opposite, but that was love in a nutshell, wasn't it?

In the morning she handed Jessie off to her husband (it was Bobby's turn to drive her to the Montessori School) and stumbled through her pre-work routine on a few hours' sleep, stopping, twice, to check her voice mail at work for messages from Thomas. Her premonitions had always tended to the gloomy side, and she held out hope, as always, that she might be wrong. Back when she was still a newlywed, with one year left in college, and Bobby was working ungodly hours for a sadistic systems manager at one of Boston's teaching hospitals, Bethany had always imagined the worst when he was running late and hadn't called, alone with her anxiety in their tiny rented house on a dead-end street in Needham. Her imagination had worked on a sliding scale of car trouble: at the fifteen-minute mark, a flat tire; at twenty-five, a severed fan belt (she didn't know what that entailed, really, but had liked the way it sounded); after thirty-five minutes and still no call, she became certain that Bobby had been run off the road by a semi truck; anything longer and she imagined her husband trapped in the mangled hulk of his Buick Skylark, upside down, in the process of being rescued—too late—by the "Jaws of Life." So much anxiety in the days before the car phone! Bobby, self-centered as always, had chosen to mistake her irrational panic for a young wife's devoted love. "Relax," he used to say, "you're so *high-strung*." She had hated her own tears, her heart palpitations, and her foolish need, once Bobby had arrived with his briefcase (which was usually empty!) and a lame apology, to be reassured with kisses in the front hallway. Later, when they had more money between them, keeping a box of white wine in the refrigerator at all times had done the job, and once the age of psychotropic drugs arrived, a 200 mg-a-day prescription of Zoloft. But now she was without a medicinal crutch, save her dwindling supply of dope, and if Thomas—dear Thomas—didn't call her soon, she would have to stop detoxifying.

They were tired from the night's alarm, and clumsy, and short-tempered: Dad complained about the lack of muffins in the house, Boy refused to tie his sneakers, Girl hurt her elbow somehow and whined—oh, could she whine!—and Mom abandoned them for the quiet confines of her car, where she assembled, from parts on the floor and in the glove compartment, the mobile phone that she never used, in fact *dismissed* for its intrusion into "private time," but now, seeing as this technological advance might help her betray her husband more effectively, she gave in to changing times. Four unanswered and metallic rings carried her past the Swensons' compound to the intersection of Route 102, where she paused at the Stop sign, turned right, and sped off in the direction of the parsonage.

She followed the Old Acton Road, a highway since the Colonial days and still the town's major artery, past the landscaped entrance to the Walden Estates; the struggling horse farm that had been cited by the ASPCA for neglect; the regional high school, where the administration had refused, despite an order from the state, to distribute condoms in health classes; the White Hen Pantry that had just been robbed at gunpoint; Hardy's Nursery complex, which was reputed to be owned by members of the John Birch Society; and the town's unsightly Public Works garage with its decaying plows, hulking diesel trucks, and enormous salt piles that were alleged to have fouled the local water supply. Near the first major intersection she came to a stop behind a row of commuters, all stuck at the scandalous traffic light, the subject of several Town Meetings, where, so far, their elected officials had refused to change the timing, forcing taxpayers on their way to Route 128 to wait in unreasonable lines, and effecting a grassroots campaign complete with bumper stickers ("Fix the Light"), bright red buttons, and a petition signed by over seven thousand residents, thanks to volunteers ringing doorbells all over town. Bethany had never shared their anger until that morning (why did everyone want to get to work so badly? What exactly was the rush?), on her way to the parsonage to check on Thomas. She even leaned on her horn when the Honda directly in front of her failed to run a yellow light, an outburst which earned her the hands-thrown-up gesture and a long, deep stare in the rearview mirror from a sinister pair of eyes. Where was his "Fix the Light" bumper sticker? Finally she entered Old Town and circled around the church, heart, once more, pounding, until she drifted up to the parsonage and it *stopped*—the note she had left for Thomas was still visible within the doorframe, untouched by his clumsy, trembling fingers, and his car, that misguided sedan produced and marketed for the young "career woman," was nowhere in sight. *Something had gone terribly wrong*, she was sure of it now, and she stayed there for a minute longer, dialing his phone number with a growing panic, watching the parsonage for signs of life and waiting for Thomas to *pick up the phone*, as if she could will him to be there with her eyes. Bethany felt herself tingle on the surface as she drove off again, and grow somehow lighter, unable to bear the distraction of the radio, or the plain fact that he was gone.

*Such melancholy*, thought Margaret Howard when she first set eyes on Thomas Mosher at the pulpit, an uncommon word in her no-nonsense vocabulary thick with the terms of her trade (like "assumable loans," "final value estimates," and "disclosure statements"), yet she could think of no other way to describe his figure as he faced the congregation with an uncertain smile and commenced the Call to Worship. Still, she thought, this was a fine-looking black man, with lightish skin and a neat appearance, and she tried to view him as a Christian, first, rather than as a member of the Board of Real Estate, although she couldn't help considering, at that moment, a worst-case scenario whereby the pastor, having received the Privilege of Call from the Search Committee, attracted the wrong following to their quiet town, causing the market to filter down after residential property changed hands and, in so doing, lose its value. She prided herself on her company's long-standing policy of doing business with any qualified homeowner or buyer regardless of race or ethnicity; indeed, if it hadn't been for that complaint to the State Commission in '89, filed—without just cause—by an African-American couple from Worcester with a history of credit trouble and a sense of entitlement (they had clearly lacked the income for the town house they so coveted), Howard Homes would have had a perfect record going back over twenty years. She had even hired Mrs. Lee on a part-time basis to make the Asian clients feel more comfortable, this after training her at the company's expense! In general, however, she believed caution was the best policy when dealing with neighborhood life cycles, and viewed dramatic changes in population demographics to be the enemy of stability. The real estate business, she insisted to anyone who asked, was really very simple, and success, she preached to her employees, was just a matter of common sense—and a little creative salesmanship. *Think of yourself as a matchmaker*, she told them, *between people and properties. We have inspectors and loan officers to run background checks. You and I are in the romance business. A house is love. A house is happiness.* She had used this speech so many times now that she almost believed it, but what else could she do? "Love and happiness!" she barked at Mrs. Lee on the broker's way out to the Lexus her commissions had already bought. "Love and happiness!" she drilled into the heads of her support staff so that anyone who called Howard Homes for an appraisal would feel special. Her territory practically sold itself, boasting excellent schools (W———'s public school system consistently ranked between #4 and #11 statewide), an almost nonexistent crime rate, and a variety of well-endowed houses of worship to choose from, all just thirty minutes from the Hub, downtown Boston. As a matter of fact, Margaret had it on good authority that the widow Hartigan was finally doing some estate planning and had earmarked a bequest in the low seven figures for the Pilgrims' Church, an astonishing figure for a woman with six children and eighteen grandchildren, although, it was true, they hardly visited the poor woman.

As she rose to sing the morning's first hymn ("Alleluia! Gracious Jesus!"), Margaret looked past Artemesia, slouching as usual, to the aisle where Grace Hartigan's male nurse had parked her wheelchair for the service. She appeared to have fallen asleep already! *If I have to go*, Margaret thought, *let me go before I lose my independence. Let me go before Jerry, so I won't have to live alone.* She elbowed Artemesia, who was mumbling instead of singing, and followed the lyrics of the hymn with flawless diction, trying to set an example for the Brooks children in the pew behind. Margaret had never understood why so many regular churchgoers seemed ashamed to sing, or answer the Assurance of Pardon with confidence, or approach the Gospel reading with a sense of professionalism. Artemesia, especially, who may have been a fragile soul, but possessed an unselfconscious piety that Margaret coveted— although she never would have revealed this fact to her devoted friend, believing it might overwhelm her sense of modesty. Artemesia sang a little clearer now and even lifted her habitually fallen chin, satisfying Margaret, who once more checked on Grace Hartigan. The widow's head, elongated with age, had dropped to her chest, and Margaret could see no evidence that she was breathing.

What if she had passed away right there in the aisle, with her degenerate male nurse out smoking in the parking lot and the congregation busy sizing up this sad young minister? What if the incompetent nurse had driven off with his criminal record to stuff his face with Egg McMuffins, and the widow Hartigan, beneath her placid exterior, was *hanging on to life by a thread*? With distinguished visitors in the crowd that morning and her generous bequest awaiting final signature?

Luckily, as the hymn was ending, the old woman came to

and even joined in the "Amen," settling Margaret's spirits in her pew. The young minister closed his hymnal and, after glancing at Jane Groom, who sat behind the pulpit beaming like an idiot, turned to the congregation gathered before him. The church was packed with worshippers that Sunday, and had been unusually silent during the Meditation. Even the children, so often prone to fidgeting and whining, sat on their hands and watched him politely. "Well, he's certainly cute," Artemesia whispered in her ear, an inappropriate comment! At the Church Meeting in a week's time Margaret hoped she would take the Call more seriously, when they would have a chance to pray together, raise their voices in an orderly fashion, and decide, once and for all, whether or not they were ready to welcome the Reverend Thomas Mosher into their community. Margaret glared at Artemesia for a moment before the minister started in: "Thank you, good people, for making a stranger feel at home in your wonderful church. First, before I launch into the sermon I've prepared, I'd like to say that, from my heart, these days I have the chance to spend among you are, in the truest sense of the word, a gift . . ."


"Molly!" the Reverend Jane Groom called out the back door to her AKC-registered bitch schnauzer and closest companion in life, "MOLLY BLOOM!" The dog, recently beset by vapors, lifted its head from the ground and refused to move. Jane had named the dog at first sight, when the man at the breeding farm had pointed her out with derision as the litter's runt, and Molly, looking just a little more embryonic than the others, had opened one crusty eye and *chosen her*, Jane thought, with an ecstatic surrender reminiscent of Bloom's wife. There in the breeder's spooky barn, kneeling before the panting mother and her litter of puppies squirming in the straw, Jane had fallen in love for the first time. Relationships had always seemed outside her province (technically a virgin at the age of thirty-four, she was inexperienced beyond a few "experimental" weekends in Northampton as an undergraduate, the guest of a precocious field-hockey player from Smith), and her biological clock, as they said, seemed not to be ticking at all; children, in the specific, seemed rather unruly, and she couldn't bear them after they began to speak, when they lost whatever mute charm God had given them to enter life. If only children could learn to be more like the infant Christ! Barking, on the other hand, didn't bother her so much, and Molly, bless her little dewclaws, didn't require a special console in the pickup truck, expensive day care, or college tuition.

"Come here, Molly!"

As a puppy she had simply curled up in Jane's lap while she was driving, but that arrangement hadn't lasted long past Molly's third month, when a growth spurt hit and didn't stop until she weighed over eighty pounds, minus her unattractive tail, which Jane, after doing some research on the subject, had chosen to have surgically docked. Molly stood in the truck bed now, weather providing, although this arrangement had been a problem earlier in the spring when she began her first estrus cycle, with mongrels of all shapes and sizes howling from their yards, or, if they were illegally unchained, running along behind them while poor Molly, in protective undergarments, on a leash herself to prevent escape, kept looking over her shoulder in alarm. *Invisible fencing,* Jane had thought indecorously, *my tuchis!* Mild electrocution was no threat when compared to a willing schnauzer ambling by like a canine beauty queen at thirty miles per hour.

"Molly Bloom!"

Thankfully a prescription for chlorophyll tablets had brought an end to the embarrassment, and since, then Jane had taken it upon herself to restore Molly to her former health, even if it meant sacrificing her involvement with the Monday Reflection Group for a while, giving veritable free rein to that intolerant Margaret Howard, who was an ardent supporter of Governor Weld, a loutish Republican even if he *was* pro-choice. Molly had simply not been herself and the trouble, already in its third week, seemed to be taking on the symptoms of a classic spiritual crisis. Milk-Bones were her only pleasure in life, and Jane had started buying them in bulk to get through this difficult time, offering them hourly, and for the smallest acts of obedience. In checking Molly's haunches each night she had noticed an alarming weight gain, but what else could she do?

"Come here, Molly!"

The dog finally ambled over, dragging her trolley leash along the state-of-the-art dog run, and climbed the stairs to rest her muzzle, with a look of resignation, in her owner's waiting palm. Jane unhooked her collar and let Molly inside, rewarding her with the giant Milk-Bone, which the dog brought over to her favorite spot, an egg-shaped plaid cushion from the L.L.Bean catalogue, a worthy resting place for such a sensitive animal, even if they kept hiking up the price.

Since six-thirty that morning, when she had crept downstairs in her spring slippers to let Molly out for the first time, Jane had been working on her poetry, a practice she took up intermittently and considered a sideline of her life's work: praising Jesus Christ. The demands placed on her by the congregation usually left little time for her own writing, but Thomas's sermon on the "infinite sphere"—in her estimation, a work of genius—had inspired her to bring out her verse notebook and attempt to finish her latest project, a cycle of sonnets based on the eight Beatitudes of Matthew. Jane had grown up in a religious house—Father a successful businessman and church volunteer, Mother a homemaker and Christian counselor—and she had been captivated, all through childhood, by her Bible study, especially her reading of the Gospels, which told of a Jesus so gentle and wise, and so demanding of goodness all around him, that the stories and parables often made her cry, even as an adult and ordained minister. *Foxes have their holes*, she would read with teary eyes, *and birds their nests; but the Son of Man has nowhere to lay his head.* Such a sad and thrilling lifestyle choice! Her parents had always consoled her when she became overly emotional about her Bible study as a child, and they had been very good at pointing out passages that might cheer her up (like those dirty pigs hurtling over the edge of the cliff, for one). By the age of twelve she had considered herself a girl apostle, secretly entrusted to spread the word among the powerless, the indifferent, and the openly hostile, starting at her elementary school, rife as it had been with conversion material—but her shyness, deepened by the many hours she spent alone with the Gospels, turned out to be a major obstacle: every time she had prepared herself to instruct one of her schoolmates on the various lessons contained in the Sermon on the Mount, so *good* it made her feel all funny inside, she balked at the last minute. Even Amy Hauser, a sad girl with a wandering eye (an obvious candidate for spiritual counseling), had scared her away. After failing in her own estimation to spread Christ's word effectively, Jane relinquished her girl-apostlehood and promptly fell into a dark phase (relatively speaking) when she listened to the Beach Boys and joined the girls' volleyball team. Her parents, who were getting older, worried about her soul's progress. Jane still went to church every Sunday, of course, but her failure to overcome her faults for the sake of Jesus Christ, she reasoned, must have been unforgivable. She had accepted communion in her pew, as was the custom in her church, with the sinking feeling that she was doing her soul irrevocable harm. So why not sin freely with the others? Smoke reefer, cut classes, fool around with boys who rode motorcycles? She hung around the periphery of the "in crowd" during high school, listening to stories about the weekend parties at the reservoir, but she was hopelessly square, and no one ever thought to invite her along. In desperation she turned back to the Gospels and found (with Joni Mitchell playing in the background) a forgiving Christ who required mercy and not sacrifice, who dined with sinners and tax collectors along with his disciples, and at once she felt an enormous sense of relief. Jesus recognized her after all! Jane grew closer to her parents again, and together they enjoyed long talks at the dinner table about the future of Christendom, or laughed about their eccentric neighbors, or grumbled about local politics— memories that would sustain her when her parents' health began its steep decline. First Mother fell ill with ovarian cancer, a terrible shock, then Father had his prostate out, and they had spent their last years, while Jane attended Wellesley College nearby, with either one or both of them in the hospital, so many sutures and oxygen tubes, catheters and dressings, their bodies wasting away and, finally, *dying* in separate semiprivate rooms one hour apart from each other—at least she had been able to inform them both about her plans to attend divinity school, and they had been lucid enough to tell her, each in their own way, that her decision made them proud. In the beginning the loss of her parents had seemed insurmountable; a combination of prayer and dedicated study helped guide her through the rest of college, and by the time she arrived at graduate school she had felt less like an orphan than a child of God, the inheritor of an enormous gift that she would share with everyone and never be able to exhaust. It seemed to her that Thomas, with his "infinite sphere" sermon, had spoken directly to her personal history, while, at the same time, describing the dialectic of *love* and *loss* that the life of Christ exemplified and that His teachings sought to answer when he preached in his Sermon on the Mount, *Blessed are they that mourn, for they shall be comforted.*

The telephone rang at that moment, spooking Molly, who stopped chewing on her biscuit for a moment and made an endearing "ruff" sound. Jane shushed her before she went into the study to answer the call. She had sold the big house when her parents died, and once she had settled at the Pilgrims' Church, bought this little saltbox in the country, formerly owned by an eccentric who had painted gold and silver stars on the ceiling throughout—which made her think, every time she looked up, of the beauty to be found in *finitude* and the fruits of human creativity. It was Bethany Caruso on the phone, a member of the church with lovely hair, a sullen son, and an ill-behaved daughter, and whose faith in anything Christian—save the pastor's sexuality, that is—Jane mistrusted on instinct. Just a few days before the Easter holiday, the usher Silva had confided in her (though she didn't necessarily trust him either) that, while changing the floodlight on the back side of the parsonage, he had witnessed something unnatural going on between the two.

"I'm looking for the Reverend Mosher," Bethany said, "and I can't seem to raise him at the parsonage."

"Well, I suspect that's where he is, Bethany."

"So he hasn't left town?"

As usual she had asked a presumptuous question about the pastor, and Jane thought it best to be circumspect. "Not that

I'm aware of, no. We do have a full calendar of meetings this week . . ."

"I thought there might be a UCC conference, or something."

Oh, that riled her! What did Bethany Caruso know or even care about the United Church of Christ? Such a familiar tone had unseemly connotations, created the perception, as they say, of intimate knowledge, and Jane was, if anything, protective of her church and its unmarried pastor. Groupies, she supposed, were a job hazard, and she felt an ethical responsibility to fend them off and preserve Thomas's virtue. "If there were a meeting," she said, trying to control her voice, "I would know."

"Oh, God," Bethany said after a short silence.

"Is there something wrong?" Jane asked, concerned for her well-being.

"It's just that I can't find him!"

"And you tried the parsonage?"

"No," she answered. "I mean, yes. I've placed a few calls."

"I suppose he could be visiting his mother," Jane tried, "which he does quite often. She lives in Annisquam, if I'm not mistaken."

"Yes, I think that's right."

Jane hesitated before she asked, "Is there something on your mind that I might help you with?"

"Thanks, but I don't think so."

"Anything at all?"

"I'm not sure if I feel right—"

"There's no need to explain," Jane interrupted, trying, charitably, to save Bethany from making a dishonest excuse. "When he turns up I'll just pass along your message, how's that?"

"Thank you," Bethany said, sounding relieved.

"Goodbye, then."

"I'm sorry to bother you at home," she blurted out.

"Oh," Jane said before she hung up, "please don't be."

"Right," Bethany answered, "right."

But her panic would not abate, and by the middle of the afternoon, with her calls to Thomas still unanswered, Bethany left work early, making the usual child-care excuse, and drove back from the office park to Pilgrims' Church, where the Boys' Choir, under the direction of Mike Flynn, was mumbling through a rendition of "Breathe on Me, Breath of God," a hymn so common in the liturgy that even Bethany, a half-hearted Christian, knew the words by heart. She stopped at the entrance for a moment and listened, gazing up at the Puritan saints in their usual gloomy light, touched by the children shyly singing of obedience to the divine:

> *Breathe on me, Breath of God,*
> *Fill me with life anew,*
> *That I may love what thou do'st love,*
> *And do what thou would'st do.*

As she started down the aisle a few of the boys, in street clothes, raised their heads from their songbooks and watched her, their words closer, now, to a wordless mumble, while Mike Flynn, an expressive organist to say the least, rocked along to the rhythm on his bench, throwing himself at the keyboard and then tearing himself back, conducting the choir with whatever limb happened to be free. Devon had lasted exactly two weeks in the Boys' Choir, calling the organist a "freak" and the singers "chumps." When they sang during Sunday service,

Devon shrank down in the pew and seemed embarrassed that he had ever been associated with the enterprise. Jessie, on the other hand, loved the Cherubs' Choir, and even lobbied to have her favorite Disney songs included in the songbook.

> *Breathe on me, Breath of God,*
> *Until my heart is pure,*
> *Until with thee I will one will,*
> *To do or to endure.*

The choirmaster was too entranced to notice her passing through the church, and Bethany was just as happy to avoid him; the man's good cheer never faltered, and his profound source of energy seemed, to her, a little spooky. He spoke the language of Rebirth and Recovery without a shade of irony and, in general, stood too close to people. The first time Bethany had come to Sunday Fellowship, Mike had intercepted her on the way to the refreshment table, and she had been forced to watch the Toll House cookies disappear over his shoulder, one by one, while he espoused his theory about *codependency* among the twelve apostles.

The church office was a depressing room off the back staircase, home to a secondhand desk, an imitation banker's lamp, ancient wooden filing cabinets, a number of uncomfortable "easy" chairs for visitors, an unreliable photocopier, a telephone (with donated fax and answering machines), and not a single human touch. Early on in her church membership Bethany had been taken aback by the modest circumstances, but then she remembered a trip she had taken to Geneva as a teenager, that strangely joyless resort town, which had included, thanks to her mother's guidebook, a visit to John Calvin's stripped cathedral, with his simple wooden chair, the throne of Total Depravity, roped off in a corner of the aisle. What a bore it had been to travel with her mother, who looked absurd in a foreign setting, and had insisted on dragging her to cultural monuments! All she had wanted to do was work on her suntan and flirt with Swiss guys (if she could find them! They seemed to spend a lot of time indoors), so she sulked along behind her mother's lead, appeased, temporarily, by an expensive wristwatch, which she then lost on a hike to see an *actual glacier* somewhere in the Alps. But the memory of Calvin's chair had come back during her course of study to join the congregation, and she recognized his spirit, she thought, in the institutional feel of the church office.

When she stepped inside, Bethany found Mrs. Safarian, the part-time secretary, and Stephen Silva, the usher, silently stuffing envelopes for a church-wide mailing. They both looked up as she crossed the threshold, Mrs. Safarian smiling in recognition, and Stephen Silva . . . well, after his wife left him in 1973, the story went, Silva had sworn never again to trust a woman. Along the way he had made an exception for Mrs. Safarian, allowing her to mother him in her natural way and scold him when he displayed his more frightening side. Together, this unlikely pair was responsible for most of the congregation's grunt work. The conventional wisdom—seldom mistaken  had the usher Silva carrying a torch for his colleague, but Mrs. Safarian's marriage, by all appearances, was a successful one, even if her husband, George, liked to grumble in public about the amount of time she devoted to the Pilgrims' Church instead of tending to him.

"Let me guess," Mrs. Safarian said, putting down her sponge for wetting the envelopes. "You're looking for Thomas."

"How'd you guess?"

"Intuition," she answered. "We've had two calls already to

complain about his Sunday sermon, and Artemesia Angelis, poor dear, just stopped by to inquire about him too."

"Has he shown his face today?" Bethany asked, trying not to sound too desperate. Her presence seemed to rankle the usher Silva. He stroked his beard for a moment as if considering the right punishment for her intrusion, then went back to stuffing envelopes with a grim efficiency.

Mrs. Safarian, on the other hand, glowed with a degree of spiritual light and enjoyment that anticipated (or so it seemed to the well-tuned members of the congregation) the joys of the heavenly world. "Well, not exactly."

"I was afraid of that."

"Usually he wanders over sometime Tuesday afternoon," Mrs. Safarian explained cheerfully, "but there are days like this one, I guess, when the Lord has other plans for him. Did you have an appointment?"

"Not officially," she admitted.

"Are you all right, Bethany? You look a little harried to me."

The usher Silva kept on peeking at Bethany's throat between envelopes. "I'm fine, really."

Mrs. Safarian moistened her sponge in a coffee mug and wiped it across the flap of an envelope. "Any message in particular?"

"Just that I stopped by?"

"Ha!" the usher Silva said out of the blue.

"You shush now," Mrs. Safarian told him.

As Bethany turned to leave, the choir was repeating the fourth and final verse of the hymn, the one about eternal life, and she wished, for the first time that afternoon, that Flynn's untalented boys would just *shut up* for a while, at least until she could put her finger on Thomas, who never sang the hymns, he admitted to her one afternoon in the country, because his ear was terrible. She missed his quiet rectitude in the bucket seat of her minivan as they escaped for a few hours, and their broken conversation while she added untold miles to her odometer, and she missed the way his resistance, refreshed by time apart, would slowly give until he fell into contemplation, and she would know, then, that they were lovers and not merely fellow congregants, because *language had deserted them*, and they were alone on a two-lane highway with their guilt and their desire, passing farm stands and self-service gas stations, circling around traffic rotaries and pulling up to rural stoplights, unable to look at each other, unable to break the silence. She missed his shyness when she found a new secluded spot and parked the family car. She missed the way his good intentions changed their nature when they sat together by the roadside.

Bethany followed the back staircase out into the churchyard, and crossed the grass with a quickening step, the sound of the organ, unaccompanied now, growing faint behind her. The windows of the parsonage were still dark, and the house itself, sagging in the middle and in need of a paint job, looked, in that characteristic New England way, as if it sheltered an unhappy family. Bethany passed underneath the branches of the apple tree, suddenly afraid of what she might find out; her pornographic note would be a test: if it had vanished from its spot beside the door latch, then Thomas, against her intuition, had come back to the church, and this period of silence had a specific meaning, was temporary, could be explained away when she finally saw him again and he accounted for his sudden absence, but if she turned the corner and found her note still waiting for him—then Thomas didn't love her anymore (how could it be true?) and his "disappearance" was merely an act of cowardice, unlike him until the very moment that he had deserted her. Partway through this formulation she began to run, brushing past the unruly hedges and emerging in the driveway, still empty, until she stopped at the foot of the entrance and looked up:

The note was gone!

Dear Thomas had come back!

He was still in love with her!

She lost her head in elation and stormed the entrance, leaning on the doorbell, pounding on the door with both her fists, calling his name to the upstairs windows . . .

But the pastor never showed himself, and soon her hope, as the doorbell went unanswered, assumed a *false and sinful aspect*. Bethany was a grown woman, after all, with a career (however hopeless), a husband (however ordinary), and the requisite two-point-three children (however confused by her marital problems)—and love, no stranger to her life, had driven her to endanger her family and *lose her composure on the parsonage steps*, in full view of the neighbors. She looked around, then, trying to make sure that no one was watching, and grabbed the door latch—inspiration! She felt the front door give, waited for a moment to make sure this portent was true, and slipped inside the parsonage.

She started her amateur search outside the pastor's private office, where she noticed first, on the windowsill behind his desk, the blinking red light of his answering machine, and counted fourteen messages* from the doorway, roughly four more than she was responsible for, and she resisted the urge to listen at first in favor of moving on to the other rooms: the kitchen with its shabby linoleum floor, cheap pine cabinets,

---

*Before the afternoon was out, Bethany would listen to the pastor's messages with her fingers crossed and then erase the tape to protect herself from suspicion. She heard the following:

"homey" wallpaper reminiscent of her childhood, although Bethany's mother, all her senses intact, never would have stood for the water stains and probably would have chucked the cast-iron skillets, blooming with rust, that hung in a depressing row above the fifties-era stove. For a moment she thought she had made a mistake and let herself into an old woman's house, but

---

"Dear Thomas . . . How many times have I asked you to change your greeting? You sound so morose, much too sad for one of God's children, but I suppose you have your reasons. It's Bethany—who else—and I'm calling because we need to talk. I'll be at the office all day. Tragically. It's Friday."

"Did I mention it's Friday? Call me."

"[silence]"

"It's Jane, Thomas. I know we shared a few words at fellowship, but I just wanted to tell you again how moved I was by your sermon this morning and how much I appreciated our little powwow about the Latin translation. Such a fascinating text for discussion! I just can't get over the image of God being an infinite sphere—I mean, the implications are endless. And such a comfort! You're a gifted man, Thomas, and I look forward to learning more about the Hermetic philosophers in the weeks to come. Bye for now."

"[in whisper] Thomas, it's Bethany. You haven't called and I'm starting . . . well, I'm starting to get a little worried. Jessie was a pill in church today and I really hope you didn't mind our leaving early, there was something in your eyes . . . I'm worried. Know that I'm thinking of you always [voice in background] fuck—not now! I'll call you when the coast is clear."

"[silence]"

"Look, Thomas, if you don't call soon I'm going to scream. Really. *I'm going to scream.* It's eleven o'clock on Monday morning, and I'm having trouble concentrating on my work, so please don't do this to me, okay? I'm trying to work some things out and . . . I'm feeling more needy than usual, and I could really use some understanding . . . That's all I have to say. Bye for now, I hope."

"Just a reminder that the Benevolence Committee will be meeting at seven-thirty tonight instead of the usual six-thirty due to the ongoing plaster work in the basement. Look forward to seeing you there!"

then she saw, on the kitchen table, the *Boston Globe* opened to the Sunday weather page, a sure sign of Thomas, yes, but also that he wasn't home. Bethany took his place at the table for a while, looking at the weather map, trying to imagine what might have been going through his mind on Sunday, the last day that she had seen him. At Fellowship they had shared a moment by the coffee urn, murmuring about the size of the crowd (why hadn't she apologized for leaving in the middle of his sermon? For losing patience with Jessie's *squirming* and her *questions* and her *greedy little hands*), and Bethany's secret knowledge of that man in the Geneva gown, on an otherwise unremarkable morning, had turned her on even more than usual. Later, when the elder widows had corralled him with their canes, wheelchairs, and walkers, Jessie had suddenly appeared, running across the grass with chocolate on her face and crumbs in her hair, asking, "Mommy, can we stay all after-

---

"You're an asshole! I can't believe you're doing this to me! Someone better be sick or dying or *maimed*, otherwise your days with me are numbered! PICK UP THE PHONE, THOMAS. CALL ME."

"Hello, Father Mosher, this is, uhh, Guy from the 'Fix the Light' petition drive? When I stopped by the other day, you told me to call you early in the week. So I am [nervous laugh]. Uhh, we could really use your help in regards to getting signatures? For the town selectmen? When you have a sec, go ahead and drop me a line at [number deleted]."

"[in tears] I'm sorry, Thomas! I'm so sorry! Can you please forgive me because now I'm worried sick . . . If you're all right, Thomas, and I'm praying that you're just, for some reason, torturing me, listen—I'm begging you, Thomas, don't leave me! Not now, Thomas! Not ever! Please, Thomas, don't leave me!"

"[silence]"

"Nothing? Oh, God—"

"[silence]"

noon?" She could be so easy, sometimes. Thomas had left early, she remembered, and now it seemed strange to her—that he would cross the lawn to the parsonage without finding her to say his usual goodbye.

"Thomas?" she called at the bottom of the stairs. "Hello? Hello, Thomas?"

Up the narrow staircase she crept to the second floor, a landing with an easy chair set by the window, a dim hallway (still no decoration) with unused bedrooms for the pastor's family, a wood-paneled alcove, and, at the end of the hallway, the master bedroom, in afternoon shadow . . . She had suspected, and now she knew, that Thomas was a saint to live in such a state of deprivation: nowhere could she find the comforts of her affluent suburbia, the carpeting that muffled footsteps and uncertainty, the ducts releasing heat or, in the summer months, air-conditioning, regulating, in a matter of minutes, mood as well as temperature house-wide, the big-screen television with channels too numerous to consider, wired to a sound system to create a "home theater," all the major consolations, in short, available to the secular humanist. Thomas lived, by the looks of it, like a graduate student, surrounded by books and papers, and Bethany felt a sense of guilt just walking in, as if she had discovered something about the pastor meant to be hidden, yet, at the same time, she was thrilled to be close to him, or at least to this reflection of his soul—that's how she thought of his bedroom as she slowly walked the circumference, such simplicity and a peculiar neat disorder, the bed unmade as if in agony, a space heater, for God's sake, who still used space heaters? Ministers of the church, apparently, which might explain the *galoshes* she had seen downstairs, once wedded to the past, she guessed, outmoded products followed suit. Bethany sat down on the edge of the bed, expecting to sink on ancient springs, but the mattress, at least, was firm; she checked the label out of curiosity, a superficial impulse (she knew) that only broke her heart when she saw the brand name "Perfect Sleeper," what an incredible idea! An outpouring of affection for Thomas sent her sprawling on the yellow bedsheet, where she grasped for his memory as if it were something she could touch, a substance like skin, a body emanating warmth and sexuality like the man himself, her lover, who had promised her once—against his will—that he wouldn't leave her, not ever. She had never been able to watch him sleep! Now all she could do was clutch his bed as if it breathed, feeling Arminian about his absence and insatiable about his *prick*, far beyond, in any secular way, missing him.

And a strange thing happened: as the minutes passed she began to feel herself in a consoling grasp, some mysterious warmth that guided her, gently, to the floor before the pastor's bed, where she knelt, elbows on the mattress, in the *prayer position*, hands clasped, eyes shut tight, mind, as it was supposed to be, swept clear. She heard a ticking in the empty room. A truck drove by the parsonage in low gear, engine whining; adolescent laughter drifted over from the churchyard, upsetting the idyll of the afternoon. The warmth had deserted her now and she opened her eyes. How much time had passed, exactly? Why hadn't she been able to pray for his return? The bedroom had undergone a change, shadows deepening, the surroundings growing less, instead of more, familiar, and she felt the chill of unwelcoming air, as if the pastor's *soul* had disappeared.

What was the source of the pastor's case of melancholy? What inner sense divided him from Christ the savior and the fellowship of other men? Was there something in his character, the members of his congregation wondered after his disappearance, that had served to distance him from the same salvation he had elucidated in his Sunday sermons, promised in so many pastoral visits, conjured during his service of the Holy Communion with the invitation *Come, Holy Spirit, come, Bless this bread, and bless this fruit of the vine. Bless all of us in our eating and drinking at this table that our eyes may be opened, and we may recognize the risen Christ in our midst?* How could they begin to read his motivation in the rituals he had performed with some clumsiness, perhaps, but always with the purpose of a true believer? What about his written profile, a document so impressive that the members of the Search Committee had overlooked their first mandate, to fill the upstairs bedrooms of the parsonage, empty for so long now, with sleeping children? How would they ever come to understand this deeply spiritual man who had, without warning, abandoned them, or begin to heal their wounded hearts with His forgiveness?

In truth they knew little about the pastor's background, just what he revealed in his ambitious sermons, filled with scholarly investigations into the traditions of their faith (his symposium on Augustine's recently discovered Dolbeau sermons was considered to have been the first disaster under his leadership, sabotaged, some believed, by members of the Council who resented paying the airfare and expenses for the guest speaker, an Augustine scholar and practicing minister from France, whose arrogance and poor language skills hadn't helped), and those personal experiences that he let slip in private consultation—most would agree that *spiritual guidance* was his real talent—in order to provide solace for the worried, peace for the ailing, and understanding for the overly self-aware and borderline despairing. The members of the church knew that his mother had encouraged Thomas to join the ministry all throughout his childhood, creating a rift with his father, an engineer, jazz buff, and practical atheist (this from a sermon about dissent among the disciples titled "All in the Family"). They also knew that his father was a man of deep political convictions, having brought Thomas, as a boy, to a number of rallies and antiwar demonstrations ("Emerson, Gandhi, and Me") and that, when he passed away from a particularly virulent form of lung cancer ("Ashes to Ashes"), Thomas and his mother had followed his instructions and organized a memorial service without speakers or a eulogy—just a quartet from the Berklee School of Music playing Coltrane's *First Meditations* suite in its entirety: "Love," "Compassion," "Joy," "Consequences," and "Serenity." They knew, of course, that his mother was black and from the South, his father had been white and from New England—and they had gleaned (and furthermore intuited from life experience) that the Moshers' decision to live together and have a child of mixed parentage had been, at the time, a matter of great controversy ("Glass Houses," a brief mention in "Epiphany Moments" and "The Jesus You Thought You Knew"). And while it made a large faction in the church uncomfortable, they knew, as much as they ever would, that racism, even in the placid and more progressive bedroom communities like W————, was still an everyday reality: early in Thomas's tenure, a young couple, also African-American, had attended the Pilgrims' Church on two successive Sundays and, feeling encouraged, had joined the congregation at Fellowship, only to be asked, during an otherwise innocent conversation with the realtor Margaret Howard, "Are you kin?" Meaning *kin* to Thomas, the entirely unrelated pastor *of her own church*, and while the couple came again the following Sunday, showing no hard feelings, and had even made an appointment with Margaret to do some house hunting in the area, word of the question spread and eventually filtered back to Thomas and had *set him off*, becoming, in local lore, the "*Are You Kin?* Incident." The pastor had made this awkward question the subject of his most controversial sermon by far ("Kinship"), examining the racial laws under the Pharaohs that had viewed all Jews as inferior—and though his delivery that morning had been far from hostile, and the tone of the sermon, in retrospect, had seemed to those in attendance to be quite conciliatory, it was said that some members of the Council—allies of Margaret Howard, who was never mentioned by name but knew full well the power of implication—never forgave the minister for using her slip-up to score a political point and imperil her reputation as a business person.

This is what the congregation knew about the Reverend Thomas Mosher's background, supplemented by the usual amount of rumor and hearsay that swirls around a public figure, aided and abetted, in Thomas's case, by his melancholy bearing, handsome visage, unmarried status, and secretive nature. What the members of church *didn't* know about their pastor would torment them in the days following his disappearance, and would lead to widespread speculation about his whereabouts, causing some (but not all) to forget the substance of his message, and to wonder aloud if they'd ever been so disappointed in a man of faith, or so indifferent—when they should, by all rights, have been in agony—about his fate in Heaven and on earth.


"Good God," Margaret Howard let out under her breath without excusing herself, waiting in the aisle with Artemesia for a chance to shake the young minister's hand and compliment him on his first sermon, the substance of which, to be honest, had not exactly dazzled her. Right after Benediction she had extracted herself from the pew and leaned down to exchange a few words with Grace Hartigan, but before the widow could answer that would-be nurse had boxed her out with an insincere "excuse me" and spirited the widow off to the head of the line. Now Margaret was growing restless and annoyed with the Brooks children, one of whom, the girl with the harelip, was whining at her mother's side, while the twin boys, both hyperactive little thugs, wrestled in the aisle right under the nose of their father, just the kind of spineless man she could not abide, not for a minute, especially with his children running around unsupervised. Artemesia, dressed, as usual, in her Sunday sackcloth, seemed lost in religious ecstasy, staring up at Anne Hutchinson's window with that heretic's look in her eye.

"Are you aware of how she died?" Margaret asked, ready, at the same time, to cuff the Brooks twins and their father for disobedience and negligence, respectively, on such an important Sunday.

Artemesia had spent the morning trying desperately not to look up at her favorite saint in stained glass, the charismatic and headstrong merchant's wife who had nearly brought down the Massachusetts Bay Colony with her heresy trial, dressed, in the window, in a simple gown and clasping her personal Bible to her heart. The Sunday before, during Jane Groom's heartfelt "activist" sermon about the importance of recycling, Artemesia had been visited by the sensation that she was being watched, and immediately checked over her right shoulder expecting to catch the elder Swenson boy, Bernie, staring at her again, only to be confronted by the Puritan martyr, animated in her windowpane, gazing down on her with a beatific smile. Of course Artemesia knew how Anne Hutchinson had died!

"Indian massacre," she whispered, bowing her head out of respect for the dead, "at Hell's Gate. There was only one survivor."

"What on earth is going on at the front of the line?" Margaret asked, craning her neck to get a look at the Reverend Mosher. "Some of us have errands to run."

"I'm going to the supermarket," Artemesia said, leaving an open invitation for Margaret to come along. The Super Stop & Shop was a source of anxiety for her, beginning with the parking lot, acres wide and long, a chaotic mess of shopping carts and sport utility vehicles where she often lost track of her station wagon, while inside was no picnic either, a hangar-sized maze of looming shelves complete with a separate pharmacy, video store, and mini–Pizza Hut. Artemesia always wound up at the meat counter, gazing at the family packs of cube steaks and chicken thighs despite the uneasy feeling in her stomach, the butchered meat all rosy under plastic and arranged to please the eye.

"Oh, no, dear, Jerry does all the shopping now. I'm afraid he's out of his element in the supermarket, though. The man is always forgetting something."

"Aren't those boys getting handsome," Artemesia remarked, referring to the Brooks twins, currently engaged in a shoving match. Artemesia's oldest son was only twelve and already he could grow a mustache just like his father. From the beginning he had been a little man, all muscle and bravado, destroyer of everything complicated, fragile, or unwilling . . .

"God forgive me," Margaret said, "but right now I'd pay a pretty penny for their matching scalps."

"You don't mean that!"

Her friend's shock chastened Margaret. "No, I guess not. I let my temper get the best of me."

"Because I think they're darling."

"And so do I," Margaret said, trying, once again, to be more Christian about the whole thing. Already the usher Silva had calmed the boys down by hissing at them through his dentures. "I'm just not sure how I feel about wrestling matches in the Lord's house."

Up close Margaret thought the minister was a little short, perhaps, just over five foot nine, certainly a handsome man and not *too black*, she noticed. In her opinion his coloring seemed just about right, and his eyes, behind somewhat sleepy lids, had an intelligent sparkle to them, a quality that Margaret had always found attractive. Say what you would about Jerry, as a young man he had been all spunk, the kind of man who could flirt openly with a married woman and charm her husband at the same time. Margaret introduced herself to the Reverend Mosher again and thanked him for the inspiring words, making sure to check the condition of his fingernails, by far the best indicator, she believed, of a man's character. Years of building business relationships had taught her a secret or two about human nature, and the ways we have of unintentionally revealing ourselves to others. The Reverend Mosher's fingernails looked fine, though his handshake, on the limp side, needed work if he wanted to inspire confidence in his leadership abilities. She saw no reason for the minister to be single at, what, thirty-one? Even if his last pastorate had been in nowheresville Rhode Island, couldn't he have found a good woman in the congregation? Without a wife at his side and a family in the works, this minister was going to be a real *liability*, and Margaret questioned the wisdom of the Council in calling him to Pilgrims' Church, still reeling from the Reverend Chambers's unexpected retirement in May and move to some kind of New Age retreat in Scottsdale, Arizona—though she had been relieved when

Jane Groom, in a surprising act of *realism,* had asked to have her name removed from the Search Committee's short list.

"I hope you're enjoying your stay," Margaret told the Reverend Mosher, meanwhile angling for the door. Artemesia's timid nature had kept them at the end of the line and she was not one to waste her life standing around.

"Very much," the Reverend Mosher answered, "thank you. You have quite a congregation here."

"Artemesia, go ahead and introduce yourself."

"If you'd given me the chance," Artemesia began.

"I'll be right outside," Margaret let her know. "Wonderful to see you again, Reverend Mosher."

"And you, Mrs. Harpswell."

"The name is *Howard,*" she corrected him.

"Forgive me, Mrs. Howard."

"Yes, of course." She reminded Artemesia over her shoulder, "Be quick, now."

*Oh, my,* Artemesia thought, feeling Godly vibrations in the company of the young minister, *this is the one! He's come from a distance to rescue us!* The church had grown quiet by then, the rest of the congregation, and its invited guests, having retreated to the lawn for Fellowship. Artemesia trembled in his company. The sunlight in the doorway, at that moment, seemed bright enough to burn through her dress and reveal her soul to the eyes of the world.

"Are you happy in Rhode Island?" she asked, having summoned the courage to speak.

"It's a good church," the minister said, "with extraordinary people. We're a few miles outside of Pawtucket. Have you been there?"

"Never," she answered, still aware of the burning light.

"I find it peaceful. The ocean is a short drive away."

"But are you happy?" she boldly asked.

The minister hesitated for a moment before he answered, "It's a depressed area. *He is the joy of the upright of heart.*"

How she fell for him at that moment! Tired of the assistant pastor with her well-meaning certainties, her love of all creatures great and small, her prayers for the woods and sermons about using the right recycling buckets, green for newspaper and magazines, blue for glass and most forms of plastic . . . Thomas Mosher had *hesitated* before he spoke to her, and in this hesitation Artemesia had sensed a great pain in his heart, the essence, she felt, of the religious experience—hadn't the Puritan Thomas Shepard of Cambridge, whose writings she had studied at the local public library when she sought to join the Pilgrims' Church, counseled his parishioners to "doubt thyself much"? Her husband doubted *nothing* about himself, that much was clear: he wore far too much cologne, applied an aerosol fixative to his hairstyle until it had the strength of a helmet, forbade talking at the dinner table so he could eat "in peace," didn't know a thing about foreplay, spent a fortune on a game for which he was ill suited—golf—and set his pager on "vibrate" because he claimed it was good for his prostate. Artemesia's trembling had quieted by now, and in the interim she had become planted to her spot, waiting for the minister's direction, her face, she hoped, showing no evidence of her inward smile.

"What a morning," he said, nodding toward the sunlight. Was that a bead of sweat running down his cheek? Had the vibrations they were obviously sharing become too much for him?

"Yes, it's lovely."

A blessed silence passed between them; Artemesia imagined her patron saint Anne Hutchinson shifting in her Colonial dress and approving of their union with a simple nod.

"I should play some politics outside," the minister told her candidly. Such an honest face! And freckles too! "Care to join me?"

"Oh, I'm afraid not. On Sundays after church . . . well, it's not that exciting, really." Oh, the shameful timidity! "I usually do the weekly food shopping for my family."

"Why don't I follow you out, then," he said, and ushered her, before she realized what was happening, through the gaping doorway and into daylight. She descended the wheelchair ramp out of reflex, an indirect route, perhaps, but while crossing over its pressure-treated frame (donated by her husband's lumberyard) she intoned a prayer for the handicapped and for the elderly, a little rushed that morning, with the soon-to-be pastor—how she hoped!—following close on her heels. Margaret had been waiting by her Cadillac all that time and motioned to her wildly across the parking lot. At the bottom of the ramp Artemesia stopped and said goodbye to their visitor.

"I hope you'll stay with us," she said, bracing herself for the inevitable, a piercing whistle that Margaret produced by blowing through her fingers and reserved for Artemesia and her useless husband, Jerry. The usher Silva had set up the refreshment table on the lawn and a much larger crowd than usual was milling around, the children having shed the outer layers of their Sunday best to ruin their appetites with cookies and play a nonconfrontational variant of tag. Artemesia's sons attended church only on holidays, and even then they usually went to the Orthodox service with their grandmother, who secreted them off to her apartment afterward to fill their stomachs with Keftedes and their impressionable ears with bile.

"And so do I."

The whistle! So sharp the young minister winced in pain and the congregation, busy renewing acquaintanceships and catching up on family news, fell quiet. A dog in the neighborhood started barking in response, and Artemesia heard someone say, "I wish she wouldn't do that." Was it Lucia Wagner, Margaret's sworn enemy on the Grounds Committee? Or Sadie Maxwell, the leather merchant, who refused to mark down her handbags after the Christmas holiday? Artemesia took her leave and suffered the humiliation of hurrying over to Margaret in front of everyone. It was a great sin, she believed, to be so full of pride as to concern herself with the opinions of the congregation, and she felt perfectly easy as she crossed the parking lot to Margaret's Cadillac, in full submission to the will of God.

 The members of the Pilgrims' Church had wel comed Bethany Caruso from the beginning, but she often wondered, during the months of her ini- tiation, if they fully practiced their Redeemer's love; in fact, the congregation's less admirable qualities had convinced her that, without her attraction to the Reverend Thomas Mosher, or, to be more accurate, their *mutual fascination,* she would have given up on her religious Awakening in its early stages and returned to life as a satis- fied—albeit medicated—agnostic. Bethany's parents had bap- tized her in the Episcopal Church, and they had taken great pains to drag her and her three surly brothers to worship every Sunday. They were a ragged, disorganized family that must have been mortifying to behold in full flower: Jonathan, the el- dest, suffered from a sleep addiction and dozed off like clock- work when their rector launched into his sermon; Nate, the "difficult" second child, refused to kneel when ritual called for it, and spoke openly of dousing the Everlasting Flame with Holy Water; quiet Lewis, tormented by hard-ons, hadn't been

able to accept communion once his hormones started firing; and Bethany, the youngest child—a midlife "mistake"—had been forced to sit between her parents for protection, and spent most of her time each Sunday morning deflecting dirty looks and fugitive pinches from her flesh and blood. Bethany's parents had divorced when she was twelve, blaming the pressures of family life and the rector of their church for his inadequate counseling, and in the difficult aftermath, both her parents, wounded by the swiftness and finality of their breakup, had sworn off organized religion of any kind. None of the children complained—Bethany and her brothers found a bitter freedom in having single parents, shuttling back and forth between the Newton house, which their mother kept in the settlement, and their father's apartment in Brookline, using one set of rules to gain concessions from the other, manipulating the strained relationship between their parents for revenge and profit. As a teenager Bethany had been polite, studious, and wild, leading a reckless life on weekends that included boyfriends from second-tier local colleges (Babson, BU, Tufts) and drinking games with Southern Comfort, the delinquent's liquor of choice at her high school, Newton South. An unattributed pregnancy—and quickie abortion—straightened her out in time for college, where, during her junior year, she met the reliable Bobby Caruso and settled down, but why? This she could never quite figure out, not then, when her friends had tried to talk her out of getting married before she received her degree, and not fifteen years later, when she found herself with two children, a troubled marriage, a job she couldn't bear but needed for the paycheck, and the sinking feeling that something essential was missing from her life, an unnamed product that no department store carried on its shelves, and no credit card, however large the spending limit, could buy.

Enter God, or at least the first New England meetinghouse she saw when she drove through Old Town, kids strapped in back, on the errand runs that filled her weekends with despair. Sleepovers, birthday parties, movie rentals, trips to the drive-thru cleaners, grocery shopping—she was forever dropping things off and picking other things up with her car running, losing one child for the night just to gain four others who were not her own, exchanging vast sums of money for disposable goods and lamenting the passage of time . . . Would she ever experience the fabled state of Peace & Quiet? A moment to reflect on her place in the world and—dare she consider it—the meaning of life? She had tried a program of meditation and beginner's Yoga at the local Women's Center and *it sucked!* Just be honest, she thought, and call it Hippie Aerobics, that way no one would be disappointed when they failed to find nirvana in their Danskins, contorted on a smelly mat beside a stranger in a strip mall. *Exhale into a spinal twist. Good, now gently turn around.* The chanting Yoga instructor with her little pigtails and perfect posture had so annoyed Bethany that she found herself slowing down when she passed the Pilgrims' Church, checking the time and subject of the Sunday sermon, posted each week on a wooden sign that faced the road.

She skipped "Summer Impressions, Part I" (10:30) because it sounded too "arty," and "Summer Impressions, Part II" (10:30) because she was out of town. Finally "A Love Supreme" (seasonal time change, 11:00) brought her to the doorway of Christendom on a rainy September morning. Bethany peered inside and let her eyes adjust to the gloom. She had come early to escape the house, and there were a number of empty pews to choose from. The few parishioners already there talked quietly while the organist worked his way through a dramatic instrumental that shook the walls. Bethany settled into a seat near the back, looking up at the stained-glass windows and recognizing the Puritan dress, but none of the grim-looking subjects. Now she knew that Carlo and Lucia Wagner had come down the aisle holding hands, as always, and taken a pew near the front; first the husband, then the wife, had turned back and caught her eye, murmuring something between them, sharing a look, it seemed, of pleasant surprise. The Swensons had arrived next and Bethany shrank a little in her seat, hoping that they wouldn't notice her right away—she had forgotten that her neighbors worshipped at the Congregational church, and she wanted to be anonymous that morning, a stranger in the house of God.

The Swensons had recently finished building a sauna in their backyard, and just the day before Bobby had brought a pair of binoculars up from his "workshop" so Devon could spy on them. "Nudity!" Devon had cried, leading Bobby to put down the newspaper, usually grafted to his hands all weekend, and join him at the kitchen window.

"That's sick," Bobby had said, "they've got the whole family in there together, even little Pele—"

"*Dad*," Devon had whined, jumping up and down with excitement, "it's *my turn* now."

The Swensons had dressed neatly for worship and didn't recognize Bethany until the church had filled to half capacity and the service was about to begin. The children waved at her in unison across the aisle; Piotr, an ageless sixty-five, fond of big straw hats and a corncob pipe, had given her a neighborly thumbs-up sign. She waved back reluctantly and lowered her gaze. And to think that Thomas had so underwhelmed her on that first morning! She had been surprised, at first, to find a black minister preaching in Old Town, and she had followed his direction as best she could, repeating her part of the Call to

Worship printed in the morning's program, mumbling her way through the unfamiliar hymns, answering, from her seat, the Assurance of Pardon, all the while watching the minister for signs of personality, the special bearing or creative spark that separated the talented clergy from the dull; he must have something special, she thought, to be leading a congregation at his age (which she figured to be thirty) and at this time, when complacency and conservatism had overtaken the politics of Massachusetts, once considered, by outsiders, a People's Republic.

But his sermon had been a snooze! Mixing recollections of his childhood with a meditation on a Psalm about the wicked, how they scoffed at their adversaries and boasted about their accomplishments, thinking that God had gone into hiding—an important point, Bethany thought, but hardly *revolutionary*, and Thomas's delivery that morning had been inept: he stumbled through the language as if in darkness, tripping over his words, losing his place on the page so that his ideas were often punctuated by an awkward silence. Ten minutes into the sermon the pews began to creak, yet the minister preached on without improvement, turning back to the nature of the Psalmist, and on, meanwhile Bethany's thoughts had turned to Bobby, or at least a version of him that she enjoyed thinking of, the tender young husband, who had insisted, one memorable night, on *going down on her* even though she had claimed she didn't like it—how could she have known?—because it seemed, well, *sloppy*, and made her feel uncomfortable; afterward, when an unprecedented orgasm had rocked her world, Bethany held his grinning face in her hands and loved him, she remembered clearly now, *loved him so much* that her feelings had overwhelmed the present tense and opened a window into their future together, when his hair, already thinning, would follow the stencil of male-pattern baldness, his cheeks would swell with pasta and prosperity, and thick black hair would sprout from places that she wouldn't want to think about—yet she had believed, then, that his transformation into middle age wouldn't bother her, not when he could bring her such a feeling of release, make such a home for her in that confusing place, her own body . . . Thomas had fixed her attention again with his conclusion, quoting Ezekiel 37:5, "Behold, I will cause breath to enter into you, and you shall live," comparing this living breath to the spirit that moved through John Coltrane (hence the sermon's title) and then, with a look of great sadness, he had stepped down from the pulpit and joined the rest of the congregation, standing now, for the singing of the closing hymn, led by the choir, which had been languishing on the balcony throughout. Bethany's bones ached from a mixture of boredom and lust, and she felt a twinge of guilt for not knowing the lyrics, when so many around her, even the children, sang clearly, if without conviction, along with the Pilgrims' Chorus.

After the service ended, an ad hoc welcoming committee, chaired by Piotr Swenson, greeted her in the aisle, and her neighbor enfolded her in his arms, purring something about seeing the light at last. She had wanted to protest, explain to him that she had come as a mere experiment and couldn't imagine a Faith or a Community that she would join—her family and job were quite enough, thank you, she had no room for God, who, come to think of it, *was* hiding pretty effectively from the world and its problems, but she had kept her mouth shut, stepping back from Piotr's embrace and greeting his wife, also named Ulla, who kissed her on the cheek, and the children, who shook her hand politely, beginning with the oldest, Bernie, with his buzz cut, and homely Elka with her hand-knit cardigan, and handsome little Pele in a pint-sized suit and tie. Others had greeted her too, although she couldn't remember them now, and it seemed as if she had been carried down the aisle by their goodwill, although someone (Lucia Wagner?) made an apologetic comment about the pastor "finding himself," and intimated that he was better skilled at offering private counsel. It bothered her that Thomas remembered the moment they met in the entryway so vividly, when she recalled almost nothing: just that it had started raining again, and she had left her car at the far end of the church parking lot, having thought the downpour to be over, and the pastor, attractive or not, had been an obstacle on her way out. "I fell in love with you *at once*," he told her much later, after the affair had been consummated in their minds, first, and then with their bodies, and their lives, once so separate, were inevitably bound. Bethany thought it strange that, while Thomas had been choosing her to dwell in his heart, and risk his standing in the pastorate, her mind had been on the weather, and it would be months before she suspected anything of the kind.

"Why are you here?"

The question had taken Bethany by surprise, and haunted her after her first interview with the pastor, arranged with great difficulty in the weeks that followed her visit to the Pilgrims' Congregational Church. She didn't know exactly what had driven her to show up for that particular Sunday sermon, other than her vague sense that something *was not right*, and she didn't know why she had called the church office twice, leaving messages on the answering machine (Thomas hadn't answered the first time), finally getting a callback at work late one afternoon, her department in the midst of a minor crisis. Because of space problems they had packed some older files and shipped them off-site, but now her supervisor needed them for an internal audit, and the storage company had no record of the transaction, or so they claimed. The caper of the missing personnel files! As if she didn't have enough useless paperwork in her life already. She had been on hold with the surly storage people when Anita buzzed her on the intercom and said, "There's a priest or something on the line."

"Can I call him back?" Bethany asked, and returned to Office Retention's twenty-four-hour hot line, currently piping in Rush Limbaugh for the benefit of its neglected callers, something she found shocking. Did they want people to hang up, or what? Anita buzzed her a minute later, and she was happy to leave the pathetic meanderings of Limbaugh's tiny mind.

"He says now is the best time for a conversation," Anita delivered with a deep sense of weariness, as if she lost a piece of herself each time she answered a call. Bethany asked her to deal with the retentive people at Retention and picked up the pastor's line herself.

"*Why are you here?*" Thomas asked in the church office, looking squarely over her right shoulder, the stairwell outside ringing with footsteps and, from the floor below, the cheerful preamble to a Debtors Anonymous meeting, one of the many services that the congregation offered to the community. Thomas sat across from her in a patterned sweater he would later call his "Bill Cosby" after its warm and fuzzy nature and prohibitive price. Bethany had been beyond the reach of subliminal messages, however, and she stammered for a moment before she answered his question.

"I'm curious," she said. "That's why I'm here."

This seemed to satisfy the pastor, who leaned back in his desk chair and continued to study the wall behind her. She turned halfway around to see what the excitement was, found nothing, and faced the pastor again. *Say something!* she wanted to cry out, but managed, out of courtesy, to keep her mouth shut. She had experience dealing with deliberate "slow talkers" at work—in fact, her company specialized in hiring men with this fatal flaw, and just one, with the attending drawl and taste for pregnant pauses, could hold her hostage for what seemed like hours at a time. But this was not Thomas's problem: his trouble with "A Love Supreme" had been the result of a temporary slump, and that very Sunday he would give a flawless sermon about truth in politics or the lack thereof (with Bethany in audience), and his uneasiness that evening, with the last of the Debtors filing in downstairs and taking full advantage of the free coffee, was not about stupidity, or a lack of professionalism, but *overwhelming love*—

"Well, that makes two of us," the pastor said, "curiosity between strangers being, ummm, sort of pronounced."

"And how are you curious, exactly?"

"You came to our church," Thomas answered, "and then you called to set up a meeting with me, so there must be something on your mind." He finally looked at her straight-on. "Am I on the right track so far?"

"So far," she said, "yes."

"I know why you're here," he announced, charming her, despite the presumption, with the hint of a smile.

"This should be good," she answered with some sarcasm.

"May I go on?"

"Why not," she told him.

"You're here," he continued, "because God willed it to be that way. An Infinite Wisdom brought you here, and that, as far as I'm concerned, is the simple part." Bethany had expected something along these lines, and she kept quiet while the pastor finished, looking past *his* shoulder now and out the window as the sunlight drained from Old Town. Soon the leaves on the stately row of maple trees behind the church would turn and fall, and the crew from Homeless Helpers, hired on a trial basis, would rake them into piles and set them aflame with lighter fluid, trying to roast marshmallows, a misguided effort that brought complaints from the neighbors and a visit from the police department; when the Helpers saw the flashing blue lights they scattered, leaving behind the sticky remnants of their ritual, and so many cigarette butts that the volunteer members of the Grounds Committee would still be picking them out of the grass the following summer. "The hardest part is yet to come. You might decide to hear another sermon, or sit in on a Bible class, or bring your family [here the wounded tone in the pastor's voice had attracted her attention away from the twilight] to the Autumn Fest for homemade apple pie. But will you come back?" The longing in his eyes! She had imagined a more confident pitch for her soul, including, perhaps, the subtle mention of some Hellfire, or whatever innuendo passed for Eternal Damnation in the age of Wellness, but this was something else entirely.

"I'm curious," he wound up, "about what I can do to make the Pilgrims' Church more user-friendly, without sacrificing the depth of our Covenant. *Bethany, I want you to stay with us.*"

After the interview she virtually stumbled out of the church office, carrying her briefcase down the aisle while the pastor followed her, pointing out the pipe organ, which had some historical significance, and the stained-glass windows, darkened now; the world outside seemed to have fallen quiet, and Bethany couldn't wait to get back outside to her car, and away from this unexpectedly intimate encounter with a man of the cloth.

"God be with you," Thomas called after her as she descended the wheelchair ramp, lit by a single spotlight.

"*Thanks,*" she said, a response that would seem lame to her when she thought about it on Route 102, stuck in late commuter traffic, waiting for the interminable light to change. What was she supposed to say? *And also with you?* The pastor had thrown her off with his disarmingly honest opening question, and from that moment on her mind had been swimming . . .

At home that night she avoided questions about where she'd been and instead gave Bobby a hard time about bringing home pizza (again), even though the pediatrician thought Jessie might be lactose-intolerant. The three of them had already eaten and made a perfunctory attempt at cleaning up the kitchen, leaving Bethany a single crooked slice of pizza in the box. Bobby and Devon were playing Nintendo Golf in the living room, while Jessie had gone upstairs to play with her stuffed animals. Bethany had carried the box of Chardonnay from the refrigerator to the table, siphoning off enough to fill a water glass. The pizza slice they had left her was missing half of its pepperoni and she considered it for a while, letting the wine sedate her first, before she forced this slab of "food" into her stomach. The longer she watched her pathetic dinner sitting in its box, the more remote her appetite felt, and Jessie, all sweetness and bodily function, saved her from having to eat by calling from the top of the stairs. "I need help in the toilet, someone!"

"Not me," Devon scoffed, lying on his belly, just like his father, eyes tuned to the enormous Trinitron. Bethany lectured them endlessly about giving equal time to Jessie, who couldn't survive without watching her Disney tapes at least once every forty-eight hours, but they never listened. Every game of Nintendo seemed to carry the weight of their entire lives.

"Should I go, hon?" Bobby asked from the other room, an offer that struck Bethany as unusually generous.

"That would be nice," she told him, closing her eyes. The

kitchen had started rotating pleasantly and she wanted to experience Chardonnay's sweet merry-go-round in darkness.

"But, Dad," Devon whined, "this is match play."

"Help me," Jessie whimpered.

"Can it wait until I finish the hole?" Bobby asked, undoing whatever good he might have done in making the offer.

"Just forget it," Bethany said, opening her eyes and standing up so quickly that she became light-headed. She grabbed the chair for balance and called upstairs to Jessie, "Mommy's coming in a second!"

"You're a peach," Bobby told her.

"Asshole," she countered under her breath.

"Hey," she heard Devon say, "nice putt."

At her weaker moments, when Bethany felt that she existed under a black cloud, that her unhappiness at work and selfishness as a wife and mother had somehow poisoned her house, she tried to remind herself of the sacrifices she had made for the sake of her family, and the areas of mothering for which she had shown unusual patience and an obvious talent. This much was true: she loved both of her children equally. Devon had been an easy baby to get along with, sleeping through the night and smiling through his waking hours almost from day one, while Jessie, to put it bluntly, had been a horror: sickly, fussy, loud, spiteful, sleepless, and inconsolable through it all. During her "terrible twos," however, something inside Jessie had softened and she became a thoughtful and affectionate child, fond of storybooks and belly kisses, bubble baths and family trips to the Museum of Science. Devon, at that age, had turned destructive and unexpectedly sour, shouting "No!" whenever he was spoken to, and bonding only with his Tonka trucks, which he would cuddle and speak to as if they were human, then toss from the top of his bunk bed or kick all the way across the backyard. Watching her children grow had opened Bethany's eyes to the varieties of human behavior, and the endless act of creativity that is childhood.

And if she had accomplished one step of their education without flaw, sent her children into the world with a single skill that would set them apart from their peers at school, it was toilet training. Simply put, Bethany was a genius with the family potty. She had discovered her talent quite by accident when Devon, at twenty months, began to show an interest in the nondescript potty seat she had installed in his room a few months earlier, hoping to bring an end to her diapering duties. On, off, wipe, on, off, wipe—it was an unending cycle, and Bobby had been an incompetent helper. From Devon's first, tentative moments with the potty seat she had followed Dr. Spock's directions carefully, letting him familiarize himself with the equipment fully clothed, and gradually introducing him to the idea that he might want to take his pants off and climb aboard whenever he heard nature's whistle call. Devon had shown periods of resistance, whining and sputtering away from self-sufficiency (just like a man!), but she had done the right thing by waiting patiently until instinct took over again and he ascended the potty without her help—and then she had showered him with grown-up compliments. My God, what a little dupe! Mother had crushed him, and within the year he was flushing happily all by himself. Jessie, too, had been a pliant student; at two years she was already familiar with the wiping mantra "front to back," and she even had a vague idea as to why ("Girls only!" she would shout). Jessie had taken special pleasure in graduating from diapers to training pants, and in the rare event of an "accident"—which Bethany took in stride—she had quietly rededicated herself to Mother's goal, that her children should lead independent digestive lives.

The experience of so many smears and stains protected Bethany as she climbed the stairs that night, unaware of what disaster she might find behind the bathroom door. In the end the emergency was minor: Jessie had been scared, more than anything else, by the way her intestines reacted to the pizza, and she had made it to the open toilet seat as soon as nature struck—and hard. Mommy's little girl didn't smell like strawberries anymore! Still she would have to be cleaned up, and Bethany instructed her to strip and stand in one place for as long as she could manage. Jessie always seemed much happier when her clothes were off (just like her father), and while Bethany, on her knees, disinfected her sensitive skin with Baby Wipes, she lifted her arms over her head and sang the chorus from Disney's "Under the Sea" in a fake-calypso voice, trying to mimic Sebastian the lobster. Anything by Disney so overexcited Jessie that soon she was running in place and squealing, and Bethany had been forced to give up.

"Thanks!" she yelled as she ran nude from the bathroom, leaving Bethany with a pile of slightly foul laundry. Bobby chose that moment to come upstairs and "contribute" to the running of the house, hovering outside the bathroom door with his usual cowardice. Anything scatological, as a rule, sent him into the garage, where he kept his *Penthouse* collection in a storage tub, or down into the basement workshop, where, she knew as a fact, he drank beer and ate Pringles on the couch.

"Can I help?" he asked, afraid to show himself.

She surprised him with Jessie's laundry, dropping it in his arms and directing him to the hamper in the mudroom. His expression told the tale of a middle manager required, all of a sudden, to do something unpleasant *himself*, and the power of speech deserted him. Bobby turned and headed back downstairs in full retreat. *It serves you right*, she thought, considering he spent the bulk of his time "managing" other people and organizing hypothetical "projects" which usually came to nothing. The company was forever sending him away for two weeks at a time on short notice, leaving her with the same job and even more work to do around the house. And judging by her workload they were forever hiring more just like him, ineffectual white men with résumés that cried out HELPLESS WITHOUT SECRETARY AND/OR WIFE, FORMERLY MOTHER while Bethany and her mostly minority colleagues in Human Resources made their lives easy, spelling out retirement plans far superior to their own in plain English, filing forms directly with Payroll, who were unbelievably rude, computing vacation days to their fullest advantage, none of which these cookie-cutter husbands with their Strip-O-Grams and Sky Pagers deserved. Okay, perhaps she was exaggerating this last part, but Bobby's face when confronted with his daughter's *shit-smeared laundry* filled her with contempt, and, more important, revealed the depth of his willed indifference to the small realities of life.

And imagine, Bobby had had the nerve in bed that night to reach across her back and pinch her nipple! She had stayed up late after seeing the children to bed and scrubbed the kitchen, then made her rounds through the downstairs picking up debris and turning off the plain blue television screen, the very essence, she reflected, of suburban life. She balled up the empty Doritos bag nearby, and, out of spite, threw away her husband's beloved "chip-clip" too—just looking at this hopeless "invention" made her heart sink even lower, reminding her of all the stale men eating crispy snacks that would only clog their arteries and further slow their reaction time. She could see Bobby already, searching through the kitchen drawers and cabinets, yelling because he thought she was in the other room, "Have you seen the chip-clip, honey?"

And this snack-obsessed *moron* had just pinched her nipple!

She had climbed into bed long after Bobby, hoping that she had lost him to his recurring erotic dream about the flat-chested lifeguard on *Baywatch* (she had forced it out of him during a session of couples counseling), but as soon as the lights had gone out and she was breathing faintly and evenly with sleep almost in sight . . . the *pinch*! What an act of utter carelessness, leaving Bethany no other choice but to give him a sharp, enlightening elbow in the side.

"Hey," he said, "what gives?"

"I was almost asleep," she told him.

"That hurt, you know."

"And my nipple is a *sex button*?"

"Christ," he said, rolling away.

"Just go to sleep, Bobby."

"Okay," he answered, "jeez."

She blamed Bobby and his unrealistic sex drive for forcing her into playing the role of "frigid wife," because she was not, by any honest definition, frigid. Her sexuality may have become, after fifteen years of marriage and two children, a wizened animal, but Jesus it was *full of life*, and subjected her, on a regular basis, to random aches, throbs, flashes, and bouts of "the itch," never mind the generalized longing that often swelled like a string section inside the theater of her heart. A few months earlier she had carried on a near-affair with Allen Weinglass, a Title VII specialist and the only decent-looking man in her department, initiated (and by him, she reminded herself) with an exchange of flirtatious E-mail messages that had made her blush even as she knew their banter was desperately unoriginal; they had consumed each message just to delete it by mutual agreement, trying to reduce the evidence, which might have brought them trouble (who knew what power was transcribing their binary conversation? The risk, she had to admit, was fairly exhilarating), and soon they were arranging awkward encounters in the kitchenette ("Just you and me," Allen would remark, standing uneasily in the doorway, his jacket shed, sleeves rolled up to his elbows, while Bethany, also jacketless, would cross her arms and lean against the dishwasher, hoping he would stay, hoping he would go away), until the near-affair took on a life of its own, and escalated beyond E-mail and innuendo to a date for cocktails at the Parker House downtown, with a room upstairs awaiting their decision to *close the deal*, as Bobby liked to say. Bethany had breezed into the lobby that night feeling, if anything, disgusted by the symmetry of the thing, and bothered by this room that Allen had booked so eagerly, without her consent; and Allen had proved himself to be a snake, rising from his high-backed chair to greet her with an affected wink, a standard compliment, and a kiss too heavy on the saliva—at that very moment it had ended, with a hotel room, a wink, and a sloppy kiss, because having an affair with Allen Weinglass, she realized, was madness: she would have been forced to quit her job rather than face him every day, and, all reason aside, though she had wanted him seriously for a while, she loathed him, yes, that was it, she *loathed Allen Weinglass*, and the attraction of an affair had worn off long before their scheduled meeting at the Parker House, which she abruptly ended in the middle of her first glass of wine, leaving him alone with his single malt and his workplace fantasy unrealized. "Hey, what's this?" Allen asked in protest, bolting up from his chair and knocking over their candle. "Bethany, what's this?" The jilted almost-lover of a mostly faithful wife causes a minor scene in the bar of a faded luxury hotel that was slated to be demolished! "Follow me," she called over her shoulder, "and regret it." The bartender had really chuckled over that one. *Life can be so cruel*, she thought, walking through the revolving door and out to Boylston Street, topcoat in her arms and her mistake regrouping in the bar, finishing his scotch and sweeping up the honey-roasted nuts he had spilled all over the table, wondering, she thought, where his seduction technique had failed him. Bethany had absolved herself from guilt by the time she reached the end of the block, and walked in a sort of daze until she found her minivan; but a stranger in downtown Boston, acting as an agent, she decided, of divine retribution, had smashed the window on her driver's side into a thousand tiny pieces, stealing the manufacturer-installed tape deck, the first-generation mobile phone that she had inherited from Bobby, her hateful briefcase (after dumping out the paperwork—foiled!), and, she would realize later, when it suddenly became vitally important to Devon's well-being, a half-inflated soccer ball. Why couldn't they have relieved her of the paperwork too? She had lied to Bobby that night and told him the break-in had taken place outside the mall, and as for Allen Weinglass, a few months later he had received a job offer in North Carolina and handed in his notice, informing Bethany in a brisk E-mail and adding that he had spoken to her supervisor and requested that his exit interview be performed by someone else.

Truth be told, Bethany didn't think of the pastor much in the days following their first interview. Work and Family quickly reasserted their dominance over God, and on Sunday morning Bethany had awakened without the intention of going back to church, and felt, instead, an old familiar tenderness for Bobby, lying on his back with his mouth wide open, not snoring so much as *inflating* and *deflating* with the sound of a balloon. Overnight he had mostly extracted himself from his pajamas, and from the peaceful way he slept, she guessed that he was languishing, at that moment, with his favorite lifeguard. A cursory search with her right hand turned up his morning hard-on and she figured, *Why the hell not?* For once she would let her husband meet the day in the throes of orgasm, and within a minute or so Bobby was wide awake (though still supine) and thanking her in a whisper, cupping her head in both his hands and making all kinds of obscene promises . . .

"Mommy!" Jessie yelled, having thrown the bedroom door open, watching as her parents quickly rearranged themselves beneath the covers. "I want pancakes!"

"The way it works, Jessie," Bobby told her, doing a remarkable job of controlling his anger, "is you *knock* first, and then, if we're feeling up to it, we invite you to come inside." He buttoned his pajama top with some reluctance. "Is that clear?"

She frowned at him.

"Are you listening to me?" he asked again, playing the stern disciplinarian for once.

"Yes," Jessie answered, still frowning, and turned to Bethany for support. "Can you make pancakes, Mommy?"

"Just be patient," she said, already exasperated by the morning's events. The suggestion of pancake batter had sent her desire crawling back into its underground system of tunnels. *Please*, she thought, *no one say* bacon. "Your mom's a little slow on Sundays, remember?"

"Pancakes!" her daughter yelled, running off in her Dr. Denton's and leaving Bethany in the unenviable position of having to face, for the second time that morning, her husband's involuntary hard-on. A tentative daylight shined through the underlayers of their custom window treatments, and while Bobby fumed and rustled in the insulated silence of the master bedroom, waiting for Jessie to reach the bottom of the staircase, Bethany prepared herself for the next request. Who knows shame and guilt so intimately, she wondered, as the dutiful suburban wife?

"Well?" her husband asked.

"I don't know, Bobby."

"C'mon, Beth, I was *so close*," he lied.

"Look, if the moment's gone—"

"Don't say that!"

"I'm sorry," she said, climbing out of bed and heading for the bathroom, "but the thought of making pancakes for everybody sort of turns me off."

"So make muffins," he suggested.

"*That* I won't respond to."

"Oh, Beth, c'mon—"

She closed the bathroom door behind her, letting out a well-earned *Christ*, and headed straight for the medicine cabinet and her Zoloft.

Halfway through the breakfast preparations, with Jessie running in demented circles around the kitchen table, Devon transfixed by professional wrestling in the TV room, and Bobby moping around the house without offering to help, Bethany was overcome with the desire to *get out* and gathered her family in the kitchen to respectfully inform them that (1) if they wanted pancakes they would have to finish making them without her, because (2) she was leaving the house for a few hours to visit a Congregational church, that's right, go by herself to a *house of worship* in order to spend an hour or so contemplating the spiritual side of life, which, she suggested, the rest of them could stand to think about more often, instead of depending so heavily on Mother for everything from grilled-cheese sandwiches (Bobby, Devon) to reassuring hugs (Devon, Jessie) to the bedtime stories that would carry them off to sleep at night (Jessie), and (3) if they had any questions or comments about her morning respite from the family, she would answer them in due time. Only Bobby looked distressed by her announcement, asking, in his most helpless voice, if she knew where he could find the griddle, while Devon had shrugged and cut out of her speech early, worried about the outcome of a wrestling match. Sweet Jessie, in her Mermaid pj's, had merely asked, "Can I come with you next time?" showing a restraint that Bethany admired as she climbed the stairs to get dressed for church, and deepening her sense of guilt—this time for going ballistic on her entire family, especially the children, who, at eleven and four, respectively, couldn't exactly be held accountable for ignoring their spiritual lives. What had she been thinking? Well, she realized, at least I'll have something to confess this time . . . After rushing through her morning cleansing rituals (skipping the makeup round) Bethany had come downstairs to find Bobby flipping the long-awaited pancakes, and trying, without much success, to normalize the situation. Jessie sat at the table squeezing a bottle of syrup over her short stack.

"How are the pancakes?" Bobby asked loud enough for Devon to hear him in the TV room.

"Mine are gooey in the middle!" Jessie offered.

"Well, I'm sorry about that. And you, Devon?"

"They're kind of pathetic, Dad."

"Dad makes gooey pancakes!"

"Just pile it on, kids."

"YUCK!"

"WHATTUP! You're POISONING us!"

Bethany was the last to arrive at the Pilgrims' Church that morning, slipping into the same pew she had chosen the Sunday before while the pastor called the congregation to worship, and bid them to rise for the opening hymn. She flipped through the hymnal trying to find the right song, but the children's choir, seated in the balcony, had already started the first verse, and she mouthed the words as best she could, looking over the shoulder of the man in front of her for the right hymn number, coming up with #122 ("God Is My Shepherd"), which seemed to be missing from her songbook. She gave up during the second verse and instead watched the pastor, who, in turn, was admiring the organist for his appearance of joy, and she was moved by the sound of these imperfect voices—some angelic, others earth-toned, one warbling out of control—joined together for the sake of a greater song; moved by the pastor's visible pride in his organist, who had *reformed* himself in the image of Christ (she would later learn that Mike Flynn, in his darkest days, had lost his legal practice after playing fast and loose with his clients' money, a fate he blamed on the devil alcohol and the "enabling" superstitions of Catholicism); moved by the worshippers all gathered in their customary pews to praise their Shepherd, undeterred by the fact that their church was more than half empty; moved by an autumn light streaming through the stained-glass windows, a welcome sight at the end of such a trying morning; and as the hymn came to an end, Bethany felt a spirit rise within her heart—could it be true?—and spread delight where there was once frustration, filling her body with a desire that she had never known before, the longing for a

*dwelling place*

as the choir promised, where

*my shepherd blesses, cares, and leads through*
*all eternity.*

The organist lifted his hands Liberace-style from the final chords, and Thomas, on perfect cue, smiled gravely from his place beside the pulpit, nodding his thanks as the children's choir, also on cue, returned to their seats in the balcony. The congregation followed suit with a collective sigh and *creak*, including Bethany, who wondered if she hadn't just experienced some kind of vision, and flushed with the possibility that God, remotest Father of all things, had made a visit to the Pilgrims' Church and noticed her, even if she wasn't singing.

A blessing!

A moment of grace and piety!

But the feeling was not meant to last, and during the pastoral prayer, with her head lowered and her eyes closed in apparent obedience, Bethany's thoughts turned back to her meeting with the pastor, how the intimacy of the encounter had surprised her, and the longing in his eyes had driven her, in a state of panic, back to her car with its four-speaker stereo and reassuring privacy—back to her children, who needed her, and her husband, who worshipped her, and their architect-designed contemporary Colonial—everything that Bethany had ever wanted in life attained (and legally) by the age of thirty-five, *yet it was all a lie*, or so it seemed to her, and she wanted—no, needed—to escape from her dull "career" and her troubled marriage, even as she coveted their security.

Why the panic, then?

Because she was afraid. Because she was . . . unhappy.

What was she afraid of?

The pastor. She barely knew him, and as a rule she didn't trust the clergy, the same way she mistrusted therapists, and contractors, and politicians—anyone, in short, who engaged in glorified fix-it work. Unlike the rest, who repaired the known, members of the clergy tinkered with the *soul*, something, as she understood it, that might not even exist! But there was something about Thomas that appealed to her, perhaps the novelty of finding a black minister in this, the whitest of communities, or his looks, which, she had to admit, caused a certain flutter below and left of her sternum, or his ring finger, that emblematic digit, hairless and sleek, unbound by gold or platinum . . .

What heresy had just crossed her mind? And with her head bowed in the act of prayer? This latest realization, in comparison to the one that followed, was nothing:

Soon the pastor wound up his morning prayer, asking for, and receiving, the congregation's soft *amen*. The familiar answer had rolled off Bethany's tongue as if she meant it. With a look of grave sincerity (she peeked) he directed them to begin the silent prayer, which Bethany had been craving since the "pancakes episode" in her kitchen, so she obliged, and in the morning stillness, with her eyes shut tight, she continued to reflect on her unquiet meeting with the pastor and his evident desire (or so she thought) to save her soul, his certainty that she had come to the Pilgrims' Church under the direction of his God, and not by her own volition. How predictable! A man who knew nothing about her belief system had casually informed her that she was living under God's control! Such *utter bullshit*, she thought, letting this profanity ring out in the silence of her imagination, hoping it would spread to the congregants in the other pews, perhaps, even, to the Swensons across the aisle, who would confront her after the service with their fingers pointed, *It was you! You put those dirty thoughts in our pious heads!* There, having raged against Divinity, she felt a little better, and waited for the pastor to break the silence with the recitation of the Lord's Prayer, the only part of the service that she still remembered from childhood.

And waited.

And kept on waiting, but the silence continued on, long past anything she had experienced as a young Episcopalian, and she opened her eyes out of impatience to find the pastor still behind the pulpit with his head bowed, and the congregation, well used to these extended moments, making prayerful use of the time. One of the elder widows snored lightly in the aisle, while her nearest contemporary (Lili Baldwin, a former pediatric nurse and fund-raiser for the Communist Party, who would herself pass away in less than a month) tugged at her sleeve in alarm. The pastor seemed to have lost himself in thought, and Bethany left the elder widows to their morning drama, watching Thomas instead, this awkward young minister in his Geneva gown, standing before his congregation wordless, alone, and in full command of a silence that grew deeper with each passing moment, and more significant, until it seemed to both reflect and answer a great collective anguish, the unspoken substance binding a group of souls into a congregation . . . The pulpit where he stood, she thought, might have been miles away, yet his melancholy (so alarming when they met) seemed to welcome her, and accept her inmost thoughts for what they were, and shelter her desire for a happiness beyond the present tense, even if, in the future, she would tempt him—and here she speculated—to violate your odd Commandment and break the church covenant to engage in sins of the flesh, because his private sorrow was that *real*, as they say, and that *intense*, and *she wanted to fuck the pastor, that was it—she wanted to fuck the pastor in her husband's bed.*

"Why are you here?" Thomas had asked unfairly to open their first conversation, and in church that morning, while the pastor gave a sermon on the ubiquity of political spin, Bethany thought of the perfect answer: *Because you will fall in love with me.* Of this she was strangely certain, and in her pew in the rear middle of the church she began to plot the unforgivable, a seduction that would—after months of the pastor's sometimes baffling Sunday sermons, the mind-numbing "Alpha" course in Christian Education, a staggering number of interminable church socials, and, most important, an *increasingly intimate* series of pastoral visits—escalate into an all-out love affair. The congregation itself proved to be a mixed bag, but she was surprised by how easily she returned to the ritual of churchgoing: rising early on Sunday morning, making sure the children dressed in time, ferrying them to Old Town with the same sense of purpose that her parents had needed to ferry her and her three brothers, cranky with a lack of sleep, to the Gothic splendor of St. Anne's in Newton. Bobby would have no part of her renewal, believing that any involvement with the church would further undermine her sexuality. Wrong again! Though the pastor was often called to visit one of Boston's many teaching hospitals, tending to the sick, or busy offering spiritual counsel to a couple in the congregation, or mediating a dispute on some volunteer committee; and though the members of the church (save the Swensons, who were, as always, loyal and generous) could be judgmental, especially the younger parents, who implied, without breaking their Christian smiles, that it was a *sin* for Devon and Jessie to have arrived in Sunday school so ignorant of the Bible; and though Thomas had seemed reluctant, at first, to spend time with her alone, pawning her off on Jane Groom, the assistant minister, who oversaw the Adult Christian Education program, or Sandy Margolis, who taught the children patiently in Sunday school—Bethany's attraction had persisted, and she finally managed to secure the pastor's undivided attention for a second meeting, at the same time of night, nearly a month after she had fled his office in alarm. The darkness outside was heavier now, and instead of Debtors Anonymous, an exercise class in the basement (taught by her greatest rival for his affections, Alessandra Palacios y Rio) provided the background din. Bethany arrived early and, finding the church office empty, took a seat to ease the pounding of her heart, which tended to race before she saw him. *All right!* Alessandra encouraged her fitness class, yelling over Abba's "Dancing Queen." *Keep it up, now! One! Two! Three!* It was Alessandra's intention to bring spinning classes to the Pilgrims' Church, and she had pledged to match any gift of one thousand dollars or more toward the purchase of six state-of-the-art machines. The pastor had come in without making a sound and closed the door behind him, startling Bethany, and she grabbed her briefcase and stood up, realizing how absurd she must have looked only when he motioned for her to sit down again. Bethany was unaccustomed to feeling flustered in the company of men—she usually brought out *their* nervous tics—and she hoped she wasn't blushing too obviously.

"Sorry about the music," Thomas said, taking a WGBH coffee mug from a rack on the wall and filling it with hot spring water from the dispensing tank behind his desk. Carefully he dipped a tea bag inside and then took his seat. He had replaced his "Bill Cosby" sweater with a button-down cardigan that she would nickname "The Priest" before she peeled it off his body in the parsonage the following spring. "Despite our limited resources," he went on, "we try to offer a wide range of church activities, some beyond the usual forms of outreach."

"Like spinning class?" she asked, trying to start things off on a flirtatious note, and slightly hurt that Thomas hadn't thought to offer her some tea.

"For a church to live," he offered as an explanation, "it needs to adapt. The world is different now than it was in 1658, or whenever the Assembly at Savoy founded our Way in England. Today we have to compete with the global marketplace, home entertainment, the media, and a creeping—" A look of concern crossed Thomas's face and he interrupted himself to extract the tea bag from his mug. Bethany watched him search for a place to throw it out; finding none, he dropped it on the windowsill behind him, a curious solution, she thought.

"Forgive me, but I forgot to offer you . . ."

"That's all right," she told him.

"Please, let me . . ."

"I'm fine, really," she answered, touched by his courtesy. "Please go on."

"Where was I again?"

"Something was creeping?" she prompted him.

"I'm afraid that's not ringing any bells."

"Spinning class!" she remembered.

"Ah, yes," Thomas said, sipping from his tea, "the Aerobics Outreach program. Not exactly my best area. Blessed are the bookish and the lame, for they end up in the ministry. Or something along those lines." Through the door Bethany could hear Alessandra's class begin to clap along to the music, a pathetic sound—there must have been five of them, and even so, their sense of timing was screwy. Thomas heard them too, and gave her what she took to be an apologetic smile. "They'll be finished soon enough."

"Oh, I don't mind."

"Good," Thomas said, leaning back in his desk chair, which gave a suggestive squeak (here Bethany's heart began to race again). "Why don't we talk about you."

But Thomas didn't mean this in the way that she had hoped! The minister, as it turned out, was only interested in her spiritual life that night, and he proceeded to grill her on the progress of her Adult Christian Education, placing special emphasis on *The Congregational Way of Life*, a dreary paperback that

Jane Groom had pressed upon her a few weeks earlier detailing the history of the church and its foundational polity. Bethany had tried reading it before bed each night, pen in hand, approaching her assignment with some sincerity, but Bobby made his disapproval quite clear, and lobbied, instead, for his beloved *nookie*; when that approach failed she had tried reading *The Congregational Way of Life* aloud to the children, but Devon, two minutes into a brief history of the Protestant Reformation, had pronounced the book "a yawn" and returned to his seat by the television, while Jessie, usually a rapt audience, kept on interrupting her to ask, "Aren't there any animals in this story?" So Bethany had given up, and later made the mistake of asking Jane, during the next education class (she arrived twenty minutes late and apologized profusely), if they had a version of the book on tape so she could listen to it during her commute—oh, the patronizing look! From a woman who had no children of her own and seemed uncomfortable around *youth*, and who couldn't possibly be aware of the demands placed on her time and sanity. And now the pastor, who claimed to be so interested in her case, had started quizzing her on *The Congregational Way of Life* as if she were a high school student, asking if she understood the implications of Christ's sovereignty, or the meaning of a "gathered church," or the importance of prayer and unanimity in the church meeting—and though he meant well, she was certain, and asked his questions with obvious care, Thomas's mini lectures on each subject (the Priesthood of All Believers, the Meaning of the Eucharist, etc.) were more than a little patronizing. If Alessandra Palacios y Rio hadn't interrupted them, glowing with sweat and dressed in some kind of Lycra body stocking, Bethany would have been forced to make up an excuse to flee.

"Pardon me," Alessandra said, clinging to the open door.

"I'm always forgetting to knock first. What a *great workout* we just had downstairs!" Though she spoke with the accent of a European émigré, Alessandra was actually from Framingham, and had returned to Boston from the West Coast after the failure of her third marriage. She had grown used to her position as the congregation's siren, and treated Bethany with some wariness. "How are you, Bethany?"

"At the moment I'm confused," she answered, with perhaps more candor than was necessary, "but this too shall pass, right?"

"It always does," Alessandra told her with an artificial warmth, still catching her breath from the aerobics. "The question is, when will our parson here join my body-sculpting class?"

Thomas stared modestly into his cup of tea. "Well, I'm not sure about that. Probably never."

"And why not?" Alessandra asked with a pout.

"My athletic career began and ended in the ninth grade," Thomas told them, "when the basketball coach, I forget his exact name, ordered me to try out for junior varsity. He found me in the library reading—and I'll always remember this—Walker Percy's novel *The Moviegoer*, my favorite book at the time, the scene where Percy writes *to be neither pagan nor Christian but this: oh this is a sickness.* Chilling words. Anyway, I warned the coach that I was useless at sports, but he didn't believe me."

"How dreadful!" Alessandra gasped.

"I showed up to the tryout in dress socks and penny loafers," Thomas continued, the lofty tone of a sermon creeping into his voice, "which my competition found amusing. But I saw an opportunity to teach the coach something, mainly that *this* black kid couldn't even dribble with his good hand. After the first layup drill they asked me to leave. I was," he admitted, "the original geek."

"That's an outrage!" Alessandra leaned one arm against the doorway for balance while she stretched her hamstring. Her age was something of a mystery to the congregation (Bethany guessed that Alessandra was in her early fifties) and there was no denying that she had a wonderful body. "You could have *injured* yourself! Such savagery!"

Bethany felt her interview was taking on a surreal quality and she listened quietly while Alessandra settled her business with the pastor and left with an insincere apology for interrupting their meeting. Bethany checked her watch and marveled, as she often did, that time should move so swiftly.

A few months into their affair, during a weekend drive that had carried them, mostly in silence, far away from the pulpit where Thomas warned against the temptations of selfishness and apathy, Bethany would remind him of their second interview, and confess that she had left the church office that evening convinced that, due to her poor working knowledge of *The Congregational Way of Life*, she had fallen far in his esteem—as well as suspecting that Alessandra Palacios y Rio would body-sculpt her way into the pastor's affections, provided that she hadn't done so already. It was springtime, one full calendar year before the pastor disappeared, and Bethany had pulled her minivan to a stop beside a muddy field in some nameless central Massachusetts town, slightly west of Route 495. Thomas was suffering from a cold that day, and had taken Bethany's advice and spread a woolen blanket over his lap. "Do you mind?" Bethany had asked, and lit a joint that she had rolled the night before while sitting in the minivan, her family snug indoors and unaware that Mom was busy in the driveway separating *seed* from *bud* on a road map of New York State. Thomas (of all people) never judged her, and this, she thought, was an unbearably attractive quality; he was a minister, after all, and therefore had a public role to play, a script to read, a chorus to reflect on his performance—and an official "modest" costume to wear on Sundays and holidays. Sometimes, watching him deliver a sermon from her favorite pew, or listening to him chat with a parishioner during Fellowship, Bethany forgot that, when they were alone together, Thomas could ignore his sanctioned lines and *become someone else*, not a hedonist, exactly, and hardly Mr. Carefree; in her company, at least, Thomas was a man first and not a minister, and left his scriptural analysis aside to sit with her while she smoked a joint beside a cornfield; or, when she demanded it, massage the areas on her neck where the tension in her life gathered itself up in knots; or, quite frankly, reach down the front of her unzipped jeans and *bring her off* with his index finger and a well-placed thumb, complaining only if she bit his shoulder particularly hard, and never when she wept about her marriage and wallowed in self-pity . . . So she smoked half of a joint that weekend afternoon, turning her back to Thomas and asking him to perform the usual massage, which he did, listening to her theories about Alessandra, himself, and the erotic possibilities of body-sculpting . . . And then Thomas answered with his own confession that his failure to speak with her openly that night, and only about her reaction to *The Congregational Way of Life*, had been a source of disappointment. He admitted, afterward, to dialing her home number from the parsonage on three successive nights, and hanging up as soon as Devon answered (she chided Thomas for harassing her children). What was this boy, an answering service? Would they ever put the child to sleep? Finally he gathered his courage for one last attempt, when, after two long rings, Bethany had picked up herself with a weary *Hello?*

Silence. Thomas had stayed on the line for an extra moment, hoping that he would find the courage to speak.

*Hello?*

More of the same.

*Give me a fucking break*, she had muttered before the line went dead. *Please.*

"This is weird," Bethany said, the vague language of the habitual marijuana user overtaking her vocabulary, "but I remember that! I was in bed trying to read that book about the church again, and I had made it to Chapter 3, 'Freedom Bound by Love,' or whatever. Bobby was down in the garage looking at his porno magazines with Devon, and the phone rang, so I picked it up without thinking—"

"And there I was," Thomas interrupted, continuing to knead her neck muscles, "your favorite heavy breather."

"You were not!"

"Well, I was breathing at least."

Bethany threw her head forward and sighed. "I *wish* you had made an obscene phone call," she said. "I mean, I had this inkling that it was you, but how could I ever get that verified? I tried to star-69 you, and the recorded voice said something about an unavailable or private line. So rude that lady!"

"The number at the parsonage is known," he explained, "but not listed in any directory."

"Like your beloved Jesus," she remarked, knowing full well that Thomas disliked unserious talk about his religion, and wouldn't take her bait. His fingers released their pressure for a moment, and just as she was about to apologize they found another knot, encircled it, and pressed down hard. "That's perfect," she said, arching her back in exquisite pain. "Please don't stop . . ."

And then he had told her: "We should really speak about the state of your marriage, Bethany."

"Oh, I don't want to! Not today!"

"An open dialogue is healthy—"

"But I'm so tired of it!"

"Another day, then?"

"Press harder," she said.

"You know I'm here whenever you're ready . . ."

"Just the back rub, please."

It was through sheer dumb luck that they had ever consummated their relationship in the first place. Bethany had been involved in awkward courtships before, but nothing touched her experience with Thomas, who, with his divided loyalties (her soul, her body), brought ambivalence to a new level altogether. Perhaps this was correct: Bethany was a married woman, after all, and Thomas was her *minister*, albeit on a trial basis, and neither of them had any practice as a sexual predator (like Allen Weinglass, for instance). Thomas would tell her, and it would come as no surprise, that he had resolved to keep his feelings a secret from her, and tried to *sublimate* his love so that it might better fuel his work as a pastor, but it didn't work! Every time he saw her in the church he felt as if he might break in two, and his thoughts, at the pulpit, were often interrupted by his terrible dilemma: whether to reveal his love to her, which was wrong, not to mention hopeless, or to keep his love a secret, which was right, but hopeless in a host of other ways (did his devotion to God preclude an earthly love? Should he reject the world of the senses like a Manichaean? According to Spinoza, wasn't all love directed toward the Ultimate Being? His love for God was not, by definition, bodily, and this had never been a problem until he first set eyes on Bethany, when his cosmology began to change: like Freud's patients in "The Most Prevalent Form of Degradation in Erotic Life," who were impotent with their wives but virile with their mistresses, Thomas felt no desire where he loved [God], and could not love where he desired [Bethany], and without some form of resolution, and soon, he feared the uncertainty might swallow him). So he decided to tell her everything at the right time, but wound up avoiding her when faced with an opportunity. The way her daughter clung to her, and stood up in the pew to whisper in her ear; and the way her son, so evidently bored with religion, slouched beside her with a blank expression, pretending that his mother, and his sister, meant nothing to him . . . And Thomas, to compound his own difficulty, refused to ask for guidance when he prayed, as he did at regular intervals throughout the day—before each meal, between appointments, whenever he found himself alone and in need of some *critical distance* from experience. Prayer was not the proper place for selfish thoughts, and his attraction to Bethany Caruso, as he saw it, was selfish to its core, not a blessed thing, a continual act of dishonesty and therefore *beneath them*, even as he measured the potential of their love, which was considerable, and fantasized about their sex life, which, as he would soon find out, was usually rushed, often sublime, and always sincere. Of course Thomas had been in love before, or at least he had thought so, but his prior relationships with women had been based on such a deep misunderstanding that he felt as if he had been single all his life, and sexually as a younger man he'd suffered from endurance problems, and had grown used to disappointing lovers with his lack of confidence, and then listening, in an unfamiliar bed (or cringing in his own), to tender reassurances that sex was just a *thing*, when he knew from experience that, actually, its importance could not be overstated, only misunderstood, too readily accepted, confused with intimacy, &c. The mythology that black men were somehow naturally skilled at lovemaking still persisted, and the fact that Thomas was merely average in bed, or even less than

115

so, seemed a great disappointment to women. All this would change with Bethany Caruso, his first genuine *lover*, whose reciprocal feelings brought out something chemical in him that cured his overeagerness and opened his imagination to acts of intimacy that he never would have considered without her influence, without her body as a foil for his descent into adultery.

Their stroke of good luck? Bobby, having just negotiated his way back into the marital bedroom following a stint above the garage, planned to celebrate his "exile's return" with a romantic weekend at home and had arranged for his parents to take the children. Meanwhile, Bethany had been trying to schedule a pastoral visit to the house (unbeknownst to her husband), and the only evening Thomas could spare fell on the Friday of their reunion weekend. Bobby had been furious! A quiet dinner with the pastor of her church, he believed, would have set an entirely wholesome precedent! And a stranger to boot! He could see it clearly: They would all three bow their heads and say Grace before the supper, holding hands in *love* and *chastity*, when Bobby, thinking ahead, had already purchased the safest and least invasive vibrator on the marital-aid market, hoping to revive Bethany's interest in her sexuality . . . At any rate Bobby had been summoned without notice to Davenport, Iowa, where the company needed his management skills to solve a "glitch" in the chain of command at one of their subsidiaries, and it looked as if he would have to stay until the following Tuesday, Wednesday at the latest. (But what about the special vibrator? The unveiling ceremony Bobby had imagined would never quite take place, and after six frustrating months he returned the package by UPS for a full refund.) Before she allowed herself to celebrate, Bethany made sure her in-laws would still be taking the children for the weekend. Oh, yes, Bobby's mother told her on the phone, the insipid theme song to *Entertainment*

*Tonight* blaring in the background, they were so looking forward to spending "quality time" with the grandkids. Which meant another trip to see Old Ironsides, because Bobby's parents were strangely obsessed with the Tall Ships. Bethany poured herself an extra glass of wine the night before, nervous and surprised that the stage for her seduction of Thomas had finally been prepared. At the office on Friday she couldn't concentrate, and spent most of her time trying to decide what to make for dinner, settling on a pasta recipe that she vaguely remembered seeing on the Food Channel. But she couldn't find all the right ingredients at the Bread & Circus, and the checkout aisles at five-thirty were a mess; and she let the vegetables overcook while she was upstairs wrestling with the zipper of a dress that made her thighs look chunky anyway, plus she wanted to seem casual, so she changed into a blouse and her favorite wide-legged slacks; and she had been lucky to hear the doorbell the first time it rang, on her way downstairs from the attic, where she had gone to find an old pair of slutty leather heels.

"I'm coming!" she yelled despite the fact that Thomas wouldn't hear her, carrying the heels in one hand and rushing, shoeless, down the staircase, a disturbing silence emanating from the kitchen, the evidence of her family, she realized much too late (winter jackets, stray gloves, a backpack), scattered everywhere.

"Just one second!"

Finally she kicked aside Jessie's bright pink snowsuit and opened the door, too frantic to worry about what she might say, how to explain the fact that they would be alone for dinner on a Friday night, when Thomas—ever wary of the unethical and the unseemly—had expected to visit with the entire family. The pastor had overdressed for the weather, wrapping himself in a greatcoat and woolen scarf despite the fact that it had been a mild February throughout New England. She invited him inside with an apology and immediately blurted out the fact that her family had abandoned them.

"I hope that's okay," she told him, tossing her pumps in the front-hall closet because she had decided against them. "There!" Bethany directed him to the coatrack and ran off to the kitchen, trying to rescue their dinner from oblivion.

Thomas would remember being left alone in the front hallway, his own heart racing with the night's potential, nearly tripping over Jessie's snowsuit, so small and pink that it reminded him of his great responsibility, and killed, for the moment, any desire he felt for Bethany. *I will live through this*, he told himself, following her through the unfamiliar rooms and into the modish kitchen, where he found her struggling to open a bottle of wine between her knees. *Here*, he said, *let me give it a whack*. Saved by the tickling of his small-talk gene! Thomas's arrival at the Pilgrims' Church had coincided with a flurry of dinner invitations, and though the congregation was relatively small, it had taken Thomas the better part of a year to visit every parishioner's home at least once, from the Angelises' mansion rising conspicuously from the stone peak of Cliff Estates, to the Swensons' modest compound just next door to Bethany (fueled in part by solar panels and heated, in the winter, by firewood), to the elder widow Margit Parmelee's one-bedroom efficiency in Kensington Meadows, the assisted-living facility just a stone's throw from Naumatuk Middle School. Slowly, with each pastoral visit, a context began to form around the faces turned so eagerly to him at the pulpit, and Thomas had gained a provisional sense of what the members of his congregation brought to worship every Sunday—just what, exactly, they kept private, choosing to confront without his help, and what they would entrust to him as their minister and *concertmaster*, as the Book of Worship put it. The range of his experience as a dinner guest was astonishing! In the unfinished baronial splendor of the Angelises' dining room, her husband working late and the children bouncing off the walls downstairs in the "rec room," Artemesia Angelis had confessed to being suicidal as a teenager, and, between dinner courses, had rolled up her sleeves to show him the areas on her forearms where she had deliberately cut herself with a razor. "Oh, well," Artemesia had sighed, "now you know my secret," and politely changed the subject to a novel she had just read by Harper Lee. After that night Artemesia had approached him with a certain shyness, and though their relations, in general, could have been characterized as cordial but distant, Thomas had often been aware of something *unspoken* between them, a bond that required no language to make it real, just a glance across the aisle, a shared feeling when he repeated the Call to the Supper: *The gifts of God for the people of God. Come, for all things are ready.*

Dinner with the Swenson family, on the other hand, had been rather hectic: first they had all donned matching rubber boots (Piotr kept an extra pair around for house guests) and carried firewood indoors from the shed; then, while the children set the table with a ruckus, Piotr had taken Thomas on a tour of the grounds, pointing out the sites where he planned to build a sauna, and an artificial bog for growing cranberries, and a pen for keeping sheep; soon Ulla had called them inside with the dinner bell, and the family crowded around the table for a feast of venison, stewed kale, and homegrown parsnips. Dag, the family Newfoundland, had taken a *special liking* to Thomas, and barked whenever he made a sudden move or opened his mouth to speak. Finally they had dragged the beast outdoors, and Thomas, beyond the point of hunger, had been able to breathe freely. After the unsatisfying dinner Piotr had brought out his "Jew's harp" for a short demonstration, to be joined by Bernie on his penny whistle, and Elka with her "fiddle," and little Pele on his toy recorder . . . Perhaps the dandelion wine had gone to his head, but Thomas seemed to remember Ulla serenading him, as Dag barked away outside the frost-covered windows, with her favorites from the Woody Guthrie songbook.

More often Thomas's pastoral visits were bittersweet, like his dinner with the elder widow Margit Parmelee, blind from cataracts and suffering from dementia, who had confided to Thomas over egg-salad sandwiches (served by an expressionless home health care worker) that she was planning to retire from Congress, and wondered aloud if the Speaker of the House, Mr. Tip O'Neill, would be disappointed in her decision. Mrs. Parmelee's husband had, in fact, represented their district in Congress for over twenty years before passing away suddenly during a committee meeting around the time of Watergate. As a boy Thomas had watched the news reports about Representative Parmelee's funeral, and he still remembered the solemnity of the Marine Guard as they gave their twenty-one-gun salute.

It was perhaps inevitable that there should have been some misunderstandings too: Take his early invitation, many times rescheduled at her own request, to have dinner with the indomitable Margaret Howard, her husband, Jerry, a virtual mute, and her disappointment of a son, Bradley, alleged to be the village drug dealer. The evening had started pleasantly enough, with cocktails and hors d'oeuvres in the sunken living room, a guided tour of Margaret's perennial beds, which she obviously took great pride in, and a helpful discussion about the strengths and weaknesses of the various church committees,

but a certain *odor* coming from the kitchen—a sickly, unmistakable combination of smells—had registered with Thomas on
the way back from the flower garden and soon became a
distraction, compounded by Bradley's late arrival on two rumb-
ling wheels, his unapologetic stupidity, clammy handshake, and
stink of motor oil and unwashed laundry; and by the way his
father, Jerry, the picture of vanished self-confidence and charm,
seemed held together by pomade, a suntan, and a thick gold
chain around each wrist. Thomas had hoped and hoped that it
wasn't true, wanted *so much* to be mistaken, yet when the time
came to sit down for dinner, Margaret had disappeared for a
moment and then, with some fanfare, laid out the very spread
that he had been dreading: fried chicken, stewed greens, bis-
cuits, and white gravy. A moment passed, and then another;
time had slipped its bearings, spun for a while, and then
lurched forward to resume its fearful pace.

"Not so bad," Bradley said, adding for the pastor's benefit,
"Thanks, Ma."

"Pretty good," Jerry chimed in. "No complaints."

"Let it never be said," Margaret spoke up, "that our village
can't roll out the red carpet for a new neighbor. I'm just sorry
that we couldn't square our schedules any earlier, what with my
workload at the office . . . Not hungry?" she asked Thomas,
finally noticing his reluctance to address the meal heaped on his
plate.

"Forgive me," he said, "but my appetite . . ."

"Are you unwell?"

"Yes—"

"Well, what is it?"

"I mean, no, not unwell exactly—"

They stared.

"What I mean to say," he resumed with more composure, "is that I've always found Southern cooking to be very heavy . . ."

"Well, then," Margaret said, "that's just more in the larder for Jerry. It's his favorite meal, you know."

"Oh, is it?"

"Yessir," he chimed in again.

She leaned in close to the pastor. "I try to make it for him every Thursday. You'd think he might get sick of it after all these years . . ."

"That true, Pop?"

"What?"

"You getting sick of this?"

"Nope."

"Coolness."

"Bradley!"

"What?"

"Not at my table, understood?" She went on, "The pastor and I have church business to discuss, so if you'll kindly put a lid on it."

"You're very good to do this," Thomas offered, to break his silence, "a busy woman like yourself . . ."

"I take great pride in my family," she said, admiring her men as they attacked her dinner. "If not me, as the saying goes, who will?"

And now Thomas found himself alone—all alone—with Bethany Caruso, the only woman in the congregation he found truly fascinating, and she had opened a bottle of Pinot Noir, pouring him a healthy glass in the kitchen and leading him, bottle in hand, to the sitting room, where she cleared away the magazines and video-game cartridges from the coffee table and asked him to sit down, running her fingers through that hair of hers, and flashing him a look of such a sultry nature that he wondered, really wondered, if all of this was really happening.

"Watch the Nintendo thing," she warned him, just before he tripped over a bundle of wires leading to the game console. "It's an obstacle course in here."

Thomas stepped over the machine and joined her on the couch, keeping a buffer zone of empty space between them, forced into an awkward reclining position by the sofa cushions. He could barely reach the coffee table to rest his glass of wine on a copy of *WWF* magazine. "So the nest is empty," he observed, feeling the force of gravity begin to work against him.

"Right," she answered, "except they always leave their junk behind. Just look at the mess in here." Bethany knew full well the stupefying power of the family couch and chose to stay alert by sitting on the edge of her cushion. The thing was like a country of its own! Every now and then she gave in to the sofa's consoling grip and lost herself in an episode of *Biography* on A&E. "You bring this stuff into your house and it just seems to multiply. I honestly don't know where some of it comes from . . ."

"Well," he began, about to launch into his spiel about the various excesses of the marketplace and the failure of late-century capitalism to address the spiritual needs of the same consumers it enslaved to the ideal of prosperity, when Bethany, sensing something along these lines, interrupted him, "And we don't use any of it!"

Thomas felt his willpower draining into the couch. He could no longer reach his glass of wine or make his legs move on command, yet he was visited by a strange serenity. "Sometimes I wonder if we aren't addicted to the freedom of choice."

"Are you super hungry?"

"Oh, just regular."

She handed him his glass of wine. "That's good news, because our dinner isn't turning out so well." She took a long sip from her Pinot Noir, noticed that Thomas was watching her, and told him, "You might as well know right now that my addiction to alcohol is *off limits*. I never discuss it with anyone and I intend to keep it."

Thomas raised his hands in a gesture of innocence. "I'm not here to judge you, Bethany. I've always believed that God provided us with wine to *gladden the human heart*, as the 104th Psalm reads. The real question is: Why are you looking for joy in a bottle?"

"It's not a crutch! Did you know they say a glass of wine is good for the digestion? Or is it heart disease? Anyway, if a *single* glass is good for you, shouldn't five be even better?"

"If it helps," Thomas reassured her, "think of this as a purely social visit. There's no need to be defensive."

"I'm sorry," she said, reaching for her wine again, "it's just that having you over makes me, well, nervous. When I was a girl, the Rector of our church came over for dinner exactly once. My parents were having trouble with their marriage, and as a last resort, I guess, they invited him over to observe the family dynamic and lead us all in prayer. Talk about looking for joy in a bottle! Our Rector was a famous drunk, and after polishing off a carafe of Burgundy by himself he *commanded* us to kneel on the carpet and beg for His forgiveness; meanwhile the Rector kept his seat at the dinner table and proceeded to inhale the better part of a roast . . ."

"It's the *arrogance* of the Episcopal clergy that I find so shocking. Imagine the *pride* of that man—"

"He was a drunk! Anyway, my father ended up moving out that weekend and we all survived the split. Divorce is not the end of the world, you know, and my parents just . . . moved on." Bethany eased herself back from the edge of the couch and waited for the warmth of the cushions to envelop her. "I hear you're in great demand as a dinner guest, Thomas."

"Who told you that?"

"Oh, the whispers . . ."

"Well, the sad fact is I never learned to cook for myself, even when I was in divinity school, and it's an important facet of my job here that I make the rounds. Although I do, you might like to know, have a very strict 'no kneeling' policy—"

"That's a shame," she ventured, diverting her eyes.

"What?"

"I wonder," she went on, "who's the best cook in all the church, Thomas?"

"Well, I'd have to reflect on that."

"What I mean to say is," she tried again, rephrasing her question to sound more suggestive, "where on your pastoral rounds have you been served with the most *generosity*?" While Thomas stumbled through a diplomatic answer about the quality of the dinner conversation and the graciousness of the church membership, Bethany inched herself closer to him on the couch—without detection, she thought—and performed her most elaborate hair flip. She waited, but her approach seemed to have no effect. *How does this work again?* she wondered, still watching him, only half listening, now, as he described Alessandra Palacios y Rio's five-course dinner, which began with lobster bisque, and then she brought him a risotto of some sort, followed by—

"Sounds catered to me," she interrupted.

"Yes, I suppose it was. I'm not a food person," he admitted, "so the effort was wasted. My lifestyle is very simple."

But he looked so delicious! Normally she didn't think this way, reduce people and their personalities to morsels for her private consumption, but for once they were all alone, and she was *lonely*, in need of loving, touching, whispering, holding, and—dare she imagine it?—some religious fucking, if only Thomas would forget about his *simple lifestyle* and make a move across the sofa! By now the children would be watching, for the eleventh time, their grandparents' home video of the Tall Ships parade, complete with amateur narration ("Don't look now, but here comes the *Harvey Gamage*! Hailing from South Bristol, Maine! Hard to believe that she was built from a traditional schooner design in 1973 . . ."), and Bobby, having just availed himself of some all-you-can-eat buffet in deepest Iowa, would be setting out in his rental car to find the nearest Adult Video store, where he would scour the shelves for a starlet that reminded him of Bethany; and here she was, languishing untouched beside her favorite minister, trying to seduce him and failing miserably! It was just her luck to fall in love with the pastor of a Congregational church, who, though single, would never violate the sanctity of a marriage vow and the trust of his parishioners, even if he loved her back, not that he could, not that he ever, ever would . . .

After her second hair flip failed to get a rise from Thomas, and the pastor, by the looks of it, seemed to be fighting off the urge to sleep, Bethany suggested they move into the kitchen. Truthfully she had given up on him, and served her seduction dinner with a heavy heart. She continued to talk easily with the pastor, smiled at the right places, even laughed once or twice, but his presence seemed hopelessly benign—right down to his flannel shirt, wide-wale corduroys, and sensible leather shoes. Thomas looked handsome in the candlelight, if vaguely troubled, hardly touching his second glass of wine, avoiding her eyes and turning the subject—when he spoke at all—to church-related business. He did compliment Bethany on her cooking and admired her choice of beeswax candles, which burned, he suggested, with a gentle light. *He's a eunuch!* she thought, longing to open a second bottle of the Pinot Noir, but resisting for now, especially after giving that stupid speech about addiction. Then Thomas asked about her experience as someone returning to Christianity, and she answered him honestly, voicing her reservations about religion in general and the Christian tradition in specific: the lack of respect for other belief systems, which, under God, must have been equally valid; the quick fix promised by so many followers of Jesus Christ; and, on a more practical level, the time commitment of joining a church, which she knew to be considerable. Thomas answered with a pitch about the democratic aspects of the Congregational Way, and his own belief (here she smiled to herself, realizing that she had reached him) that religion was not about inherited ritual or tradition but *love in the here and now*, love for the Son of Man, first, who died for our sins, love for each other, and obedience to the Holy Spirit, which was love distilled, and the graceful acceptance of difference, including the variations of belief, because Christ taught, and His children must practice, a doctrine of *acceptance*, and the Congregational Church, the pastor insisted, as the only church He ruled with absolute authority, had a mandate to accept His children, all of them, no matter what stage they had reached on their "spiritual journey." This last phrase made Bethany wince.

"Thomas," she told him, "you don't have to talk that way to me, not when we're alone like this. I mean, there's candles burning. We're in the kitchen."

The pastor seemed taken aback. "I'm not sure I . . ."

"Who do you think I am? *How* could you say that to me?"

"I don't understand," he said simply. "Tell me how I'm supposed to talk to you. Please."

"Like a human being! I'll allow you that I'm not a great student of theology, but when someone casually informs me that I'm on a *spiritual journey* I have a hard time keeping a straight face. Frankly you're above that kind of thing. I don't think twice when I hear the others talking about my *spiritual journey*, but you of all people!"

"Bethany, I appreciate what you're saying, but—"

"Does my journey begin at the Burlington Mall or over at the Pier One Imports? Or in the parking lot outside my office building? Did you know, Thomas, that the company I work for makes, among many other overpriced consumer goods, satellite-guided *missiles*? Half the people in this quaint New England village work for an arms manufacturer, including myself and my dear husband, so forgive me if I'm not ready to explore my *spirituality* to its fullest."

"Yes, but—"

"And the journey itself! I wonder if my neighbors realize that their little trip to *Heaven* might not go off so smoothly as their last vacation at Sugarbush. The car's all packed and the house alarm is set and the kids are in back fighting over the Game Boy in their mittens . . . What will they say when they realize the *end is near*? Who will they call first, their team of lawyers? Their broker? What will they do when they find out their *spiritual journey* has been taking them in the *wrong direction*?" Bethany, to her own surprise, had been fighting off tears throughout, and with this last observation she began to cry—but only for a moment, and without the wailing and sobbing that sometimes reduced her to a puddle of nerves.

After a long silence Thomas said, "I'm sorry, Bethany."

"You have nothing to be sorry about," she answered, still in shock from her unexpected outburst. She wiped her face dry with a paper napkin. "I'm the lunatic at this dinner table."

"You spoke your mind," he told her with some reverence, "and I appreciate that. So few people bother with me . . ."

"And blew out a candle in the process," she observed, watching the single beeswax candle burn. "I'm glad that's over. *Phew.*"

Perhaps it was a residual effect of their argument, or the fact that, after surviving an uncomfortable hour, they were beginning to warm to each other's company, or perhaps the mention of *love in the here and now*, forgotten during her outburst, had freed their deeper motives from shyness and hesitation, because, at that moment, they began to act as if some foreknowledge had brought them together on this very night, for the sole purpose of coming together, freed from the constraints of moral agency, and Bethany, for one, would not let this opportunity escape them. "Drink your wine," she instructed Thomas, and in his own good time he would, watching as she tied her hair into a twist, held it behind her head, and let it slowly unravel on her shoulder, shining with an incandescence that outmeasured his capacity for language, that would quiet his urge to describe her the next day, when he wrote in his journal, *I looked at Bethany and forgot myself. Already she is everything*, and this realization, paired with an overheated caution about being found out, would compel him to throw not just that day's entry but his *entire journal* in the kitchen rubbish. For her part Bethany was picturing her bedroom upstairs, which she had prepared in a fit of optimism; earlier she had vacuumed the carpet free of Bobby's footsteps, drawn the window treatments for privacy, set the thermostat to a comfortable 68°, turned out the overhead light and aimed her reading lamp directly at the king-sized bed, made with her best linens—the marital suite so precious to her husband (and the builders) was in perfect shape to be defiled, and if Thomas, at the threshold, even thought of backing out, she would let it drop about the French embroidered underwear. But there was no call for such drastic measures. Thomas, who was not usually prone to explicit sexual fantasy, had been unable, for months, to stop imagining their first encounter in some detail, and while he did manage to govern his daydreams inside the Pilgrims' Church, where the Puritan saints ruled more sternly, even, than Christ himself, an image of her trailed him on his daily rounds, reminding him, as he climbed into his Ford Probe for another hospital trip, that in his heart he was a *sinner*, born from his parents' love for each other and from their brave idealism, yes, but also from *lust* and *human vulnerability*. Bethany was not to blame! He was fascinated by her beauty, her intelligence, her frustrated ambition, and though she may have tempted him to act (that tank top she had worn to an unnaturally hot Autumn Fest, the phone calls after hours, the urgent dinner invitation), final responsibility for breaking the church covenant rested, Thomas believed, with him alone. He had found no cure for his attraction, not through reading, prayer, and other religious exercises; nor would he find relief in friendly contact, private consultation, or—and this was the lowest—the practice of *onanism*, because he fantasized about her most vividly in the parsonage, when, following another night of work, he climbed the creaking staircase, undressed in silence, and prepared himself for bed, laboring under the weight of his loneliness, his old familiar loneliness, which had always, until now, provided *comfort* in his chilly bedroom, and he was always *cold*, no matter what the season, shivering alone in that drafty room, the covers piled high, the space heater humming and clicking . . . Was it sinful to imagine her with great affection on those nights? To share a pillow and feel her bodily warmth, to laugh as her imaginary double rolled on top of him? Oh, but she tormented the pastor in the a.m., finding him in the crawl space between dreaming and reality, seeming to be so material, and so intent on making love, and again, and again . . . What about the actual seduction? Bethany, in fact, was much less of a romantic by nature, and even though she (arguably) had more at stake in the affair—more to lose, she believed, while Thomas didn't bother with such calculations—she chose the right moment to approach him: they had finished all the wine in the house, hashing out their religious differences until 1 a.m.; they had just traded deep, end-of-the-week yawns across the kitchen table, and Bethany, feeling drunk and weary enough to do something *really bold*, had suggested to the pastor that their night, so long delayed, had reached an end. "I'm wrecked," she had claimed. "Let me see you to the door." She thanked him for his indulgence and advice in the gloom of the front hallway, and stood nearby while he draped himself, once again, in his protective winter clothing. (Bobby had just placed his last call to her from Iowa, but she had foreseen his concern and turned off the ringing function on all the telephones. *Call me in the morning*, he left on the voice mail, *or I'll start to worry, okay?*) Thomas was certain that their night would end in sorrow! That he would drive back to the parsonage drunk on wine and *heartbroken*, wrestling with what he might have done to change the evening's course, the charm he might have summoned from—where?—to make her laugh *at least once*, and replaying the moment, in candlelight, when he should have confessed his love and risked offending a married woman for the chance, the slightest chance, that she had prepared a confession of her own. In his mind he was already following the dark road home, past the horse farm, the high school, the nursery, the Public Works garage, and heading into Old Town, but then Bethany, taking some initiative (she knew he never would) approached him from his blind side, grabbed the lapels of his greatcoat, pushed him back against the wall, and kissed him on the mouth *without apology*, holding him in place, daring him to try to resist. The pastor let himself be kissed, thinking of a line from the 106th Psalm: *And a fire was kindled in their company; the flame burned up the wicked.* She began unbuttoning his greatcoat, revealing, in a whisper, that she *wanted him*, and wanted him profoundly, not in the manner of some bored and unloved housewife looking for a thrill, because, she told him, she was *never* bored, *always* loved, and still she wanted him, *so badly, Thomas, you have no idea.* There, pinned against the wall, his eyes half closed and his coat half open, the pastor answered, *I do.*

Second Part

With still no word from the pastor by noontime on Wednesday and not a sign of him emanating from the parsonage, the Reverend Jane Groom, assistant minister of the Pilgrims' Church and acting chairperson of God Loves Animals, Inc., an experimental hospice program for ailing pets, after consulting the congregation's part-time secretary, Mrs. Safarian, about the vagaries of Thomas's schedule, made the drastic step of calling Caroline Abbey, the youngest of the elder widows, to begin spreading word of the pastor's disappearance over the Pilgrim Prayerline. Mrs. Abbey was home to take Jane's first call, in fact she rarely left her house at all, ever since the Bridge Club had fallen into disarray and the nice checkout girl at Stop & Shop had told her about the home delivery service for Seniors, which she swore by, even if the boy who brought her packages was surly and ungrateful for his weekly tip, a brand-new dollar bill. Mrs. Abbey's phone had become a mostly inert object in recent years, ringing only with bad news and telemarketers (they were always trying to fleece her out of something), and

she received Jane's message about the pastor's disappearance with some distress but total comprehension, taking Jane's dictation, by reflex, in Gregg shorthand, which she had last used professionally in 1972:

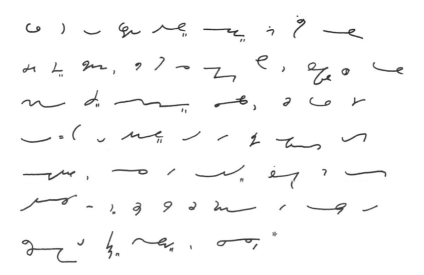

Mrs. Abbey relished the chance to play a role in something—anything—other than a game of bridge, and after hanging up she consulted her phone list, sealed in a plastic sleeve and stored with her bills and winter gloves in the top drawer of her dresser in the front hallway. The name just below her own on the Prayerline was Alma Acevedo, and she dialed Alma's number with a sense of urgency. The Acevedo woman she hardly knew, only that, like most females of Spanish ancestry, she was

*Pray for our pastor Thomas Mosher, who has been missing since Sunday afternoon. If you have any information about his whereabouts, please call Jane Groom immediately. We pray for the well-being of Thomas and the swift resolution of this mystery. May the Lord help us walk together in His ways as we follow the life and example of Jesus Christ. Amen.

small in stature, sweet in temperament, quite round, and worked as a part-time domestic for a number of families in the village. And she used an answering machine! The means of this newfangled appliance stymied Mrs. Abbey, and it took her three attempts, interrupted by the various beeps and pauses, before she could be certain the message would reach Alma in its entirety. In order to keep the Prayerline moving Mrs. Abbey skipped to the next name on the list, Adams-Edwards—as in Bob and Connie from nearby Acton, a lovely couple with a teenaged daughter who ran with a rough-and-tumble crowd, according to Cynthia Moss, whose niece was that teen-outreach counselor, Lisa Darling. To ensure a connection Mrs. Abbey phoned Connie at her work number—what was she, a lawyer? and after informing the secretary that, yes, this was an emergency, a *church* emergency, she insisted that Connie raise herself from her meeting. Mrs. Abbey repeated the message from Jane Groom, adding the fact that Thomas had skipped a meeting the night before of the Benevolence Committee, an unusual oversight on his part. "I suppose he'll turn up," Mrs. Abbey guessed, "and we'll look foolish for worrying."

"Maybe he's gone out on retreat," Connie said, copying down the last words of Mrs. Abbey's message.

"Or has someone in his family taken ill? Anyway," Mrs. Abbey told her, "I think you'll agree it's worth the risk."

"I'm disturbed, Caroline."

"Keep the faith, darling. He'll turn up."

"It's just not like him at all," she said, "not at all."

"I know it," Caroline answered, "say what you will about the content of his sermons, the man's been awfully reliable."

Connie sighed. "Who's next on the list? Artemesia?"

"That's right, Artemesia Angelis."

"Thank you," Connie said, suddenly aware that she was

needed in the conference room. "I'd better keep this ball rolling."

"Be gentle with her, darling."

"She's a fragile one, isn't she?"

"Amen to that."

Connie, the Adams to her husband's Edwards and therefore, she believed, a brilliant problem solver, asked her secretary to prepare an E-mail message for delivery to every church member with an Internet address. (That fall, in a rare moment of visionary thinking, the Council had approved a four-part course in on-line basics for church members, taught on a volunteer basis by Harry Meade's son Timothy, a student at MIT.) Connie buzzed the conference room to buy herself a few more minutes, and then she phoned Artemesia, who took the news about the pastor quite hard, nearly fainting in her kitchen. With all the hammering and other sounds of light construction, Connie couldn't tell if her Pilgrim had lost consciousness or if she was merely being histrionic.

"Are you all right?" she asked. "Artemesia, are you there?"

"Yes, I'm still here."

"You're not alone in the house?"

"I think the men are building something . . ."

"Good. Now just sit down for a minute, can you do that for me? Find a chair and plant yourself."

"Or maybe," Artemesia said, sitting on the floor and leaning back against the unfinished cabinets, "they're knocking down a wall . . ."

"You just pull yourself together," Connie told her, "and I'll call your Pilgrim for you, okay? But first I need your help. I need you to find your copy of the Prayerline. Right now."

"I can do that," Artemesia said, the music of three hammers bringing her back to her senses, although nothing short of

Thomas reappearing safe and sound, she knew, would restore her mental health for long. Artemesia put down the receiver and went to retrieve her phone list, coming back a minute later—the hammers now quiet—to give out Richard Babson's number and resume her nervous breakdown on the kitchen floor.

And so it went on throughout the afternoon and evening: from one Pilgrim to the next the news of the pastor's disappearance spread, by telephone, answering machine, voice mail, E-mail message, and chance encounter in the supermarket; from Caroline Abbey, elder widow, all the way to Henry Yu, computer consultant and father of three, who received the message on his alphanumeric pager at six-fifteen that evening, courtesy of his wife (PASTOR MISSING LITTLE HENRY FEVER CHICKEN OK? CALL HOME); for her part Bethany Caruso heard the news from Sam Cabot, an investment banker who conducted all his business, no matter how personal, on the speakerphone, and made a habit of snubbing her when their paths crossed every Sunday. Perhaps it was unfair, but Bethany suspected that Sam was an alcoholic—what with his bright red skin and perpetually windblown hair, the rage in his eyes, and his wife's timidity, her summer hats that dangled ribbons, the pallid children who escaped to boarding school . . . After hanging up the phone Bethany took a moment to gather herself, closing her office door and turning the flimsy lock; she hadn't slept the night before, alone in her bedroom and *frightened for Thomas*, opening her eyes at every thump from the heating ducts and rustle in the trees outside, climbing out of bed to check on the children four separate times between midnight and sunrise. For a long time she had wanted the morning to come and end her uncertainty; then, as daybreak arrived and it became clear that, yes, she would survive, she wished for more uncertainty, another day of being in the dark about his where-abouts, surely *not* knowing was better than its opposite, final knowledge that Thomas didn't love her anymore. As Bethany drove her daughter to school that morning the sky had seemed impossibly overcast. Jessie hated to be late for anything, especially school, and her goading and whining had driven Bethany to question the wisdom of teaching children how to tell the time. "We're running late!" she kept on reminding her mother. "Hurry up!" As a result, Bethany had committed the Montessori sin of leaving the drop-off area before Jessie and her hand-bag were safely inside. Now she stood by her office window and took in her first-floor view: a remote area of the parking lot, some kind of electrical transformer behind a fence, a ragged Dumpster, evergreen hedges singed brown with acid rain, a rot-ting pile of mulch. In one of his most ambitious sermons, Thomas had talked about the conquest of nature, the human wish, as he had put it, to *know the world beyond all recognition*, and it struck her that this small corner of the New England landscape, flattened with asphalt and littered with in-dustrial by-products, gave proof to his argument. He is the soul of the place, she thought, and now he's left us. Or rather, He's missing, even worse than gone. Anita picked that moment to buzz her over the intercom, and she ignored the terrible sound, *Like a dying breath*, she thought, *or am I only being morbid?* Finally she picked up and said, "Anita? How about leaving the intercom alone for a while. Make some personal calls or some-thing. Or better yet, *go home early*. Anything to keep you from pressing that button!" It was the rudest thing she had ever said to a secretary! But the moment had demanded it, and she would have weeks, even months, to make it up to Anita—flow-ers, an expensive lunch in Boston, &c.—before she filed her an-nual Grievance with the Senior Officer. Bethany admired the dedication that Anita brought to being a disgruntled worker, and the ease with which, each year, she threatened legal action against a company that paid her a decent salary for playing Solitaire on her computer. The day she filed was something of an event in Human Resources; one year there had even been an office pool to predict the exact date Anita would ready her Grievance, button her silk jacket (she dressed for the occasion), and march across the floor to hand in the paperwork. But there were no secrets between adjoining cubicles, and Anita had intercepted a tally sheet and foiled them, picking an obscure Tuesday afternoon in mid-January when most of the junior managers had been required to attend a seminar on changes to the company's benefit packages. After she had been to see the Senior Officer, just to show that there were no hard feelings, Anita had opened a Tupperware container of homemade mini-cupcakes and offered them to everyone on the floor.

"If that's the way you want it," Anita answered, and clicked off with an alarming force. Bethany could tell that lunch at Legal Sea Foods wouldn't do this time, and she would have to spring for something more extravagant, like the executive buffet at the Swissôtel near Downtown Crossing, where Anita had hosted that surreal brunch for her son when he graduated from high school. She would never forget the sight of Anita's extended family huddled around the prime-rib station, coaching the poor attendant while he tried to carve . . .

Bethany never spoke directly to her Pilgrim (the accountant Raymond Claffey) and delivered her message, instead, to his male assistant, Ron, a stickler for detail who asked her to repeat the "May the Lord help us walk together in His ways" passage twice. "It's a prayer," she explained to Ron, who seemed dubious, and answered, "You're asking Mr. Claffey to *pray?* He's a very busy man, and I can't promise anything until he leaves this meeting around three o'clock . . ." She hardly listened to Ron, and didn't care if Raymond Claffey's meeting brought the Prayerline to a grinding halt. Thomas was missing! She herself refused to close her eyes and pray for his return, certainly not in her depressing office, with the tropical fish on her screen saver floating away and sending up slow-motion air bubbles. At two-thirty a "sensitive" exit interview was coming in and she had forgotten to pick up some lunch—not that she was hungry, the thought of anything solid in her stomach brought on deepest nausea. That morning she had fallen to her knees in front of the toilet bowl and retched for a while, but since she hadn't eaten properly since Sunday, nothing had come up. *I'm either pregnant,* she had thought, staring into the Caribbean blue water, *or I'm still detoxifying.*

Later, in need of supplies for her interview, Bethany had passed Anita's empty cubicle on her way to the stockroom, an oversized closet with tall industrial shelving perpetually lined with the products of her undoing: Post-it notes in neon colors, rolls of Magic Tape and extra black dispensers, shipping labels, box-bottom hanging files, manila file folders, premium double-top file folders (letter and legal size), corrugated storage boxes, three-ring binders, clear-front linen report covers, a heavy-duty paper trimmer (arm locked shut), and an electric three-hole punch . . . This was the stuff of requisition forms and color catalogues as thick as phone books, the office worker's bane and joy and only natural right. The unspoken code of white-collar crime allowed her (1) to order new supplies at will, (2) to consume them at rates so high that her productivity actually fell, (3) to clip whatever she could carry *without guilt,* (4) to distribute her bounty to family members at her own discretion. The atmosphere in the stockroom bordered on the Holy, and whenever she stepped inside, hushed by the sight of the worker's reliquary, Bethany remembered a line that her Rector had often quoted from Thomas à Kempis's *Imitation of Christ*: "Do not despair, brother, of making spiritual progress; there is still time and the hour has not yet passed." But how could this be true? With so much wasted time and effort, the hours lost to corporate handiwork, the tasks themselves so meaningless they might have been designed by an enterprising Devil? Inside the stockroom Bethany could hear the chatter of all Human Resources, information shared in a brisk, conversational tone ("Here's those 401(k) forms you wanted, sugar"), the lives recounted in confidence over cubicle dividers, women talking about their weekend plans, phones cradled between shoulder and cheek, while their counterparts in other offices along Route 128 kept them "on hold." There was no time for anything, not anymore, and spiritual progress had become a dream and even worse—a joke! Despair was everything; the hour had passed long ago. Maybe Thomas knew this, she thought, and his disappearance was a sign in Christian code for all of them to *stop* and take a reckoning of what they had become. She had spent the night before thinking of their time together, trying to recount their most recent conversations for a small or subtle hint that might have illuminated his state of mind, but his nature was so secretive that she came up with nothing! Since the beginning of Lent they had been unable to sleep together, separated by the Easter holiday, a stroke (Jerry Waddle), a heart attack (Al Neuhaus), and the premature arrival of Martha Proctor's baby boy. At times like this she burned for him, and resorted to techniques to grab his attention that were *less than subtle*, like her latest pornographic note. Once she had even slipped out of her underwear before taking Jessie to Cherubs' Choir practice, hoping to corral him into the parsonage for a moment or two, only to discover thanks to Mrs. Safarian that

Thomas and the other members of the Council were meeting with their financial consultant behind closed doors . . . There, alone in the stockroom, as she rested uncomfortably on the middle rung of a step stool, Bethany's mind began to circumvent the larger problem of the pastor's disappearance and fixate on her missing love note—unsigned, thank God—which had either blown away in the suburban wind (she deemed this unlikely) or had been taken by another congregant. Someone else who loved him? Or a Judas who wanted to see him ruined? At times it seemed there were impressive numbers in both parties, and Thomas, trusting as he did in the Word to inform our reason, had returned their admiration and enmity alike with the Perfect Indifference of His Love. Whatever thief had stolen her note from the parsonage steps might know something about his disappearance, and just as every act of Will is decided by a Motive, as Thomas might have put it in a sermon, God's absolute and certain Foreknowledge of events would eventually compel this moral Agent, in an accident of Grace, to come forward.

Later that same night Bobby Caruso fumbled with his keys at the front door, having returned home after a brutal skull session in the conference room, preceded by a depressing progress report from Davenport, Iowa, and an upbraiding by his boss, and through it all—the bitter cups of coffee, the peaks and valleys of adrenaline, the constant threat of layoffs—*not a single phone call from Bethany*, whose love for him seemed to be waning with every night they spent apart. If the alarm goes off, he thought, they've seen the last of me, but it never came to that: while Bobby stooped to pick up his key ring (a Bud Light bottle opener), the front door miraculously swung open and Ulla the Remarkable, as Bethany had somewhat meanly dubbed her, swooped down and restored the keys to his open palm, lifted him upright by his shoulders, and ushered him indoors. Before he had the chance to thank her properly, Ulla had run off in the direction of the kitchen, calling into the TV room, "Turn it off, Devon, your father's home!" Such a brisk understanding of what kept a household running, and pale white knees that, emerging from the fringed holes of her blue jeans, seemed to have been carved from Nordic stone! Long nights alone in the fornicatorium had increased his sexual appetite; his imagination was alive to every woman in his orbit, from Miranda Levy, a colleague in project management, who, until now, had always reminded him unpleasantly of Michael Ovitz, to Ulla herself, a natural subject for sexual fantasy, but *guilt* had always held him back, along with his suspicion that Bethany would somehow intuit his attraction to Ulla and fire her on the spot. He avoided fantasizing about Ulla for the sake of the children, and in the hope that Bethany, noting his exemplary conduct with this Swedish bud, would invite him back into the master bedroom for—at the very least—a night of erotic massage. Bobby had never forgotten a strange joke that had circulated about a classmate of his in high school: *Why does Stephen Hardy suck his own dick?* Answer: *Because he can.* Aside from marking Stephen—a nice guy who meant well—with an indelible image, the joke had haunted Bobby ever since with its suggestion that sex was a selfish act, when he believed the opposite: that frequent lovemaking was the root of all generosity, the highest form of communication yet devised by man, machine, or lonely whale. He saw no reason to talk endlessly about *feelings* and *the relationship*, especially in front of some marriage counselor wearing the wooden beads of her destructive tribe, well known to be the leading cause of upper-middle-class divorce! Sex was far superior to arguing with the help of a stopwatch, or switching "roles" two nights a week to build "empathy," or separating on a trial basis—the therapists could barely control their glee when they suggested *that* one, knowing full well that once the wall of familiarity fell, there would be no reason for anyone to go hunting close to home. It was a proven fact that the only way to save a relationship from trouble was *to have sex, constantly*. Now that was empathy! As he used to say to Bethany: If you knew what it was like to sleep with you (here she sighed and rolled over), you would sleep with me more often. *And now*, she had answered once, *a word from the horny philosopher*.

The scene at the family dinner table that night, no less hectic and confusing than his workplace, only deepened Bobby's sense of gloom. Ulla had interpreted a recipe for pot roast quite freely and bathed the thing in a currant cream sauce. The children loved it ("All dinner should be pink!" Jessie pronounced) while Bethany, looking pale and distracted, ate only a few of her overcooked vegetables. Of greater interest was her glass of wine; she kept on leaving the table to fill it at the refrigerator, coming back, each time, with another layer of glaze over her eyes. Did he hear her talking on the phone? And muffling her patented sobs with that dish towel she was carrying around? Jessie had finished her dinner already and, with Ulla's encouragement, began singing a song from Sunday school: *Yo tengo un amigo que me ama, me ama, me ama, me ama, ama, Su nombre es Jesús*. When she had finished, Devon called her a "Jesus freak," adding, "You're like indoctrinated, yo."

"Shut up, Big Poppa!"

"You shut up, Jesus freak."

"Big *what*?" Bobby asked, jumping into the fray.

"Jesus loves me!" Jessie shot back at her brother. Ulla tried to calm her by suggesting a time-out, but she had already passed the point of no return. "Devon changed his name to Big Poppa!"

"Shut up, yo!"

"It's true! He said if I don't call him Big Poppa from now on, he'll kill me in my sleep!" Ulla lifted Jessie from her chair to console her and, at the same time, gave Devon a deeply disapproving look, bringing him to the verge of childish tears.

"I never said that!"

"You did!"

"Listen up," Bobby said, trying to regain some order (usually this was Bethany's department, but she seemed to be sitting this one out). "No one's killing anyone under *my* roof, understand? And as for changing the names you were born with forget it. Your mother and I thought long and hard about this subject, and I think we did all right by both of you. Devon comes from your mother's side of the family, where I can assure you there are no Big Poppas—"

"It's not *real*," Devon interrupted.

"What does it mean, Big Poppa?" Ulla asked, balancing Jessie on her hip. "Anyway, it doesn't suit you."

"Nothing," Devon said. "It means nothing, okay?"

"Then we're settled," Bobby announced. "No killing, everybody keeps his given name, and we finish our dinner in peace and harmony, am I right? The argument is over now. Everything," he wound up, turning to Bethany for some support, "is nice and normal here."

But his dream of a peaceful family meal was interrupted by the doorbell, and Bethany, animated for the first time all night, held Ulla off (naturally she had already started for the door) with a firm "I'll get it, thank you."

For a moment she allowed herself to hope for the unthinkable, that Thomas had reappeared on her doorstep with a logical excuse and an apology for the confusion, perhaps his mother *had* needed him in Annisquam, or he had forgotten to tell Jane about the congregation in New Hampshire which had asked for his guidance in extending the Call . . . She opened the door with *expectation* and the feeling that she might, after all, have been dreaming this terrible episode, only to be confronted with the smiling face of Bradley Howard, amateur Hell's Angel and her sometimes dope dealer. There was more of his mother in Bradley than either Howard would have admitted in public, and because of this family resemblance, his habit of dressing head to toe in black leather, and his open leer, Bradley gave her the creeps.

"You paged, Mrs. C?"

"Oh, right," she said, "I didn't hear you coming." Being stupid, Bradley usually visited his "clients" on his infernal Harley; after setting off every car alarm on her street during his last delivery, Bethany had suggested that he try visiting on foot. "Why don't we get this over with."

Bradley produced a small Ziploc bag from his leather trench coat. "A fine, full-bodied smoke for the working mother, smooth aftertaste, organically grown. I'm giving it my rasp-free guarantee. Any trouble with your pipes, the next dose is on your dealer." He waited outside while she grabbed her wallet, whistling "Mother's Little Helper" through his teeth. "Just so you know," he said when she came back, "I've been having *mucho* problems with my main supplier, a guy down in Texas, and I've been forced to, well, raise my prices, ummm, accordingly."

"Just give me a number," she said, picking through receipts and banking slips in search of legal tender.

"For you," he answered, "add another deuce."

"A *what?* Oh, you mean a twenty. Here, let me see . . ."
Bethany quickly found the right amount of money, knowing
that, at any moment, her husband might appear to find out
what was keeping her from the table. She took the Ziploc bag
of dope from Bradley, whose leer had settled on her blouse, and
asked him, "You know I'm familiar with your mother from our
church, right?"

"Ummm, yeah?"

"Do you think she approves of your chosen profession?"

"Fuck if I know, lady."

"Does she suspect?"

"Don't think so," he answered once he caught her drift.

"Before I pay," she told him, "I want a solemn oath that
you will *never, ever* sell drugs to my children or any of their
friends, even if they offer you top dollar. I've seen your Harley
parked around the middle school, and I don't approve of your
recruiting methods."

"An oath." He laughed. "Yeah. Whatever."

*Bethany,* her husband called from the dining room, *is everything all right? Do you need me?*

She yelled back, "It's the Fix the Light people again! I'm almost finished!" Bradley's leer had grown so intense that she
nearly called the police right then and there. "I want an oath,"
she repeated, dropping her voice to a near-whisper, "that your
*product* will never foul the lungs of my kids."

"I promise?" he said, focusing, at last, on her money instead
of on her blouse.

"That's good enough," she told him, handing over eighty
dollars, "thank you." Bradley stuffed his take in the pocket of
his trench coat, checking over both his shoulders with a dramatic flourish before he left her in the doorway. The smell of
wood smoke was in the air that night, reminding her of winter,

and up and down the length of her street Bethany could see the pale blue glow of her neighbors' television sets, filling the windows in every house with a common shade of loneliness. She felt a dread much greater than the village landscape just outside her door; the orderly spread of her housing development promised *respite* from the high-technology highway where many of them worked (there, just through the woods, see the golden arches of McDonald's tower like a radio beacon, pale in daylight, shining at night), and yet here she was, on the threshold of her own eleven rooms, and she felt abandoned! As Bradley walked away he could have been a Savage from the woods or, even worse, the wayward child of intolerant Settlers, spreading their beliefs like smallpox all throughout the wilderness. And what was she, the village dope smoker? An adulteress in search of spiritual depth? Another hapless victim of suburban *ennui*? Bethany was about to close the door on her transaction when Bradley said, out of the darkness just beyond the floodlight's reach, "Hey, I heard the Reverend Brother Mosher packed his bags and split the church."

His voice had taken her by surprise. She had always found Bradley's drug-dealer routine more theatrical than sinister, but now he was proving, just like his mother, to be a malignant influence. She had to squint to make out his shape at the end of the walk; a pair of moths flew frantic, intertwining patterns in front of where he stood. "Word has it the Right Reverend's been ballin' ladies all over town—married, single, made no difference to the man. I say more power to the brother. Rainbow! That's what I say."

"Check your sources," she told him, readying the door for a furious slam, "and get off of my property."

"I'm getting," he said. "Take it easy, hey."

"And don't come back here, ever," she warned him.

Bradley only laughed. "Yeah, yeah, yeah. Thanks for signing my petition. Crazy *bitch*."

Snug in her saltbox, shaken by the day's events and trying, as an enlightened optimist, to believe that Thomas would return, Jane Groom kept vigil at her kitchen table with a kerosene lamp (she appreciated the simple light it cast) and her mother's King James Bible open to the Gospel according to Mark, near enough to the telephone should the pastor materialize, and mindful of her companion Molly Bloom (still ailing) in the midst of an evening nap beneath the table, and beginning, in her endearing schnauzer way, to snore. Jane had been struggling with apprehension and self-doubt since early that morning, when she had awakened suddenly from a strange dream about Thomas—that he came to her during the night, sat politely at the foot of her bed, and tried, in a gentle voice, to explain his absence without the aid of Scripture, saying, *I no longer depend on the Bible, Jane.* While the ease of his manner in the dream had set her mind at rest, she had wanted to ask, *What have you chosen instead?,* but hadn't dared, even in her dream state. Upon waking, she had felt obliged to spend an hour or two engaged in silent prayer. As helpful as this was to her, she knew from practice that her Lord was not a micromanager (she was reminded of this fact as she read Christ's parables in Chapter 4 of Mark that night. Imagine having Faith enough to speak in parables to the multitudes! And entrust the mystery of the Kingdom of God to such a motley group of disciples! She understood their fear as the storm rose and tossed their tiny ship while Christ slept on His pillow, shared their amazement when He rose from his sleep and commanded,

*Peace, be still. And the wind ceased, and there was great calm,*
and she prayed for the same safe passage to the other side of
this uncertain sea). Soon after resorting to the Pilgrim Prayerline to raise the alarm, Jane had been visited by the image of
Alexander Haig, President Reagan's power-hungry Secretary of
State, stating, at the first press conference following John
Hinckley's assassination attempt, "As of now, I am in control."
She remembered watching him and thinking, *Madness!* His unhealthy satisfaction at that chaotic moment, the way he seemed
to welcome the violence and disorder of an attempt against the
President's life . . . Of all the lawless men Ronald Reagan had
empowered in Washington during his two administrations,
Alexander Haig, with his icy stare and not-quite-hidden
agenda, might have been the most dangerous, and Jane sin-
cerely hoped that by taking some initiative she was following a
blessed path, and not falling prey to whatever earthly ambition
God had placed in her heart expressly to remind her that all
achievement was transitory, and success in this world without
the temperance of His salvation would only lead to failure and
calamity in the next. It was precisely this belief that had com-
pelled her, once the Reverend Chambers had informed her of
his retirement plans, to withdraw herself from consideration
for the position of senior minister. She had looked into her
heart and found a *great uneasiness* with power; and when
Thomas had arrived in the village, promising a new progressive
era in the history of the church, a *social and spiritual awakening*, she had come to view her selfless act as a gift from God
and the handiwork of the Holy Spirit.

*Know ye not this parable?* Jesus asked his disciples. *And
how then will ye know all parables? The sower soweth the
word.* But Jane's concentration suffered that night, and she was
astonished at herself that she *could not sow anything*, not with

the help of her third-favorite Gospel, which she had turned to for its treatment of the Messianic Secret; not in the glow of her kerosene lamp, usually so conducive to clear thinking; nor with Molly snoring peacefully at her feet, one of her favorite sounds in all the world. The lamp's wick badly needed trimming, and as a consequence the flame flickered higher than it should have, sending up an oily smoke that stained the chimney. To her distress the telephone refused to ring, and more than once that evening she had left her seat and picked the receiver off its cradle, checking for a dial tone, only to discover that her phone was working perfectly. Why would no one call with information about the pastor? Or just to commiserate with her, show concern and loving kindness to a fellow church member? Jane found the silence from the congregation most alarming—that Thomas, who had offered them patience, understanding, and imaginative guidance as a teacher could *vanish*, and no one apart from Margaret Howard (she had called immediately to suggest involving the Police), the members of the Council (over a somber conference call they had decided against notifying the authorities until Thomas missed the Membership Committee on Thursday), and Mrs. Safarian (as his secretary and a lay leader she knew Thomas intimately, and during tearful conversations with Jane throughout the day, she had assured Jane, again and again, that Thomas hadn't said or done anything out of the ordinary) cared enough to *help her solve this mystery*. Of course, there was the possibility that the members of the church were suffering from a collective case of denial, or they could have been in shock. And it was true that ever since Jane had delivered her sermon on the Jewish tradition of *midrash* and its relationship to the Gospels (she had properly credited her ideas to Bishop John Shelby Spong), a certain element in the church had been indifferent to her Sunday greetings. She had heard the unkind whispers about the series of dramatic skits she had organized for Lent, culminating in Easter Sunday's "An Encounter at the Tomb," and endured an unreasonable request from the Grounds Committee that she keep Molly off the church grounds—as if she were the only dog to ever soil the lawn! As if her stool weren't natural and biodegradable! The intolerance of Jane's peers had sometimes brought to mind the factionalism Paul faced in Corinth, and in times of controversy (which was often) she turned to his Second Epistle for guidance, especially the passage: *While we look not at the things which are seen, but at the things which are not seen: for the things which are seen are temporal; but the things which are not seen are eternal.* Thomas had been her ally in so many minor disputes of procedure and matters of governance, and over time that had established a biweekly routine of sharing their thoughts over a cup of tea in the parsonage—Orange Pekoe for Thomas, Lemon Zinger for herself. During these intimate and candid meetings they had often remarked, with a sense of weariness, that the Pilgrims' Church resembled a Christian country club more than it did a house of worship. They had agreed to pick up their meetings again once the ordeal of Easter was over, but Thomas, after the holiday, had seemed even more distracted and remote than usual, putting her off when she raised the subject. He was always so tired in her company! Jane, not wanting to apply too much pressure, had resisted mentioning their meeting schedule more than once, and now that he was *gone* she regretted her timidity, wondering if his latest period of withdrawal hadn't been, as Lisa, the teen-outreach counselor liked to say, a *cry for help.* The "infinite sphere" sermon, too, had begun to haunt her: It was hard to explain, exactly, but ever since completing her cycle of sonnets based on the eight Beatitudes of Matthew, inspired by the vision of Love in Thomas's sermon, she was having trouble remembering the substance of his lesson, only the sphere, that loving sphere, expanding outward through space and time . . . And it had begun to seem as if his "infinite sphere" sermon, once spoken, had outlived its very purpose like some rare, native flower that, in blooming, dies . . . and in dying, shares a brief, unaccountable joy to all who witness its life, though they can't, with any accuracy, describe what they saw, and words fail, utterly fail, when they try . . .

Rather than prolong her losing battle with the Gospels, Jane roused Molly from her nap and lured her out back for an evening run with the help of a dog biscuit. An episode of *inappropriate barking* that afternoon had clearly worn her out, and when Jane hitched her collar to the "trolley" leash outside, Molly showed none of her usual enthusiasm for the great outdoors. She kept on looking back at the house with longing in her eyes; Jane clapped her hands and told the schnauzer, "Go, Molly," and she obeyed, trotting off reluctantly to do her business. The weatherman had raised the possibility of frost that night, but it felt warm to Jane. She stood on the back porch and watched Molly sniff the ground in circles, squat gracefully in the darkness to pee, and lope off in search of another, more interesting spot. *Heaven and earth shall pass away,* she was reminded, *but my words shall not pass away. Take ye heed, watch and pray: for ye know not when the time is.* "Good dog," she murmured to herself, and began to cry! The words had come from her mother's Bible, signed on the inside cover in her youthful hand, *Margaret Constance Perry.* Another name from a life that Jane knew almost nothing about, save an envelope of old photographs, mended with disintegrating Scotch tape, and the few family stories that had survived in her memory. Was her mother back in that lost world now, conversing freely with her relatives? Would the Kingdom of Heaven see the reunion of all the families in Christendom and beyond? *But we had the sentence of death in ourselves,* Paul wrote to the Corinthians, *that we should not trust in ourselves, but in God which raiseth the dead.* As a girl these words had frightened her silly, but now that Jane was older and an orphan, she took great solace in the idea of death's certainty. The silence of the night sky! It seemed the Heavens were a great protective tent, the stars a kind of unifying wisdom, blinking with their chemical eternity, reflecting all the hope of Science, all the genius of Creation, their very multitude an order that human beings, so small on earth, could only stare at from the ground with a sense of wonder and *accept*, with gratitude and awe, as the Ultimate Design. Was this a version of his *infinite sphere?* Where was Thomas underneath the stars? Was he alive? She thought of her dream the night before, trying to regain the peace that she had felt with Thomas at the foot of her bed, and instead she was newly troubled by his confession: *I no longer depend on the Bible, Jane.* Generally speaking, she did not believe in visions, miracles, or portents from above, and suspected, instead, that her subliminal mind had begun to work through the problem of his absence (although she would never underestimate the influence of the Holy Spirit). Jane couldn't help wondering if her dream, so vivid in her memory, had unearthed an important secret, and her tears gave way to a fierce determination to face this crisis with a Faith befitting one of His disciples. *They shall take up serpents,* Christ had promised, *and if they drink any deadly thing, it shall not hurt them; they shall lay hands on the sick, and they shall recover.*

*I shall recover,* she thought, and knelt to greet Molly as she came back on her trolley leash, wiggling her behind and panting. Jane accepted her wet kisses in the darkness, grateful for this attention from another living being. "Good dog," she murmured in her ear, "yes, Molly, you're a good, good dog."

"What about foul play?" Bobby asked, sitting across the table from Bethany and scanning the *Globe*'s sports page for photographs of female athletes, preferably Monica Seles in mid-grunt, or Steffi Graf returning a backhand with a Germanic look of concentration, or Rebecca Lobo, the college basketball player from UConn, with her arms around one of her smaller teammates, like that perky little guard with the ponytail who was always pumping her fist in the air. How he admired sportsmanship among women! After one last minor argument Jessie and Devon had been excused from the dinner table, and Bethany, her voice trembling, had confided in him that no one had seen the pastor of her church since Sunday afternoon. "At the first sign of trouble," he advised her, "always call the State Police. They're professionals, Beth, not like these rent-a-cops in the village. All they do is give out parking tickets. I wouldn't trust them with a stolen bicycle."

"But his car's not in the driveway," Bethany told him. She had come back to the dinner table feeling terrible about paging Bradley, and had immediately exchanged her glass of wine for ice water. Chemical dependency was becoming a burden on her psyche, and if not for the trouble with the pastor, she might have considered attending her first Tuesday night AA meeting. "There's no sign of a struggle in the parsonage. It's like he just *left*. I mean, the answering machine is full."

"Who told you that?"

She clutched her water glass in both hands. "Jane Groom, the assistant minister. At least I think it was Jane. Anyway, you have no idea what a rotten day I've had." Ulla glided in from the kitchen to clear the last of the dishes, blissfully unaware, it seemed, of anything beyond her wholesome aura. Bethany had decided against mentioning the pastor's disappearance to the children just yet, thinking it might frighten them. She eyed the label on Ulla's blue jeans and quietly hated her for having the body of a fifteen-year-old boy.

"My Volkswagen's on the blink," Ulla said, reaching across Bobby's newspaper for a stray butter knife, "so I'll need a ride back to Somerville." But he was studying a photograph of Lindsay Davenport (always a disappointment when she played well, he thought, why not Mary Pierce? With those big French-expatriate eyes?) and missed his opening. Bethany was listening, though, and volunteered her husband as a taxi service. "I'll be ready in ten minutes," Ulla promised, heading around the table. Unless Bobby was mistaken, she had given his shoulder a little squeeze on her way into the kitchen.

"Are you okay?" Bobby felt his scrotum tighten in anticipation of his time alone with Ulla, but his powers of sexual prediction had been deceiving him lately. It was only a few nights before that his "package" had given him the full alarm, and he had waited for Bethany's knock at the fornicatorium door, lying still so as not to disturb the signals. By 2 a.m. he had given up hope, and fell asleep in the disenchanting glow of soft-porn on cable.

"I'm fine," she said, "just a little shaky."

"When I get back, I could spend the night—"

"Nice try, Bobby."

"It's just that you seem upset—"

"NO."

He waited in the car while Ulla said her goodbyes to the children, who treated her departure, each time, as if it were permanent, especially the girl; she usually tried everything in her arsenal to convince Ulla to spend the night (tears, wailing, fist-pounding), while the boy maneuvered shamelessly for a good-night kiss—one on each cheek, in the European style. At least in his admiration for the female form, Bobby thought, the boy was like his father. Now if Devon could only control the blushing problem and stop identifying with his mother, he might turn out to be a real Lothario. Ulla finally emerged from the house with her backpack, turning back to wave before she reached the driveway. It was a touching scene: the Caruso family gathered to see their favorite nanny off, Bethany watching her leave with envy, Jessie squirming and crying in her mother's arms, Devon reaching through his pocket to adjust his boner, and Bobby, the faithful husband, checking the progress of his receding hairline in the rearview mirror, anxious to look younger and more virile to his passenger, so modest that she would never know—or even suspect—just how much she meant to them, that she represented maturity to the children, youth to the parents, and *deliverance* from the prison of the family unit to them all. Bobby opened his passenger door and she climbed inside, dropping her backpack on the floor and letting out a slightly foreign sigh.

"I have thirty quizzes to grade tonight," she said, "and my roommate's boyfriend is here from Denmark. Niels is obsessed with television shows by Aaron Spelling, do you know him?"

"Sure, the *Love Boat* guy."

She unzipped her backpack. "At home Niels is very serious, but when he comes to visit, he turns into a couch potato." Ulla spoke English with a spooky perfection, indeed there was a hint of accusation in the way she pronounced "couch potato" too correctly, as if to say, *Your language is a fool's paradise, but I've mastered its every nuance.* "He just sits in front of the TV eating Pop-Tarts!"

As Bobby pulled his car out of the driveway he felt a twinge of jealousy for this interloper. He imagined a tall Danish graduate student with a scruffy beard and serious eyes, a ratty couch facing a secondhand color television, an open box of Pop-Tarts on the coffee table, and Ulla, left alone with him for the night, having to cross in front of the TV on her way back from the shower, draped in an oversized towel, leaving tiny wet footprints behind her . . .

"Plain or frosted?"

"Who cares? They're both foul," she answered, taking a cassette tape out of her Walkman, "so many chemicals. I can't believe Americans let their children eat the stuff." She ejected Bobby's tape from his stereo and checked the label, asking, "Who's *Boston?*"

"No one," he explained. "Here, let me see that," and he took the incriminating evidence from her hands, tossing the tape in the back seat. "Just a blast from the past."

Ulla popped her own tape in. "Do you like Prince?"

"Absolutely," Bobby claimed. "Talk about multitalented."

"Then you must know *Come,*" she said, pressing the rewind button. "It's my favorite CD in the world. Don't the lyrics just blow your mind? He's got such a natural idea of human sexuality. Prince is very big in Sweden right now."

. . . And an hour later, as she's drinking herbal tea in her bathrobe, candles burning on her windowsill, the quizzes spread across her desk and her hands beginning to cramp from correcting so many undergraduate mistakes, there's a knock on Ulla's bedroom door and she answers, "Yes, come in," without thinking, and the door opens to reveal the Danish boyfriend, Niels, who tells her that *Melrose Place* is over, sitting down on the edge of her bed, the candles flicker and their eyes meet, and she drops her pen . . .

On the highway Bobby tried to calm himself by thinking about traffic accidents, and when that no longer worked (still during the title song, "Come") he thought about the potential for his friendship with Ulla to result in marital disaster: fumbled kisses on her doorstep, an invitation to her bedroom, an hour of bliss in candlelight followed by the guilt, an accusation, his anguished confession, tears and anger on both sides, a phone call to a lawyer, divorce papers, a lecture from his parents, the children's refusal to see him—and the entire village, thanks to Bethany's church connections, would know every detail: how Bobby took advantage of a homesick *au pair* and lost his family, his well-paying job, and his self-respect, ending up in a group home for recovering sex addicts, forced to go door to door in the surrounding neighborhood and say, "Hello, my name is Bobby Caruso, I'm staying at the local men's shelter and I'm a sex addict. Please keep an eye on your daughters." Ulla seemed unconcerned about the fact they were alone in the car, and listened without expression to her favorite CD, staring out the window as the rural scenery along Route 2 gave way to suburbia (protected from the sounds of the road by concrete barriers) and, just as the highway came to an end at the Alewife "T" station, a peculiar urban blight. Ulla looked up at the Rindge Towers, windows lighted in the random language of high-rise living, and asked, "Are those housing projects?"

"I'm pretty sure," Bobby answered, and immediately saw himself in an apartment on the lower floors, standing at the window and watching traffic curl around the rotary, missing his family, repeating to himself, *I never should have made that lunge for Ulla.* It wasn't until they had reached Fresh Pond Circle that she reflected, "You treat poverty like it's a crime here."

They argued for a while about the relative merits of America's welfare system, Bobby claiming that the tax burden on working people was too high already, Ulla countering that higher taxes meant better services for everyone, and that he, as a wealthy American, had a moral obligation to contribute what he could for the betterment of every family. She had a blunt debating style that he found attractive, and as they traversed the back streets of West Cambridge for lesser Somerville, Bobby felt his scrotum tightening again, aided and abetted by Ulla's favorite CD, which, if he was not mistaken, included the recording of a woman having an orgasm. First Bobby promised himself never, ever to listen to that Boston tape again (no matter how much "More Than a Feeling" reminded him of promiscuity in high school). Then he resolved to be strong, and ignore the signal emanating from his groin for the sake of his troubled marriage, no matter how long it had been since Bethany had *let him in*, and how deeply Ulla tempted him with her idealism, close-cropped hair, and perfect knees that promised perfect legs, and perfect ankles, and perfect feet that he would praise with language and his tongue, surprising her with his taste for the unusual, and perfect hands to hold, fingers interlocked, while she pinned him with her pale blue eyes and told him, *Fuck me.*

"Here we are," Ulla said when they had reached her house, just the three-story tenement that he had pictured halfway up a hill, a mass of bicycles chained to the porch railing at the top of the front stairs. "Thanks for the ride, Bobby." She pronounced his name like *couch potato*, and looked up at her apartment windows wistfully, as if she didn't want to go inside.

*Kiss her!* his scrotum signaled, but he kept his hands on the steering wheel and told her, "Good luck with your quizzes."

She zipped her backpack. "Don't remind me, please."

"Hey, don't let that Niels guy get you down. I say just ignore him." What an idiot! Ulla made a face that he couldn't decipher, and in the moment before she left the car, backpack in tow, she threw her arms around his shoulders, squeezed him tighter than he thought possible, and reassured him, "He's half the man you are."

Then she was gone, slamming the car door behind her and climbing the front steps with an unselfconscious grace that he hadn't seen since Bethany was a sophomore in college and he was a senior with a 2.8 GPA and only vague plans for the future, watching this beautiful stranger climb the staircase in his fraternity house and thinking to himself, *There goes my wife.* Now, over fifteen years later, Bobby was still admiring Bethany from a distance, forced, by virtue of their marital problems, to plot his way into her arms. How some things never changed! He waited until Ulla was safely inside the apartment building, watching for a final wave or smile, but she merely vanished into the darkness of her entryway. Bobby shifted his car back into gear and started up the hill, dazed by Ulla's compliment and jubilant when he discovered, quite by accident, that she had left her favorite tape behind. Was it a gift? he wondered as the music cued up again. A way of telling him that he was welcome, after all, to think of her as a sexual being? To imagine her at night when he was alone in the fornicatorium? And would she, in turn, be thinking of *him* that night, the candles in her bedroom extinguished, the quizzes all corrected, her duvet cover pulled up to her chin and sleep eluding her, trying not to listen, through the adjoining wall, to the sound of her roommate fucking Niels? *Niels!* Bobby imagined as he drove faster on the way home, replaying his encounter with Ulla and feeling, if anything, closer to his first love, Bethany, because *she* was his ideal, *she* was the mother of his children, *she* was his wife and co-participant in the most improbable fantasy of them all—a working marriage—and if he ever had to choose between them, neurotic wife or placid nanny, there was no choice: *Bethany* had climbed the staircase in his fraternity house in midwinter, wearing an olive-green overcoat from the army surplus store off-campus, unaware that he existed, unaware that she would one day marry him. Bobby remembered everything about that night! Turning to his half-friend Louie (they only hung out at parties) and asking, *Who's that girl?* and Louie, overconfident despite his clownish looks and deadly-smelling feet, said, *Dunno. Looks psycho to me.* Was it strange that an average encounter between two friends at a fraternity party would change the course of Bobby's life? No more unlikely than a Swedish graduate student with torn blue jeans reminding him how much he needed his wife, or a sequence of events whereby Bethany, after fourteen years of silence on the issue of religion, decides one Sunday morning to begin attending church, joins the congregation in search of *wholeness*, she claims, *wholeness, what a word to use with me*, and then slowly, imperceptibly at first but later more rapidly, she *changes for the worse*: sure, their marriage had been rocky from the start, but never quite like this: always they argue, one or another is brooding, they communicate by not communicating (except where the children are concerned), finally, at her request, they separate *for the third time in as many years*, choosing this well-worn and temporary solution over divorce, a word that she has spoken first—how could she!—and a concept that he refuses *absolutely* to consider. Once spoken, the word torments him, especially at night, alone in his unfinished room above the garage and floating on his leaky water bed, adrift from his wife, their marriage, and the bedroom he had chosen from the building plans for its intimate layout. *Divorce*, he thinks, *the ultimate* no, he would rather hear a doctor say *prostate exam* than listen to Bethany spit *divorce* in a late-night fury, and he doesn't blame himself for this predicament, or even blame his wife, whom he considers to be hysteria-prone, *he blames the church* for stealing her soul away from him and making promises that no mortal husband can ever keep, *he blames the pastor* for taking an interest in his wife and daughter (he only met Thomas once in passing, picking his daughter up from choir practice, and he was shocked, when the pastor shook his hand through the open car window, to feel his scrotum *clinch*), *he blames religion* for ruining his marriage, and though he knows better than to say a word to Bethany and upset her fragile nerves, he believes her pastor is a common wife stealer, and Bobby welcomes the unexpected news—yes, *welcomes* it—that the Reverend Thomas Mosher has disappeared from the village.

"Is that you?" Margaret Howard called from the top of the stairs, sealed in flannel for the night and wearing Acorn slippers, the only way to keep her toes from going numb after dark (her circulation had always been poor) no matter what the season, "Bradley? Is that you, dear?" She hadn't heard her son's motorcycle pulling in the driveway, and a thumping at the door had brought her from the upstairs study, where, at her rolltop desk, she had been looking over the appraisal report for her latest coup, a striking Queen Anne that she had managed to poach from one of her competitors in Sudbury. The intruder must have been Bradley, because he headed straight for the refrigerator, although there had been that unsolved rash of food-related B-and-E's in '87, widely attributed, in the local paper, to delinquent teenagers. Bradley had been away at Colorado College then, taking hallucinogens and skipping all of his classes, frittering away his potential—not to mention a generous allowance—on *experience*, as he had put it, meaning drugs, his first motorcycle, and dope-crazed women. What happened to the boy who used to give her a homemade Valentine's Day card every year? Red construction paper cut into a heart, a doily in the middle decorated with his crooked handwriting, *Be My VaLentine Ma*? Bradley was thirty years old and had moved back home after Christmas, claiming his landlord had illegally evicted him; he was able-bodied and refused to look for steady and respectable employment, not that anyone would hire him without a single marketable skill and hair down to his waist (at least he'd shaved those awful sideburns); he certainly smoked and probably dealt marijuana, though she didn't want to think about it; and tonight he had come home past his negotiated curfew and immediately started rifling through her refrigerator!

"Hey, did Pop drink all my beer?"

Margaret could hear him combing the shelves for a snack, just the way his father had done not an hour earlier. First they complained about eating leftovers again, and then, after licking their plates clean, they insisted on making mashed-potato sandwiches! What had she done wrong to be cursed with such useless men?

"Hey, Pop!" he started yelling. "POP!"

"SHHH!" Margaret hissed. "You know he's sleeping at this hour!"

Bradley quieted down. "Then where the fuck's my beer?"

"Honey, I have no idea." She didn't tell him that an hour earlier she had come downstairs to check on Silvia's cleaning job and make herself a cup of tea, and the depressing sight of his Budweiser "tall boys" *blighting* her Sub-Zero had moved her to pour them out in the sink. To cover her tracks she had taken the empties out into the garage and crushed them under her slippers. Such a satisfying act of vandalism!

"Be careful down there," she reminded Bradley. "Silvia just cleaned the kitchen."

"You'd better tell Pop I'm on to him," Bradley called upstairs, rousing Jerry from his slumber (no small miracle) to ask Margaret from the bedroom, "What did he just say?"

"Nothing, dear, go back to bed."

"POP," Bradley yelled, "WHERE'S MY BEER?"

"What is he saying, Margaret?"

"MY *BEER*! IN THE *FRIDGE*!"

Margaret had heard enough. "Someone in this house still has work to do," she informed them both, "so if you'll kindly *shut up* and let me run my business. Jerry, you go back to sleep." His favorite words! Earlier in their marriage she had complained about his fondness for sleep, thinking (and rightly so) that it would hold him back in life, but during their middle period, when Howard Homes was first taking off, she had learned to use his circadian rhythm as a tool for control. One word from her now and Jerry nodded off like some kind of magic trick. "Bradley, mention your missing beer again and you're evicted from this house. You need to learn that there are more important things in life than motorbikes and liquor, not that your pride and joy out in the garage, that *Harley Whomever*, is ever running correctly." He muttered something in response, but she ignored him. "And don't forget who pays all the bills around here either. Am I clear?"

"Whatever, Ma." She could hear him messing up the kitchen counter with his late-night snack.

"Silvia just cleaned!"

"I know, Ma."

"There's a sponge on the sink, dear."

"*I know*, Ma."

"And don't forget to turn the lights out when you're finished!"

Back in her study Margaret put aside the appraisal to brood on her condition, still fuming from her latest encounter with

Bradley, and, though she might have been loath to admit it to anyone but Artemesia, saddened by the pastor's disappearance. The Reverend Thomas Mosher had never been her favorite man on earth; in fact, she had warned the congregation, during their deliberations two years earlier, about letting a social agenda dictate their choice of a new minister. She had been careful, of course, to voice her objections in the broadest possible terms, mentioning Thomas's obvious qualifications and the fresh approach he would bring to the pulpit, still there were those in the church, taken with the idea of historical novelty (while black ministers had sometimes been invited to visit the Pilgrims' Church, their choice in leadership had always been more traditional), who had never forgiven Margaret for that speech! And let's not forget the *Are you kin?* incident, an innocent question to strangers at Fellowship that had been seized on by her enemies as evidence that she, Margaret "equal opportunity" Howard, was somehow a *racist*! She was one of the few who seemed to remember a simpler time when the Reverend Chambers's wife, Vicky, was still alive, their three girls were little and the church held yearly Easter egg hunts on the grounds, and outings to the Topsfield Fair, and "movie nights" in the basement of the church . . . Bradley had developed a crush on the youngest Chambers girl, Emily, and had teased her relentlessly in Sunday school, pelted her with colored eggs, and pushed her down the staircase at the old grammar school . . . So family life wasn't always hugs and kisses, but the Reverend Chambers had brought a father's wisdom to his ministry, taking an active interest in the progress of all the congregation's children, even Bradley, who had kicked him in the shins that time during rehearsal for the Advent play, after the Reverend Chambers, trying to raise Bradley's self-esteem, had cast him in the difficult role of Joseph, opposite his daughter Sofia—now a professional actress on Broadway—as the Virgin Mother. Back then the Pilgrims' Church had been a sanctuary for parents, helping them to raise their children in a world that was quickly going to Hell in a handbasket. And the Reverend Chambers had been devoted to his wife right up until the end and then some, sharing the pain of Vicky's illness with the congregation as if it were a gift; she would always remember his first sermon after her diagnosis, the shock in every pew that soon gave way to tears, the outpouring of affection for this shrew of a woman who had always turned up her nose at them, and had spent most of her free time lobbying the Council for expensive renovations to the parsonage. (In one widely circulated letter she had called the residence a "hovel, clearly unfit for a Christian family.") Not once in his twenty-odd years had Margaret heard a peep about any of this bachelor's funny business! Let the Catholics have their pedophilia, she had always thought, the Episcopalians their cocktail parties and extramarital affairs—at the Pilgrims' Church we know right from wrong, and we don't need a priest in glad rags to stand between us and our Lord, thank you very much. We're perfectly capable of naming our sins and confessing them on our own! It was no secret that Margaret believed that her church had made a grave mistake in extending the call to the Reverend Thomas Mosher, and if the *crisis* of his disappearance weren't evidence enough, she had something else, a concrete exhibit, to prove that her suspicions about his character had been warranted:

Dear Rev. Mosher,

I am in a dilemma. Coming to your church makes me very horny. I have tried the route of self-pleasure in the pew but found it disappointing. After the sermon this Sunday, will you fuck me?

True, there was no mention of an open invitation, or of any sexual history between the pastor and his suitor, but this vile note *did* prove, and candidly, that the Reverend Mosher was more than just a melancholy man of God. From the beginning she had not trusted his wounded-lamb routine, or his scholarly air—and his nomination to the Grounds Committee had been a disaster, simply put. She disliked his know-it-all sermons, and his endless rendition of the silent prayer, and the pretentious way he intoned "Praise ye the Lord" at the end of the Assurance of Pardon. Apparently the parsonage was a pigsty, and he refused to lift a finger to clean it. Still the women in the church were all aflutter in his company, surrounding him at Fellowship, volunteering for every committee in sight, and siding with him on every issue *for the wrong reasons*, exactly what she had feared when they invited an unmarried minister to lead the church. And now it had come to this! The pastor on the run from unseemly complications, a desperate love note waiting for him on his doorstep (well, not anymore), that useless lesbian cohort of his the congregation's only hope . . . Just one more scandal, she thought, and that was it: she would follow through on her ancient threat, revived at least once a year on the Grounds Committee, to leave the members of the Pilgrims' Church to their squabbling and become a Presbyterian.

Margaret gave up on her appraisal report for the night and lifted the love note closer to her desk lamp, examining the handwriting for clues about the pastor's chippy. Graphology was another area where, for the sake of Howard Homes, she had become something of an expert. One of Margaret's lauded "personal touches" was to ask each prospective buyer to write out a personal statement in longhand describing their ideal home, neighborhood of choice, and hopes and dreams for the future, &c. Couples were allowed to collaborate on the answers, but Margaret required a written statement from each spouse (the husbands, being men and therefore entirely incapable of an imaginative leap, often left the "hopes and dreams" question blank; she had known women to run out of room on the answer form and continue writing on a supplemental sheet). While this exercise helped her clients to narrow their parameters, making the broker's job much easier, the written statements also provided Margaret with an accurate psychological profile of her buyers, and this, in the long run, saved her an untold amount of time and grief. A single sentence of handwriting revealed so much about its author! The pastor's love note had been scrawled too quickly for spacing to be an issue, and the lack of a signature—a real pressure point—would make a final judgment difficult. Still, she could identify a clearly inclined angle in the first line, evidence of a repressed personality; the reclined personal pronouns came as no surprise (the author's feelings were often a mystery to herself) and the erratic baseline indicated that our secret admirer was prone to moodiness. While the piece of paper itself was small, torn hastily (rough edges) from a notepad, there was enough room for Margaret to notice an overly wide right margin—meaning the author lived in the past. What could this possibly mean? When in doubt, Margaret thought, *make a list*, and she produced a yellow legal pad from underneath her appraisal report, writing along the top of the first page ALOOF, FEELINGS MYSTERY, MOODY, STUCK IN PAST. She studied this profile for a moment, and then, beginning on the line below, made a preliminary accounting of the pastor's groupies, BETHANY CARUSO, SADIE MAXWELL, ALESSANDRA RIO, LUCIA WAGNER. After a moment's hesitation she added ARTEMESIA. With the profile in mind she crossed out Sadie Maxwell, whose feelings were not a mystery to anyone who visited her leather shop, and

Alessandra Rio, a classic extrovert who signed everything in sight with a flourish, and Lucia Wagner, who fit the profile exactly, but was obviously devoted to her husband—even Artemesia, not one to judge her fellows, had remarked one Sunday that the Wagners seemed attached to each other at the hip . . . Leaving Bethany and Artemesia as the two most likely candidates, although there might, of course, have been someone she had overlooked, like that poet Martha Proctor? Whose husband was an art professor? No, she had just given birth to a boy and named it *Amo* or something, making an after-sermon dalliance in the parsonage beyond even him.

Poor Artemesia! She had been crying all afternoon, placing desperate calls to Margaret on her cell phone, the last as she toured the Queen Anne with the witless young couple who were selling it and running off to California in search of sunshine, easy living, and a catastrophic earthquake. It was a fact of life that in a seller's market (this latest boom in the New England economy seemed to have no end), everyone, even the Yuppie flakes, could make a killing in real estate. Margaret had been short with Artemesia, pretending that she was someone from the office, but what else could she do? The Yuppies were proudly showing off their *turret* overlooking Concord Avenue, decorated in a hideous style that Mrs. Flake referred to as "Bloomsbury" (the drapes would have to come down before Margaret showed the property). Once she had delivered her speech about the benefits and liabilities of an "open house," especially for such an exclusive property, Margaret had asked for a moment alone. She placed a quick call to the office first, making sure that Mrs. Lee, her Asian specialist, had reached her client in Wellesley (the woman was always getting lost, proving, to Margaret, that there was something to this stereotype about Asians and driving). That worry solved, she called Artemesia at home, apologized for being short, and listened helplessly, with rising frustration, as her best friend bawled her eyes out over the pastor's fate. She hadn't heard crying like this since Kitty Dukakis admitted to swallowing rubbing alcohol on national television! All she could do was listen, interject a "There, there," every now and then, or "Take a deep breath, dear," tender words she had rarely spoken since the days when Bradley was small and Jerry still delivered his halfhearted spankings. She was afraid they had failed their son in the discipline department—among others, judging by the way he turned out (what was he *doing* downstairs? Ordering more movies up on the Direct TV? At least he wasn't calling those 1-900 smut lines anymore, like the time they went away to Florida and came back to a $400 phone bill). In her own defense, hearing Bradley howl over his father's knee had been enough to break a mother's heart in two. Round about her fifth "There, there" and without any end in sight for Artemesia's tears, a light had switched on in Margaret's head, and for the first time she suspected that there might have been something to Artemesia's irrational admiration for the pastor: that her reaction might not have been a product of her hysterical nature, that her feelings might, on the most basic human level, have been *encouraged*, or even *reciprocated* . . . And then it dawned on Margaret that she had never seen her best friend's handwriting, except, perhaps, for her signature on a sign-up sheet in the church, or on the traffic light petition, and it was entirely possible that she had written the note herself! Until now Margaret had avoided this realization, and had offered her friend one last "Take a deep breath, dear" from the chilly turret before begging off her duties as listener, slipping her mobile phone back in her purse, and joining the Yuppies downstairs for a détente over decaffeinated cappuccino served in *bowls* instead of coffee mugs.

Margaret had forgone the pretentious ritual, asking for a simple cup of tea instead. How it hurt to pair Artemesia with the likes of Bethany Caruso! But drastic times, as they said, called for drastic measures, and if life in the church was ever going to be normal again, *someone* would have to get to the bottom of it all—namely, Margaret thought, yours truly.

"Bradley," she called from the top of the stairs, crossing her arms in her flannel nightgown, "are you there?" She could hear the television in the sitting room and resisted the urge to nag him about taking off his motorcycle boots, which left hideous black marks on the hardwood floors. To her surprise, she heard the jingle for *Headline News* instead of professional wrestling, his passion since the age of twelve. "I have something very important to talk to you about, Bradley."

"What *now*?" he asked with his mouth full.

"Are you decent?"

"Sort of . . ."

"Good, because I'm coming down." At the bottom of the stairs she took note of the kitchen's state, which was much worse than she had feared, but Margaret bit her tongue and concentrated on how best to manipulate Bradley. "I promise this won't take forever."

"Look," Bradley said, slouching in the leather Eames chair and stripped, for the night, down to a ratty black T-shirt and his Jockey shorts, "when I'm finished eating, I'm gonna clean—"

She raised a hand to shut him up. "I'll worry about that later, dear." Bradley looked at the female newscaster as if for help (that explained his interest in current events) and then back at his mother, unsure of what to do. "After all these years of being a *deadbeat* and a burden on your mother, there's finally a way that you can make yourself useful."

"What's that?" he said, blinking stupidly.

"Turn off that useless box," she instructed, and he did with the remote control. Margaret sat down on the end of the couch and asked her son, "Can you keep a secret?"

"Yeah, I guess."

"That's what I thought," she answered. "Now surprise me. *Make me proud.* Tell me everything you know about Bethany Caruso."

### Maundy Thursday

Thomas had been washing feet in the yearly ritual to commemorate Jesus' act of humility in John (13:4–20), using a natural sponge, a plastic bucket, Epsom salts, and a touch of dishwashing liquid from the kitchen (purely for the suds effect), girded, like the savior, in an irregular Fieldcrest bath sheet from T. J. Maxx, plenty absorbent for the job of drying off all twenty-four (two for each disciple) and blessing every owner with the words *He that receiveth whomsoever I send receiveth me, and he that receiveth me receiveth him that sent me.* To speed the ritual along, Jane had asked for volunteers before the service, and falling short by two disciples, she had been forced, along with the usher Silva, to bare her fallen arches to the eyes of the church, and let Thomas, in an act of professional intimacy, dip her toes in the communal water. She had never been as nervous to face the congregation, her good shoes stashed behind the pulpit with the others, kneesocks balled inside, slacks rolled up to the knee, her feet looking pale and out of place in the bright light of the service, somehow larger than usual . . . She watched the other disciples go before her one by one, an unpleasant heat gathering beneath her gown, thinking of her schnauzer for comfort, who sometimes licked her toes after she had taken a therapeutic bath in the evening and then scurried away, knowing full well that she had done something *forbidden*. Thomas was kneeling on a mat borrowed from the exercise class, looking solemn about his charge, she thought, and when her dreaded turn arrived he chose her right foot first, and then her left, washing them with the natural sponge that she had purchased herself at the Food Co-op. But Jane was *ticklish* in that area, and any emotion that might have swelled from the pastor's loving abasement of himself was soon outweighed by the funny tingle of his touch; the drying process was a kind of torture, and though she tried to control herself and swallow her pleasure, the towel's pile found all her *weak spots* and she burst out in a laugh, audible to everyone. Thomas, thanks to the repetition of his work, had been deep in thought, worrying about Bethany and her absence from the church that night, hoping that she wasn't struggling through an epic fight at home, but Jane had lured him back into the moment with her unexpected laugh: her bare feet in his hands, his towel dampened from the others, laughter spreading through the crowd, though sparse, to warm the atmosphere inside the church, his melancholy lifting with his eyes to have a look at Jane, whom, he expected, would be *mortified* by her outburst . . . Instead they shared a smile that even the usher Silva, the next in line for a footwashing, couldn't begrudge, and to protect himself from laughing, too, Thomas dropped his head and intoned the blessing, *He that receiveth, &c.*, then gently motioned Jane to move along.

At first sight of the usher's feet he cringed: a little toe was missing on the right, and age, use, and possibly arthritis had curled the nine toes that remained until they were clawlike; one ankle had a purple patch; he imagined corns, heard the word as if whispered in his ear: *Bunions.* Silva was the last to go, and Thomas had been lucky, he realized, with the first eleven pairs to cross his station: all had been groomed and healthy, exemplified by Sadie Maxwell's feet, slender and elegant in the grip of his powder-blue towel, soles rubbed smooth with pumice, nails trimmed and painted with mother-of-pearl enamel. They were *proud* feet, perhaps too proud, giving proof to the whispers that Sadie had *designs* on him, a rumor he ignored because he was not interested in her, no matter how she tried to win him over with belts and wallets from her leather shop, or how attractive she might have been (and it was shocking, actually) from the ankle down. Thomas was chastened by the poor state of the usher's feet, which spoke of time and suffering, and touched by Silva's humility that evening, the ease with which he offered this imperfect part of himself to be cleansed and blessed before the congregation that he served so faithfully on *nine toes*, years of pacing the aisles of the church with the offertory plate, sweeping the carpets, moving chairs and boxes in the parsonage, and stuffing envelopes—all performed with his precise Yankee impatience and a scowl that he should have *trademarked* for its power to correct and repel. Who among the members of the church, over all that time, could say they really knew the usher? Who had known that he was missing something basic, like a toe? *Such feet as these had borne the cross,* Thomas thought, and at once it struck him, rubbing Silva's callused heel with a sponge, that he was not worthy to bless these troubled feet, that without the ritual to bind him to the task he would rather not meet Silva without his shoes, he would rather not kneel in front of the cantankerous usher and supplicate himself, he would rather kneel for Bethany and their selfish pleasure than for the duty of his calling, and since he could not kneel for her in marriage, which was sanctified, then everything, including his love for her, the vow he had repeated at his ordination, and the blessing that he spoke today, Maundy Thursday, was a bold-faced lie. The usher cleared his throat, signaling that it was time for Thomas to finish up the service and send the congregation home for a hearty supper with their loved ones. He obliged, blessing Silva, the last disciple, with words that he didn't quite believe, and stood to face the gathered church with the feeling in his heart that he was lost, and undeserving of their faith in him to be a worthy guide.

After the service had ended with Mike Flynn's original organ piece "Blessed City, Heavenly W——," and Thomas, feeling queasy with dishonesty, had done his usual meet-and-greet at the entrance, shaking hands and grabbing shoulders, mixing up a name or two and cutting Sadie Maxwell short with an "excuse me"; after Artemesia Angelis, whose boundless faith and insatiable curiosity, instead of being a source of *wonder*, filling him with pride as her pastor and spiritual adviser, made him feel *weary*, asked for a moment in the church office because she had something *very important to tell him*, another vision, she claimed, this time about his *sorrow* (at this he had grown rigid), and he had deflected her attention by suggesting that she call Mrs. Safarian for an appointment; after Jane had gone outside to free her schnauzer from the cab of the pickup truck and water her, and Silva, shod again with the rest of the disciples, had made an accounting of the night's donations, filled the treasury box, and locked it away; after the church had emptied and the only echoes were his own footsteps, Thomas pulled off his gown and hung it in the office, left his Bible on the desk, turned off the banker's lamp, and locked the door on his way out, heading down the back staircase in the direction of the parsonage, where, the pastor knew, he would spend another night alone. Easter weekend would follow Daylight Saving Time that year, and the church grounds were still glowing, at that late hour, with the remnants of the sun. Thomas stopped outside the back door and watched Molly run in wild circles on the lawn, trailed by Jane with a bowl of water. The dog was in heat and wearing some kind of diaper for protection, a subject that Jane never tired of discussing in gruesome detail. Soon Molly had caught sight of Thomas and charged, covering the ground between them in a matter of seconds and leaping to a sudden stop. She wagged everything that moved, including her undergarments, and seemed to be waiting for a sign of affection, however small, before she pounced.

"Someone likes you," Jane said, passing underneath the branches of the apple tree, which had yet to show its buds. The Grounds Committee had recently approved a motion to hire the tree doctor for another visit, and Thomas had angered Margaret Howard, the longtime chairwoman, by abstaining from the vote. Margaret ran her pet committee with all the charm of Joseph Stalin, and in truth he had abstained, claiming ignorance of the natural sciences, to protest her use of strong-arm tactics.

"Is it all right to move?"

"That depends on your opinion of dog lips," she warned him, fending her dog off with the command "Stay, Molly."

Thomas kept still while she hooked the leash to her schnauzer's collar and encouraged her in baby talk to drink from the water bowl. Once Molly was slurping away he relaxed some and remarked, "Still in heat, I gather?"

"Oh, yes. The pills are a godsend, though."

"Are the strays still waiting at your door?"

"And howling all night long? No, not really." She sighed and scratched her arms. "Not since the chlorophyll."

"I know you worry, Jane," he said, the closest thing he could manage to an expression of fellowship, which seemed in order, somehow, after washing her feet. Jane seemed to feel the same way too and answered, "We're both prone to it, aren't we?"

"I guess we are, Jane."

"I look forward to our next afternoon," she told him, meaning their regular bull sessions that Thomas had been ducking since the spring began, choosing, instead, to close himself in the parsonage, let the phone ring as it may, and think of Bethany. Even the television was no distraction from her absence; every time he turned it on, it seemed, some camera was gliding over the surface of a pizza, narrator waxing poetic, as if Domino's delivered parcels of the Alaskan frontier in less than thirty minutes. The endless loops of commercials for fast-food and corporate identities only reminded Thomas of a deeper hunger, the one that Kierkegaard described as the foundation of Christianity in the individual, *Grief after God*. "I've missed the *connection* to you, Thomas."

"I apologize for that," he said, "what with Holy Week . . ."

"Oh, I know."

And now Thomas felt like dear Søren himself when, in the last throes of his love for Regina Olsen, he wrote in his journal, *Oh, I will throw everything overboard to become light enough to follow you*. What a fantastic dream! To delight in the pleasure of the journey, as Augustine wrote,* and find enjoyment in

*From "Teaching Christianity": "Supposing . . . we were exiles in a foreign land, and could only live happily in our own country, and that by being unhappy in exile we longed to put an end to our unhappiness and to return to our own country, we would of course need land vehicles or seagoing vessels, which we would have to

his faithful use of Bethany, as well as in her faithful use of him, the idea of God's providence no more than a murmur underneath their vessel, the sound of speed on water as they begin their life together . . .

"I promise to call you," he said to Jane, "and soon." Another lie! The truth of the matter was, he couldn't bear to spend another afternoon "connecting" with her. So why not say it? "After Sunday, my schedule looks quite clear."

## Good Friday

Thomas had been looking for her since the crowd began to filter into the church, breaking his usual protocol by leaving the office every few minutes to check the seats for Bethany, or whatever aspect he saw first: an angle of her face, the gleaming of her hair, a single shoulder as she turned to greet a neighbor, or tried, without much success, to extract Jessie from the crawl space underneath their habitual pew. The rumor mill had increased its output of allegations lately, and Bethany, never a favorite in certain quarters, had mentioned a noticeable *shunning*, though she claimed not to care about the opinions of the small-minded members of the church. It was true the seats around her pew seemed less popular now, and Jessie no longer basked in the adulation of every mother as she came speeding down the aisle in one of her Sunday outfits. "Mommy!" she

---

make use of in order to be able to reach our own country, where we would find true enjoyment. And then suppose we were delighted with the pleasures of the journey, and with the very experience of being conveyed in carriages or ships, and that we were converted to enjoying what we ought to have been using, and were unwilling to finish the journey quickly, and that by being perversely captivated by such agreeable experiences we lost interest in our own country, where alone we could find real happiness."

had cried the week before. "We're having brunch! In Sunday school we're having *brunch*!" *Shhh!* someone had hissed, enforcing the instructions printed in each program: *Many people find God in quietness; please do not unthinkingly disturb their meditation.* Thomas had watched from the stairwell that morning as Bethany soothed her daughter, whispering in her ear until her frown was replaced by a look of strange composure, as if the two of them had come to an understanding that they lived apart from the others, and always would, and this fact was an unavoidable symptom of the universe. (Bethany would later explain that she had promised a trip to Toys "R" Us on the way home.) This forbidden quality only made her more attractive to him, and Thomas craved the moment when they would catch each other in a dangerous stare across the church, Bethany, most often, mocking him by sitting primly in her seat (she had told him once that churchgoing did wonders for her fantasy life), Thomas trying to avert his eyes at the last possible moment, turning his attention, in a kind of penance, to the elder widows gathered near the center aisle, who responded to his respectful nod (or not) depending on the quality of their eyesight or the level of their medication. The wheelchairs parked in the aisle reminded Thomas, as he strode past the members of the Council in the front row, that he would not grow old with Bethany. Most Sunday mornings he climbed the three steps to the pulpit feeling *stung* by the circumstances of his calling, nodding in deference to Jane, who, by tradition, came out to face the congregation first, and in annoyance to the choirmaster Flynn, banging away on his organ like a pious Elton John. It had come to pass that the only pleasure Thomas felt in performing his service derived from Bethany: knowing that she had come to watch him (and sometimes wore silk underwear to increase the pleasure of her thoughts); and endured his sermons

184

out of loyalty, even though she questioned the substance of his "modern" message; and continued to want him despite his inability, more than half the time they sinned together, to bring her all the way to orgasm.

During the winter she had started showing up at his back porch, stopping at the parsonage on her way home from work and knocking at the storm door, which rattled, claiming, when he found her there in her full-length parka, that she couldn't help herself, and promised that she would only stay a minute . . . She had done the same at 6:15 p.m. on the last Tuesday before Lent—Thomas knew the time because he had just come back from an interminable "coffee" meeting with Skip Waterbury, and, while putting on the kettle for yet another cup of tea, had checked the clock to figure out how many hours he had wasted listening to Skip's plans for an interfaith racquetball league (roughly two, with travel time included). Thomas knew her knock well, though he had not been expecting it, and he resented the fact that she had come without calling first, disrupting his evening's order: a cup of tea, the rest of the newspaper, a list of phone calls that he should have returned over the weekend, but Ed Brooks, the school administrator, had fallen into another one of his depressions, and his wife, Candace, had reached the end of her rope, calling Thomas every few hours with an update on his condition. Ed's denial was so deep that, when his wife mentioned the possibility of seeing a psychopharmacologist about treatment, he had insisted to her that he was just overtired and feeling a little "blue."

"Happy to see me?" Bethany asked when he let her inside as far as the hallway, and he struggled to find an answer sufficient to the task, resorting to a simple "You know I can't invite you in."

How many times had they made out like teenagers in this

narrow hallway, a bare lightbulb hanging from the ceiling, the walls covered with cheap paneling, a stack of bundled newspapers waiting to go out to the curb, and the blue recycling tub at their feet, filled with empty aluminum cans and plastic bottles? Every shabby detail was invested, now, with an erotic significance, and Thomas felt an indescribable vacancy on recycling day, when the housekeeper, if she remembered, cleared the hallway of his rubbish and lugged it to the street.

"Wait, the newspapers," Bethany said, and pressed her leg against the bundled copies of the *Globe* before she pulled him in for a long kiss, choosing to leave her overcoat on for that heightened "quickie" feel. "Okay, I'm set. You can go ahead and feel me up."

Thomas preferred to start more slowly, unpinning her hair from its system of barrettes and touching her soft face, feeling the nape of her neck, nibbling at her ear and pressing his forehead against her own, smelling her in the unfragrant hallway and taking in her natural scent, murmuring in her ear, *In one of the front sections, right behind your knee, there's a long article about the Big Dig and its environmental impact—*

"Say it again," she gasped.

"The Big Dig," he repeated, pressing her against the paneling and letting one hand find her sex, the other leaning against the wall for balance, lifting a knee between her legs.

"Good, now go on—"

*There's a stack of Metro Regions touching your calf, now that Mike Barnicle's gone it's a vastly improved section, what an idiot that guy—*

"Dead end," she warned him.

"Maybe we should stick to the Dig," he suggested with his eyes closed, his hands inside her wide-legged slacks now and trying to roll her underwear down. The fact that Bethany was

186

wearing panties at all meant she had come on a whim, and his resentment about her visit had subsided around the same time she had invited him to feel her up.

"Softer," she instructed.

"Sorry, it's just that I—"

"Did you just hear something?"

"No, did you?"

"On the porch—"

"It's your imagination—"

"You're right—"

"Playing tricks—"

"Gentle, Thomas."

He obeyed, releasing the pressure and letting his fingertips glide, placing his other hand, for support, in the small of her back, and tasting the bitter residue of her workday on her neck, that lovely neck, holding steady in this pattern until she gasped, "How deep is the Ted Williams Tunnel?"

"Ninety feet at the East Boston interface . . ."

"And how much concrete?"

"Twenty-six thousand linear feet of steel-reinforced concrete slurry walls . . ."

"Oh, that's a lot!"

"Yes it is!"

"And the dirt!"

"Thirteen million cubic yards . . ."

"By the truckload! Tell me by the truckload!"

"Five hundred and forty-one thousand, give or take . . ."

Afterward Thomas stood at the kitchen sink, waiting for the hot water so he could wash his hands, while Bethany, her clothes impressively disheveled, sat at the table and sipped his cup of tea, adding milk to cut the strength after it had steeped for the duration of their encounter—in real time fifteen minutes, long enough for both of them to be suffering from the physical exertion, forced, as they were, by impulse and necessity, to make love quickly and in semipublic places—the back of her car, an unused hallway in the parsonage—a compromise that made it so much harder, when the moment came, to say goodbye. Thomas could feel the blood seeping from his shoulder and he didn't mind; the scab would last a week or two and remind him of her visit, leaving a faint but permanent scar.

"You do know," she said, "that we could avoid all this by going upstairs. You do sleep on a bed, don't you? Or do they only give you a pallet?"

"The walls have ears," he answered, drying his hands on a dish towel, "or at least it seems that way. You know that."

"This is hopeless," she observed, "truly hopeless."

"I won't argue with you," he said, already thinking of the next recycling day, when he would hurry outside at dusk and rescue his empty tub from the sidewalk. Life had brought him to such a strange juncture: in divinity school he had imagined his first pastorate with a kind of longing, believing that the ministry would challenge him in ways that graduate study never could, but his years in school, as it turned out, had been the high point of his spiritual life. *Judge me, O Lord*, he used to whisper in his prayers, *for I have walked in mine integrity, I have trusted also in my Lord, therefore I shall not slide* (Psalms 26:1). And now that he had been ordained? Forget sliding, O Lord, he had plunged to the bottom of Psalm 36: *There are workers of iniquity fallen: they are cast down, and shall not be able to rise.*

Bethany was staring into space over the rim of her teacup, the flush already draining from her cheeks, a sadness touching her that Thomas recognized, or so he thought, as his own. "I'm pathetic for coming over here so often, you know."

"Please, let's not—"

"It's not that I check the hours until the day's over, Thomas, I check the *minutes*. Right there on the computer screen, that little Windows clock? I'm its slave! And when I leave my desk, I follow this strategic path that takes me by every clock on the floor, just so I can keep on watching the minutes go by, and if I'm stuck in a meeting or something, God forbid, I check my watch."

"You're bored," Thomas said, "and you're better than your job, which is more than I can say. We've talked about you looking for more meaningful work—"

"It's not the work," she interrupted. (*Why is she always cutting me off?* he thought.) "Don't you see it's you? I'm waiting for *you*, Thomas, so I can rush over here and lose what's left of my dignity. That is, if you're even home. Or if *Jane* isn't over for a prayer meeting, or one of your other admirers hasn't shown up at the door with *osso buco* and a bottle of red wine."

"Unfair," he protested.

"Well, it's true, isn't it?"

"It's not my fault! She took me by surprise!" Was it Sadie who had brought the osso buco, or Alessandra? Either way, one of them had brought the veal on a weeknight, and the other, catching wind of it, had shown up on Friday with a platter of Icelandic salmon and a bottle of Alsatian white in an ice bucket. Luckily, the charity boxes for Honduras were being picked up by the shippers on Saturday morning, and Thomas had forgone the second romantic dinner to count Beanie Babies and fold thermal blankets with Mrs. Safarian. "Do you know what it's like to live without privacy? With the phone liable to ring at any moment? And Silva constantly lurking around? This isn't my home, Bethany. I'm an invited guest, and if I outwear my welcome with the Council, I can always be replaced. Let's not forget that."

"Hopeless," she repeated, "just hopeless."

"Anyway, it's difficult."

"I'm late," Bethany said, leaving the table and heading for the bathroom. "They'll be waiting for me. Ulla's finishing a computer model or something, and last I checked Jessie still had her stomach bug. I had to let Devon stay home from school and take care of her today. I'm sure he played Nintendo from dawn to dusk. When I get home, he'll be in his aggressive zombie mode. You should write a sermon about boys and video games, I swear they take over the male mind . . ." She left the bathroom door open and kept on talking, dropping the toilet seat and telling him, over the sound of her efficient stream, about the relative merits of frozen dinners and the intricacies of Jessie's twenty-four-hour flu, pausing only for an unselfconscious *flush* before she launched, next, into a tirade about the state of his plumbing, really, she thought, the Council should invest in water-saving toilets, they were a dream as long as you avoided the hydraulic suction: once Jessie had forgotten to stand up before she flushed and they had nearly lost her, sweet beast, you can't imagine the scream! Thomas knew she would be straightening herself out in the mirror, trying to erase the effects of their fifteen minutes in the hallway, tucking here, yanking there, combing her hair out with the brush she carried in her handbag; she asked him, through the open door, if he could find some time for her late on Saturday afternoon (maybe), and what did he think of her going back on the Pill (her decision), all the while Thomas was considering the fact that he felt married to her, and could have listened to her voice in his bathroom until the end of his days, yet their affair, at that moment, seemed less a reflection of love than a compromise between two desperate people, one who had grown weary of loving only Him, the other who had found the limits of a loving family, and wanted, through him, to experience the infinite consolation of being loved by God.


*Easter Sunday*
The morning of His resurrection that year was darkened by an ominous cloud cover, just as Thomas had feared the night before, watching the loathsome weatherman describe, in sunny terms and a ridiculous Italian suit, the advance of tropical air from the southeast and its eventual collision with an onshore wind along the New England coast, the classic recipe for STORMY WEATHER, a screen graphic had promised with an animated downpour, prompting the pastor to sigh, lift himself from the easy chair, and switch off the television. (His sleep would be shallow at best, his dreams strange and feverish, and twice during the night he would rise and head downstairs in his bathrobe to appease his sweet tooth with a slice of low-fat pound cake from the supermarket, washed down with a glass of tap water.) The first raindrops roused the usher Silva from bed at half past five to pull on his foul-weather gear and do his best imitation of Paul the tentmaker, erecting the congregation's candy-striped shelter (an ancient donation from the Country Club) on the green behind the church, a three-man job that the usher insisted on performing by himself, pounding in the last of the iron stakes by seven-thirty. After months of fiscal austerity the Council had splurged for the Easter holiday, approving funds for a museum-style banner at the church entrance, more floral arrangements than anyone could remember, and, most surprising of all, colorful new gowns for both the choir and the clergy: royal-blue satin with a diagonal yellow stripe, an extravagance only partially offset by a 30 percent discount on the material. Just an hour before the service was scheduled to be-

gin, with the choir running through a final rehearsal under Flynn's direction and Molly barking in the stairwell, Thomas and Jane were modeling their gowns in the office for Mrs. Safarian, who had played an instrumental role in convincing the Council to open their purse strings for the holiday.

"Oh, my," she purred, looking festive herself in a pink Chanel knockoff with matching patent-leather heels, "what a special morning for all of us. This *is* something new."

"I feel like it's Prom Night," Jane commented, surprising the others with her reference to dating rituals. "A wrist corsage, a chaperone, the whole bit." It seemed from her sermons that Jane had been born into God's service, skipping the formative experiences shared by everyone else in adolescence, like shopping for a prom dress or having a crush on the English teacher. "Not that I attended my senior prom, mind you. I stayed home and helped my mother with a batch of sugar cookies."

"How's the fit?"

"Just perfect, really."

"I couldn't believe it myself," Mrs. Safarian told Jane, "but for his prom last year my grandson hired a stretch limousine. Three of his friends went in together, fifty dollars each, and his father made up the difference. Needless to say, I was against the whole idea."

"It's such a waste, isn't it?"

"According to the boy, a limousine on Prom Night is becoming *mandatory*. That peer pressure is an awful thing."

"Well," Thomas said, looking down his chest at the expanse of satin, "it's certainly blue."

"And the yellow! My heavens it's bright!"

"Yes," he remarked, "that's yellow, all right."

Mrs. Safarian was overcome by the sight of the two ministers in such finery, even in the gloom of a rainy morning. "I never, ever thought I'd see the day," she said, fighting back the tears, "such a beautiful banner waving outside, so many tulips and lilies, and the two of you looking so colorful . . ." Mrs. Safarian struggled to compose herself. "I hope you'll excuse me," she asked, and dabbed at her eyes with a tissue.

"Yes, yes—"

"Of course, yes—"

"It's just the emotions of the day," she explained, "and the choir, you see they're practicing my favorite canticle . . ."

Later, after Mrs. Safarian had gone off to consult with Silva about the flower arrangements, and the choir, chatting and giggling about their Easter gowns, had filed through the hallway on their way out back for some refreshment underneath the tent, Bethany interrupted Thomas's morning with that singular knock and peeked her head inside the office, asking, "Have I picked a bad time?"

"We're just consulting," Jane told her, taking the initiative, "please, come in." Bethany ushered her children inside the office to wish the ministers a Happy Easter, an uncomfortable moment for Devon, who refused to make eye contact with the adults. His mother had forced him into wearing his clip-on tie and corduroy suit for the holiday; on the way to church that morning he had insisted on lying down in the back seat, paranoid that one of his friends, out for a morning bike ride, would catch sight of him.

"I have a purse!" Jessie yelled, showing off her oversized accessory to Jane. Her outfit that morning—a yellow dress, white tights, black patent-leather flats—was enhanced by a bright smear of jelly across her chin. "See?"

"Well, aren't *you* grown-up," Jane told her, "a purse all to yourself? What do you keep inside?"

"Animals?"

"You don't mean *real* ones, do you?"

"Stuffed animals! And once I hid a cupcake!"

"And you" she said, turning to Devon in an effort to give him equal time, "don't you look handsome in that suit. Can you believe it, Thomas? Why, if I didn't know any better, I'd swear you were a young software executive with *oodles* in stock options. Just look at you!" The child's attendance at the church had been slipping ever since he quit the Boys' Choir, and Jane wanted to let him know, on this special morning, that God's love for him had not diminished.

Thomas stared at the boy and thought he should say something, remembering the time when Devon, a year or so younger and in the first throes of his hip-hop obsession, had asked him at Fellowship, "Before you became a minister, were you an Original G?" Thomas had laughed at the suggestion, having learned a thing or two about Gangsta Rap from his former congregation, and the boy had been offended; since then, they had existed in an uneasy standoff. It was no surprise to him in general that Devon's attendance at church should have fallen off so drastically.

"Yes," Thomas finally said, "you're looking like a real NASDAQ trader. I suppose your company is about to go public—"

"He hates that suit!" Jessie cried, unwilling to give up the spotlight. "He said so this morning!"

"Jessie, enough," Bethany told her.

"Corduroy's for chumps! That's what he said!"

Devon had commenced to blush and squirm, mumbling something in reply to Jane and looking to his mother for help, who (quite deftly, Thomas thought) sent the children off to save their seats before another family claimed them for the service.

"If I could," she said humbly to Jane, "I'd like one word with Thomas, just for a minute."

She answered, "We are consulting here."

"Only a minute," she repeated, "I promise you."

Such a persuasive woman! Soon the assistant pastor had gone the way of the children, albeit reluctantly, leaving the door open wide behind her in what Thomas chose to interpret as a warning, which Bethany ignored—closing the door once Jane had reunited with her dog and walking straight to the windows, where she drew the shades, collapsed into the nearest chair, and brought her fingers to her temples, a dramatic gesture that he assumed, from experience, meant trouble on the home front. Once she had assumed the "crisis" posture he explained to her, in his most understanding voice, that Easter Sunday was not the best time, strategically, for the two of them to be alone together, and he begged her to save her thoughts for another day, when the church was less crowded and his mind was uncluttered by the responsibility of delivering a sermon—

"This can't wait," she insisted, "trust me." Outside the members of the choir were milling around the tent, trying to ease their preperformance jitters with laughter and orange juice from concentrate. Thomas could hear Flynn's voice rising above all the others: *The phrasing of the final verse is much improved, people! Christ is risen! Remember to sing with all your hearts! Sing until the Heavens hear you!*

"Is it something I've done?" he offered, trying to speed the conversation along.

She answered by shaking her head.

"Bobby? Does he suspect something?"

"Hardly."

"Is it the children, then?"

"Sort of," she said, and sniffled.

"Bethany," he tried, "in a few minutes I'm supposed to stand in front of a room full of people and talk about the *resurrection*—"

"Can I have a tissue first?"

Thomas pushed his box of Kleenex across the desk, watching her reach for a tissue with the patience of a designated listener. The church had gone astray, he believed, in trying to compete with easier forms of consolation, and at times it seemed that his only function was to fill the pastor's chair, look engaged, and, when the time was right, offer up the tissue box.

When Bethany finished blowing her nose into the pink Softique she said, "It's Jessie's handbag that has me so upset, the one my mother gave to her when we were cleaning out the Newton house, just before we dumped her in the nursing home . . ."

"I didn't realize," he answered, and fell quiet again. How could he often be so wrong about what bothered her? Why was her emotional life such a mystery to him?

"I haven't seen my mother in months," she went on, "and I feel incredibly guilty about that. I mean, Jessie's so proud of that purse, she carries it everywhere, but she doesn't even realize what *happened* to her grandmother. Just the other night she asked me, 'When's Gramma Kit getting better?' So I started explaining that the answer, basically, was *never*, but she got scared when I mentioned the nursing home and made me promise that I wouldn't move there too."

"I'm sorry, Bethany. I had no idea."

She blew her nose again. "And my brothers! They never bother to tell me what's happening, so it's really up to me, the family fuckup, to make sure she's being treated well, like I have the time and energy to head over there and see this *woman* who isn't my mother anymore, half the time she looks right through me, the other half she screams for help . . ."

Jane rapped on the door. "*Fifteen minutes.*"

"I hear you," Thomas called to her. "Just give me five, please."

*"Can I lend a hand in any way?"*

"No, thank you, Jane."

*"Five minutes, then."*

"Am I a horrible person?" Bethany asked once they had given Jane a moment to wander out of listening range. "I want you to tell me honestly, as a minister and not my lover. Objectively, as another human being. *Am I a horrible person?"*

"Of course not," he told her. "That's absurd."

But the answer wasn't good enough for her. "I don't think it is absurd," she argued, "because I *feel* like a horrible person, and that's evidence enough. Or would you rather I listed my faults? First there's the fact that I'm unfaithful to my husband of fifteen wonderful years, second I'm having an affair with *you*, which is really something in itself, third—well, that's hard to say. I *am* an absentee mother most of the time, and don't forget my talent as a daughter, letting my mother die slowly in a semiprivate room, cared for—if she's lucky—by dropouts and ex-convicts. She's all alone, and do you know why I never see her? Do you?" She didn't wait for Thomas to answer. "Because I'm *afraid to visit.*"

"That's not unusual," he assured her, ignoring everything that had come before her insight, including the disturbing emphasis she had placed on *you* ("I'm having an affair with *you*"), which he forgave as an unintentional slip. "Of course you're afraid to visit, Bethany. She's changed."

"So have I," she said, pausing to blow her nose again. "Everything's changed, and I'm not sure if I can cope with it."

The rain had grown heavier outside, trapping the members of the choir underneath the tent and causing a small commotion as they ran for the back door in pairs and small groups, encouraged by the vocal choirmaster: *Careful now, people! Watch your step!* In a few minutes they would file into the church and take their seats, collective spirits high and their gowns streaked with rain, part the covers of their songbooks and lead the entire congregation in songs of praise and wonderment. Bethany had brought the tissue box into her lap and consoled herself with fistfuls, asking Thomas, once her sobbing had subsided a little, "Aren't you going to share your wisdom?"

But what could he possibly say? That he loved her? That it was perfectly natural to be afraid of visiting her mother in the nursing home? That her mother wouldn't know the difference anyway? That she was selfish and emotionally dependent and probably was an absentee mother herself? That her children, over time, would learn to resent her selfishness, and would carry this resentment with them like an open wound? That her husband resented her selfishness too? That he would eventually tire of her self-dramatics and file for divorce at the first sign that her looks were fading? That her children were bound by family logic to repeat her mistakes in adulthood? That she had a greedy soul? That she was fascinating and flawed, and like no woman that he had ever known before? That her tears bored *him* to tears? That she had replaced his religion and silenced God? That he was leaving the church? That she was close to God if she would only see it? That she was close to God?

Jane knocked on the door again. "*Five minutes.*"

Bethany let out a bitter laugh. "Nothing. I tell you everything, and you tell me nothing."

Again, what could he possibly say?

"Here I come," he called to Jane, and stood up to signal the end of their meeting, giving Bethany the lame excuse, "This isn't the best time. I'm sorry."

She left the box of tissues on her chair. "No, I should have known better. It's Easter Sunday, and you have work to do." The choirmaster had begun playing the morning's first piece,

Olivier Messiaen's "Prayer of Christ Ascending," a late and much-debated addition to the liturgy. Thomas walked her to the door, giving her arm a last affectionate squeeze before their joint appearance in the hallway. She smiled faintly and told him, "I never pictured you in blue satin, Thomas."

"Nor did I."

She whispered, "Love the yellow stripe."

Thomas opened the door on Jane, who greeted them with a worried smile and informed him, once again, of the time. The organ's peaceful rumble shook the hallway's posts and beams, and the members of the choir, faces composed (though one or two snuck a peek at the pastor and his favorite congregant), shuffled past the office in a single line. *Deus est sphaera infinita cuius centrum est ubique, circumferentia nusquam.* "I'm aware of the time," he said to Jane, more interested in watching Bethany slide past the assistant pastor with her head bowed, trying, no doubt, to hide her swollen eyes.

*Deus est sphaera infinita.*

"Goodbye, Thomas," he heard clearly as the sound of the organ rose a melodic step, and then another, ascending to the rafters in beautiful obedience to Christ. Later it would seem to Thomas that he had never known her better, or loved her more, than on that rainy Easter morning when he failed to comfort her, and watched her walk away as if into the arms of God.

*Deus est sphaera.*

Goodbye.

For some time after the pastor's disappearance the leadership of the church would face the persistent accusation that the Council hadn't acted quickly enough, that a foolish caution and the fear of bad publicity had somehow overwhelmed their responsibility to look after Thomas, just as he looked after their souls according to the Ordination Service. Not until Thursday morning, four days after he delivered his "infinite sphere" sermon, did a delegation organized by the usher Silva, who had been collecting the pastor's daily *Globe* to maintain the appearance of normality, enter the parsonage and find everything in order, if a little grimy; indeed, one of the shaken volunteers would later remark to the press that it seemed as if the pastor had run out for an errand and simply *vanished*, leaving everything of value behind—from the notebook computer on his desk upstairs to the three good suits in his closet, from his pocket-sized Book of Worship resting on the bedside table to the leather-bound album of family photographs lying face-down on a bookshelf. Four days and no reasonable explanation for the delay gave rise to the opinion that a mostly hidden *prejudice* had clouded the Council's good judgment, reinforcing the body's tendency to shrink from any crisis until the most drastic and thoughtless action had become their only option. *Forgiveness Is All*, a banner hanging in the basement classroom advertised, but many church members interpreted the Council's caution in Thomas's case as indifference, and refused to forgive their failure to initiate the Prayerline when the pastor's absence was first noted on Tuesday afternoon, or support their decision to wait before involving the police until it looked certain that Thomas would miss the Membership Committee meeting on Thursday, leaving the officers assigned to the case little recourse in their attempts to find him. (The police had adopted a wait-and-see attitude within an hour of searching the church grounds, intimating to the usher, who passed the word along to Mrs. Safarian, that all the evidence pointed to suicide.) With the pastor missing under mysterious circumstances and the congregation in unprecedented turmoil, some among the membership wondered openly if the Pilgrims' Church, active continually since its founding in 1850 by a group of wealthy Abolitionists, would survive the trauma of *losing* their young minister, compounded by the chaos and recriminations of the "emergency" church meeting called by the Council in accordance with the Bylaws, the most painful gathering, insisted Sam Cabot, the trembling Church Archivist, in the congregation's one-hundred-and-forty-seven-year history. As Sam would later write in his "Chronicle of Church Life," commissioned to be the centerpiece of the Millennium Time Capsule:

We thought ourselves called to pray together for His guidance in our time of trouble, and instead descended into bickering, profanity, and harsh reproof. Such an event may be sufficient argument for the continual folly of man, and the ever-present need to feel humbled, as we were not, by divine Providence. We must learn the error of our ways, so that a plentiful effusion of the blessed spirit will descend upon us. We must reclothe ourselves in Christ and give thanks for His dominion in the universe. The Lord gave us as clear a message as when He sacked the Temple of Jerusalem, and we must obey His loving wrath. All praises due to the Lord who would save us from ourselves.

On the night of the church meeting Bethany was numb with grief and suffering from dizzy spells: still she had managed to arrange for Bobby to look after the children (Thursday was one of Ulla's off nights) and conduct back-to-back interviews at five and five-thirty before dumping her paperwork on Anita's empty desk and joining the northbound traffic on 128, running late as usual and desperate to reach Old Town in time for the opening prayer. One moving violation later (to the tune of $135) she found a space in the church parking lot, and followed Bob and Susie Guan, who looked to be in mourning, up the wheelchair ramp, preferring not to greet them; she did her best to ignore the police cruiser parked near the entrance, shining in a sinister way, and she reminded herself, as the Guans stepped sadly through the doorway, that while adultery may still have been a crime in Massachusetts, the Blue Laws of the Commonwealth were no longer actively enforced. At the top of the ramp she took a moment to steady herself, thinking of Thomas in his royal-blue gown—how absurd!—and whispering, *I need your help*, unsure, in the end, if she meant to address her beloved or his God. And again, *I need your help*. She entered the meeting-house in the middle of the silent prayer, a perfect opportunity, she thought, to slip inside unnoticed, and she traversed the rear aisle with her head down, stepping lightly so as not to break the silence, choosing the only empty seat that she could find with the church at near-capacity, a forgotten row where the usher Silva stored damaged or outdated hymnals. She settled in beside the well-worn books and closed her eyes to join the prayer. Someone coughed nearby, a *creak* sounded from above, a parishioner started grumbling about *getting on with it, already*, and a child, dragged to a church meeting that she couldn't possibly understand and would remember for the rest of her life, asked, *Is this why we're here, Mommy? Is this why?* The assistant pastor led the congregation in an *Amen* and cleared the sadness from her throat, repeating her announcement for the sake of late arrivals that child care was strongly encouraged and available in the basement, arranged, on short notice, by the ever-resourceful Mrs. Safarian. Bethany kept her eyes closed throughout Jane's opening announcements, gathering, as the silent prayer gave way to whispers and opinionating, that her arrival had drawn the attention of the crowd. *There she is*, she heard in a not so careful whisper, *praying like Young Miss Jesus herself. Can you imagine the gall?* She had expected the commentary on her presence and it hardly bothered her. More painful was the way she missed Thomas, completely, and her realization that, for herself at least, religion was over. Thomas had tried to share his faith with her and it had come to nothing! All that trouble just to fall in love with Thomas and to lose him! All that for another absence! For *nothing*, and the deepest loneliness that she had ever known!

Just one aisle across and seven rows toward the pulpit from where Bethany was seated with her eyes closed, Margaret Howard, having completed her inquiry into the pastor's disappearance and come to a satisfactory conclusion, was itching to get a word in edgewise, waiting for that fool lesbian to finish her opening statement and introduce the officer in charge of the investigation (of all the nitwits on the force, who should be present but the Maldonado boy, a former playmate of Bradley's and mastermind of their bike-stealing ring back in junior high school), who looked about nineteen and spent most of his time "on duty" visiting his child bride at the Fudgery in Old Town, where she worked afternoons behind the counter weighing bricks of the sickening product and selling what used to be penny candy for outrageous prices; waiting for the "witnesses" to finish making themselves feel useful by revealing the last time they'd seen the pastor before he "vanished," if that's the proper word for what cowards do when life gets difficult. At the supermarket last week buying breakfast cereal and a dozen eggs . . . At the video store renting that mythology series by Bill Moyers . . . Leaving Fellowship on Sunday with a box underneath his arm and entering the parsonage through the back door . . . Amateur sleuths, all of them! (Strange how Bethany Caruso wasn't saying a word! Margaret had kept an eye out for her entrance during the opening prayer, which, as usual, went on far too long, and of course the devious woman had picked a spot that she could hardly see without risking permanent damage to her neck, still tender from overdoing it on that hopeless flower garden.) Beside her Artemesia was crying her eyes out, dripping fat, childish tears on that burlap top of hers and gazing up into the rafters as if the Lord could be of any help with a predicament made by men (or rather, a weak man and a woman on the prowl), and paying attention to the meeting only when Piotr Swenson, the Swedish pervert, stood up and made the brilliant suggestion that the congregation form a human chain and *comb the woods* for the pastor, an idea that seemed to meet with some approval, even from the Maldonado boy, who nodded and copied the suggestion in his POLICE TACTICS 101 notebook. With that piece of organic homegrown stupidity Margaret decided that she'd heard enough, and she searched through her handbag for the envelope marked "Evidence," instructed Artemesia to pay attention, and stood up, waving her envelope in the air and announcing, "I have something here that might shed light on our discussion!" She found the buzz that met her announcement gratifying, even if Artemesia, her best friend, looked as if she had just discovered the Holy Spirit was a ruse.

"I know what some of you are thinking," she began, launching into the speech she'd outlined in her office that very afternoon, instructing her secretary to HOLD ALL CALLS, "and before I share what's in the envelope, I'd like to start by saying a few words about my history in the Pilgrims' Church. I won't dare to put a number on how many years I've been praying in this building, but let's just say that times were different when I moved to the village from up North. Over the years I've served on every church committee we have here at least once. Some of them, like the Grounds Committee, didn't exist when I first stepped through those doors—so I followed procedure and turned to the Council for help, and together, with everyone's support, we founded them. Sometimes it seems like I've rotated *off* the Council more times than I can count, and maybe Sam will enlighten me one day about how many times I've served on that body."

"Four terms," the Archivist piped up from the front row. "One more and it's a modern record. And let's not forget you were the first woman."

"Thank you kindly, Sam," she said, relaxing a bit. "Love me or hate me, that's where I'm coming from. Now, for the majority of that time we were blessed to have the Reverend

Chambers with us, a man whose leadership was a mighty thing to behold. I think we can all agree that Hal possessed rare qualities as a minister, and he made our church feel like one big happy family [a murmur of assent]. I for one miss him terribly, but people do retire and move to Arizona and whatnot, and that's just the way life is. Finding a replacement for Hal was not an easy task, and you might recall that during the process we encountered some differences of opinion. There's a *perception*, let's say, that I didn't like Thomas Mosher for my own reasons, that I never welcomed him as our pastor, and I've paid dearly for some words I mistakenly used in front of the Search Committee. You all know what I'm talking about, and I'm truly sorry that I let my temper get the best of me on that occasion. And this *perception* was only furthered when, as you might recall, I made a friendly comment to some visitors at Fellowship that was consequently blown all out of proportion. Yes, I did not appreciate being made an example of in this sacred building for *political purposes*. Who would? Let me repeat that question for you. *Who would?* I'll freely admit that I had some differences of opinion with the man. But right now, I'm standing before each and every one of you and telling you that I learned to care about Thomas, I really did, and I'm as sad as anyone about, well, this recent turn of events. I've been praying for his safety, just like you, and I'm sure that, wherever Thomas is, he's being watched over by our Lord the Shepherd."

"Amen," the assistant pastor added, and the crowd murmured in agreement, *Amen.*

"I'll need my reading glasses," she instructed Artemesia, who immediately began looking through her handbag. "Not that case, dear, the other one. That's a girl. Now pass them over here." Once Margaret had donned her half-glasses she tore off one end of the envelope and explained, "Earlier this week I found the following note attached to the front door of the parsonage. Naturally, since the pastor had gone AWOL I thought it might be of some importance. Little did I know"—she paused and bit her lip—"what a *shock* I had in store for me. Before I read this work of vile pornography [a gasp from the crowd], written by someone in this very room tonight, I need to apologize in advance for uttering such rotten language in the Lord's house. Let me assure you that I'm offering this evidence in the spirit of *open inquiry*, and I hope my breach of etiquette will be forgiven [stunned silence].

"Okay. Here we go. *Dear Reverend Mosher,* the note opens, *I am in a dilemma. Coming to your church makes me very horny* [shocked ripple]. *I have tried the route of self-pleasure in the pew but found it disappointing. After the sermon this Sunday, will you* . . . Brace yourselves, ladies and gentlemen, because what follows isn't pretty . . . *Will you fuck me?*" The pandemonium that broke out in the meetinghouse was worse than even Margaret had been willing to hope for, and she refused to sit down again until she had finished her speech in its entirety. "There's more," she promised, "if you'll give me the floor for one more minute! Just another minute, please! People, I have more to say!" She managed to catch the usher's eye in the front row and, because they had reached an understanding, Silva climbed onto his pew and motioned for the crowd to quiet down. While Artemesia, it was true, looked as if she were about to have a *conniption*, the thought of Bethany Caruso suffering through this moment made Margaret a very, very happy woman. "Good people," she went on, "as I mentioned to you earlier, the woman who wrote this vile note is with us in the church tonight [another ripple]. Who knows, she might be sharing a pew with you and your loved ones. But I won't speak her name out loud. Snitching is not my chosen line of work in this life. Passing judgment is the Lord's business, and as many of you know from experience, I'm in Real Estate. Connecting people with the properties they covet. *Right now*, I say we give this troubled soul the chance to come forward and reveal herself before her peers. The Lord already knows, good people, but the rest of us deserve an explanation, *yes we do*. The time is now! Stand up! The Lord knows who you are, and I suggest you meet your maker. I've got all night, good people, and I hope you do too."

Opinion in the church would differ about the order and magnitude of the strange events that followed in the wake of Margaret Howard's speech. Some in attendance that night, like Lucia Wagner, would swear that the antique light fixture hovering over their proceedings like Ezekiel's wheel, already an item on the agenda for the next Council meeting, had shown signs of acute instability during Margaret's speech; indeed, Lucia claimed to have heard a lurching sound from above that distracted her from her knitting, placing the first signs of the fixture's collapse *before* the elder widow Caroline Abbey's first rebuttal, when the lights began to flicker out; *before* Artemesia Angelis rose to give her dramatic confession of sin, and Margaret Howard, trying to salvage her performance, questioned her sanity before the gathered church and disavowed her part in their friendship—at which point the first lightbulb exploded into dust and the fixture plunged from its great height down to the floor of the meetinghouse, falling with the most remarkable noise upon the heads of those who sat underneath. Others in attendance that night agreed with the assistant pastor that the fixture's descent had been inaugurated by a *clap of thunder*; the whole had been so sudden that many of the victims, in their various states of shock, knew nothing of what had befallen them, including the usher Silva, who had checked the fixture's anchor in February, as he did each year, and had declared it sound; and the young police officer Phil "Candy" Maldonado, whose experience on the force had been limited thus far to traffic accidents, petty larceny, domestic disputes, lost pets, and missing "suckers" at the Fudgery; and Arthur Norregaard, a second-generation physician who preferred to sit in the rear of the church because of the acoustics, but had decided, that evening, to sit up front for a change of pace, and was nearly *crushed* . . . None in attendance could provide a rational explanation for the calamity, or of how, given the dangerous circumstances, every life should have been preserved (while some, especially the elderly, suffered minor scrapes and bruises, *not one bone* was broken or dislocated from its rightful joint among the injured). This much, however, was clear: With her vituperative speech and unseemly recitation of the stolen mash note, Margaret Howard, an admired figure for her contributions to the church and for her undeniable success as Realtor, yet loathed, by a certain faction, for her reactionary politics, had intentionally, and with premeditation, *disrupted the equilibrium* of the church community, and it was no wonder, then, even to those who shared her outrage about the alleged goings-on in the parsonage, that the Good Lord had found a way to *censure* the congregation for the tone of their proceedings, and return their collective thoughts, once the church members in attendance had been counted, the injured had been cared for, and the usher Silva, with the help of volunteers, had cleared the meetinghouse of debris and assessed the damages on paper, to the sad and disturbing mystery of Thomas's departure.

But first the remarkable event itself:

Margaret's mood had begun to sour just as soon as she

wound up her comments and took her seat to enjoy the reaction, half expecting Artemesia to pull out of her devotional trance and throw her arms around her ample shoulders, grateful that she had shown the courage to confront this sinner among them and restore order to a church badly in need of a *spiritual realignment*, to quote the Reverend Chambers, who, with characteristic charm and wisdom, had often referred to the periodic need for a church to renew itself in Christ. But Artemesia had refused to acknowledge her, in fact she *turned her back* to Margaret and concentrated on crying quietly (at least her sobs had not been audible above the din), and had even *shrugged her off* when Margaret reached out—with her bad arm, no less—to offer some condolence to the fragile woman. Such a lack of gratitude for all she'd risked by standing up to speak, for the years of unbroken friendship, for the hours she had spent all week (and time is a precious resource to a busy woman) talking Artemesia through her feelings about the pastor's disappearance! Not a peep! Not a *wonderful speech, Margaret*! Not even one of Artemesia's brittle smiles that revealed (and she would have died to know it) her missing molar on the right side! Margaret's disappointment gave way to a rising fury when the first woman to stand and face her challenge was *not* Bethany Caruso, the known adulteress and root cause of the pastor's undoing, but Caroline Abbey, the youngest of the elder widows, who took the trouble of shooting Margaret an angry glance before she claimed the floor and launched in:

"You can all calm down now, because I'm not Margaret's mystery woman, but I guess that's pretty obvious. I've been a widow for seven years and, believe me, I'm lucky if my late husband comes to me in a dream, God rest his soul. I do have something to add here, though, and I hope you'll hear me out [low, agreeable murmur]. Good. I'll get right to it, then. As a longtime member of this church, going back even further than Mrs. Howard, I might add, I think what we've just heard tonight is *entirely inappropriate*, and I'm not talking about that damn fool note, either! Given the source and all, I tend to doubt the note's validity, but I guess that's just something we'll have to sort out later. I don't need to remind the membership again of the furor surrounding the 'Kinship' sermon, do I [another murmur]? And even if the note *is* real, it wouldn't be the *first* time we had a clandestine affair in this church. That's right, and I venture a guess it won't be the last, either. In her rush to judgment, here, if I may borrow a phrase, Margaret seems to have forgotten that our *pastor is missing*. We don't know if he was *kidnapped*, or if we drove him to suicide for Heaven's sake, or if he's down at the Pequot reservation playing slot machines and taking in a show. We just don't know yet! Maybe he'll come walking through that door tonight and inform us it was all a lesson! A demonstration that God is an *infinite doorknob*, or whatever he was talking about last Sunday! Now, I've never played bridge with the man, but it seems to me that Thomas Mosher was a conscientious pastor, a good neighbor, and a thoughtful friend, never mind if he's Afro-American, Indian chief, or one-half Japanese. Thomas was a good man— *is* a good man, let's pray—and I think we owe him some loyalty. In case anyone in this room has forgotten, that's a *virtue*, and an awful important one, I might add. That's it. That's all I have to say."

Meanwhile Artemesia Angelis had been staring through her veil of tears at Anne Hutchinson's darkened stained-glass window, hoping that her patron saint (and sentenced heretic) would animate and show her the way to enlightenment, lift her pearly eyes and button chin and shape her thin white lips into words of wisdom, telling Artemesia, in her faux-Colonial voice that even she knew to be an artifice, the truest way to confront Margaret's public accusations and protect her beloved pastor's reputation from the slander of her former friend, delivered with such cruelty not two feet away from Artemesia's wounded heart—a curse that it should keep on beating, and beating, and beating!—and without remorse or even a shade of affection for the melancholy man of God who had traveled north from Rhode Island to save them. Yes, to *save them*! She had been trying to see the pastor since the early days of Lent and confide in him that *she knew where his pain was*—it had come to her on Ash Wednesday after she had slipped inside Grace Church and received the mark of the cross on her forehead, *remorse* and *penitence*, such hopeful concepts, yet so difficult to live by . . . Back in her station wagon, waiting to pull out of the unfamiliar parking lot, Artemesia had caught sight of the ashen mark on her forehead in the rearview mirror and thought of Thomas and his furrowed brow, and then, all at once, *she knew where his pain resided*: God had filled his heart with so much love that it became a burden on his soul, an emptiness *without bottom*, she knew because she had struggled with a variation of this pain herself for years on end, though she had only recently, and with Thomas's help, come to realize the nature of her unhappiness . . . and her epiphany regarding the pastor had only been deepened by his "infinite sphere" sermon, delivered with such low-key grace to the indifferent multitudes, which she had immediately recognized as a *Christ-like parable* about his sadness (and her variant), and the responsibility they shared as true believers, having been chosen for this blessed servitude by God . . .

Artemesia's tears had rarely fallen so copiously or tasted

more bitter on her tongue, and her sister confessor and secret weapon against hypocrisy, dear Mistress Hutchinson, had never appeared more remote in her persecution.

*MY GOD, MY GOD, WHY HAST THOU FORSAKEN ME? AND YOU, ANNE HUTCHINSON? WHY ME?*

Artemesia was so engaged in trying to make the picture *speak* that she hardly caught a word from Caroline Abbey, believing that she, like Margaret before her, had risen from her seat to speak *against* the pastor and his alleged deeds; she sobbed and stared and prayed for some deliverance from the terrible scene, and when none seemed imminent, she wiped her eyes with the back of her hand and rose to her feet, burning, inside, with a newfound sense of purpose, eager to answer these foul allegations with the purity of martyrdom.

"It was me!"

"Sit down, Artemesia!"

"It was my fault! I forced him into it!"

"She's obviously confused, good people!"

"I'm the horny one, not Thomas! Never Thomas! He's been chosen!"

"*Sit down*, Artemesia! Medic! She's having a breakdown!"

"It was my fault!"

In the last moments before the ceiling cracked open and the great wheel came hurtling down to earth, Artemesia would remember casting a glance in the direction of Mistress Hutchinson and seeing a light flicker on within her, a soft white glow that belied the *wickedness* of her expression, just as if she had awakened from a dream of goodness with a devilish idea, and she distinctly remembered thinking, *Yes*, and hearing her Mistress answer, *It is finished.* Then came the strange suggestion to *throw thyself to the dirt* (and she did) followed by the disputed clap of thunder, and then all she remembered was darkness, the splintering of wood, and the shrieking of the injured.

And what about Bethany Caruso? Where was she throughout the events set into motion by her love note left recklessly at the parsonage door? Withering in her seat? Contemplating her sins and preparing for a dramatic confession of her own? Was her pew situated beneath the tumbling light fixture that night, or was she spared the injury and grief by chance? By divine preservation? During the speeches—how was she able to breathe? There beside the damaged hymnals (such an untainted smell despite the use) Bethany had been thinking to herself, *I will survive this*, keeping her eyes closed as if the silent prayer had never ended, unable to pray, unwilling to open her eyes to the ongoing spectacle, unsure if she could manage to flee the building without being seen, and convinced that Margaret Howard would *crush her* beneath the business end of her high heels and bury her remains in the flower garden with the tacit approval of the Grounds Committee, ensuring a profusion of blossoms for years. Bethany had kept her eyes closed throughout the body of Margaret's speech (hearing her playful words for Thomas repeated with such *bile* had been heartbreaking) and on through Caroline's rebuttal, which she had appreciated; through Artemesia's deluded confession and Margaret's stern rebuke; through the sound of exploding lightbulbs, cracking plaster, and the dolorous cries as the fixture tumbled from the ceiling. Is it any wonder, given the nature of her week, that Bethany was not surprised to hear the sky fall? That she was not afraid to die? That she *accepted* the accident from the safety of her undamaged pew? She waited patiently for her fellow congregants to come to terms with their misfortune ("Is anybody hurt?" "My hip! My hip!" "Don't move!" "What happened?" "The lights fell, I think!") before she opened her eyes on a chaotic scene that she might have predicted in a dream, lifted herself calmly to her feet, and walked off toward the bright red EXIT sign as if nothing strange had just taken place—as if an evening recital had come to an end, her spirit had been moved in a limited way, and she was rushing out because she had promised her family that she would pick up some dinner at the nearest drive-thru.

"How'd it go?" Bobby asked with his aggressive male innocence as soon as she walked in the door, refusing to wait until she had taken off her coat, stowed her briefcase in the hallway, and poured her first glass of wine, which she planned on supplementing with a few drags from a joint as soon as the children were safely in bed and Bobby had slunk up to his room above the garage. The family was gathered around the TV for an episode of a raunchy sitcom that Jessie and Devon probably shouldn't have been watching, but Bobby was an indulgent father, and Bethany had given up trying to fight him on the minor issues.

"Hon? Any news?"

"I'm not sure how to answer that," she called from in front of the refrigerator. The box of Chardonnay was almost out, and she would have to remember to ask Bobby to bring a new one up from the cellar.

"Big Poppa stole my purse!" Jessie reported cheerfully.

"I already gave it back, stupid."

"I'm not stupid!"

"That's right. You tell him, Jessie."

"Big Poppa's going on a field trip tomorrow! To ride the Freedom Trail! And visit Paul Revere!"

"Shut up, yo!"

"I will not!"

"Dad, will you tell her to quit it, please?"

Bobby joined his wife in the kitchen at the next commercial break, pointing out the take-out Chinese on the counter (he knew that she found Chinese food unsanitary yet insisted on feeding her children with it anyway) and complaining about his workday with an annoying specificity, recounting an argument with his boss and how it related to the future of the "project" he was working on, complete with a thumbnail sketch of the issues at hand, proper names that she was supposed to but didn't recognize, a catalogue of personal slights and unreasonable expectations. *Either shut up about your co-workers*, she wanted to say, *or take the plunge and move in with them*, but she didn't have the energy for a confrontation. "Really," she kept on saying, and "Hmmm," trying her best to seem interested in his depressing career. The act must have worked: in mid-sentence Bobby snuck up behind her for a marital squeeze and seemed deflated by her brush-off tactics, retreating to the cabinets for another stack of cookies. Bethany sat at the kitchen table and gazed at her glass of inexpensive wine, feeling as if her true self, leading her real life, were somewhere far away—out there in the world with Thomas, she imagined, wherever he was or wasn't at that moment, or maybe in the past: inside a lovely hour they had shared in the parsonage, unable to keep their hands off one another, or an entire afternoon in her minivan, driving past the borders of the village to a countryside where no one knew them, no one cared to know them, and the *reality* that kept them apart was inconsequential, nothing compared to the vulnerabilities they exposed together, the parts of their bodies they touched, stroked, and tasted, the conversations that seemed to have no end . . . Bobby asked about the church meeting again, and she told him haltingly about the strange events: how the police were on the case, taking statements and interviewing witnesses, but the meeting itself had been interrupted by an accident, when, evidently, a piece of the ceiling had collapsed and landed in the middle of the church—

"But you're all right," Bobby said, "aren't you?"

She thought about it. "I'm definitely feeling weird."

"Was anybody hurt?"

"Well, that's hard to say."

"An ambulance, Beth. Did you see an ambulance?"

A squall was rising in the TV room, threatening to topple the furniture, and Bethany, to her distress, found that she was having trouble forming a sentence. *Quit it! Quit it, Devon!* "I don't know," she answered honestly. "It happened so fast, everyone was hysterical, and I just sort of . . . left."

"You *left*?"

"Yes," she was forced to agree.

"You walked away from the scene of an accident?"

"The police were already there," she tried, "and the place was crawling with, you know, physicians and dentists, there's even a chiropractor in the church, so I didn't really think—"

"Jesus, Beth."

*Quit it, Devon!*

"What? What was I supposed to do?"

"I don't know exactly, but *leaving the scene?*"

*Devon! I'm watching this!*

"Thank you," she said, rising to send the children to their separate rooms for the rest of the night, "for your expert advice on how to be a Good Samaritan. What an asshole you are sometimes."

Bobby threw up his hands. "There she goes again."

"No, I mean it."

"Is this a PMS event?"

"Asshole!"

"Say it a little louder, Beth."

"*I mean it!*"

When she came downstairs half an hour later Bobby was waiting for her in the kitchen, having taken her seat at the table and rolled up his sleeves for a no-holds-barred discussion about the state of their marriage and his increasingly marginal role in the Caruso family. Bethany was unwilling to apologize for calling him an *asshole,* but she would listen to a series of complaints about her attitude, devouring an entire order of vegetarian lo mein that tasted, to her, like garbage, while he listed her faults (and quite accurately, she reflected): she was selfish, self-involved, terminally distracted, cold, ungrateful, dismissive of their marriage, unappreciative of him, lacking in sexuality (wrong there), and, generally speaking, an unpleasant person to be around, period.

"You forgot my drinking problem," she said, getting up to rinse her plate and stack it in the dishwasher. "Which reminds me, when you think of it, could you bring another box of wine up from the cellar? This one's almost spent."

"Sure," he said, "*when I think of it, okay?*"

"Thank you," she answered. "Proving, I guess, that I'm grateful for some things in this life. Just maybe not the important ones, the things that really matter, like . . . well, I seem to be drawing a blank."

"You know I love you, Beth."

"I know that, I do."

"I just wonder sometimes how this happened," he told her, his voice no longer colored with anger, "and how much longer

I can stand to go on, you know, like *this*. Either we patch things up and make this marriage work, or we give up and go our separate ways. I can't go on fighting you on every little point. It's now or never, Beth."

"I know," she said softly.

"Now or never," he repeated.

"Yes."


On Friday morning, acting on a tip from Bernie Swenson, who had dutifully reported to the police seeing a car that fit the description of the Reverend Thomas Mosher's pause and turn left onto Mill Pond Road the previous Sunday evening (the new wheels for his skateboard had needed some breaking in), a team of scuba divers began scouring the bottom of the pond for the pastor's Ford Probe, just the second time in recent memory that frogmen had stirred the murky depths of this dying body of water, once an integral part of village life and now a cesspool choked with weeds and thick with algae, the final resting place for diseased livestock, excess building supplies, broken refrigerators and other major appliances, stolen cars, oil drums, worn radial tires, and, according to the police diver interviewed by the local press, "what looked like a small airplane, but who knows. We had a job to do and performed it to the best of our abilities. Frankly, once we'd covered the bottom without finding the automobile in question, we were happy to get out of the drink. The debris can be very hazardous for the hoses and whatnot, and God forbid you get an ankle stuck. It's an obstacle course down there. The way people just toss things in the drink is sick." That stone turned to no avail, Piotr Swenson proceeded with his plan to "comb the woods" nearby and mustered a group of volunteers largely made up of family members (excepting little Pele, whom they left home with a sitter) to cover the nature preserve around the Mill Pond, keeping track of each other by calling out at regular intervals, "We're here, Thomas!" Elka stumbled onto an abandoned shopping cart, Dag the family Newfoundland charged a deer, and Piotr, with the help of his Field Guide, noted three different species of edible mushrooms, but otherwise their search was fruitless. That such a troubling week should end with the pastor's disappearance still unsolved lent a special fervor to the congregation's Friday evening prayer session (called for by the assistant pastor) and a sense of collective guilt to their hearts, bringing about much *soul-searching*, periods of *distraction* from important daily tasks, and a widespread *contemplation* of sins committed in the past, especially the sin of impatience regarding the pastor and his style of governance, reviving insensitive comments, rude queries, and unspoken thoughts about his race that might previously have been *shelved* as minor, or rationalized away. How the members of the congregation suffered! How they prayed for an end to their ordeal! Perhaps their condition was best described by Sam Cabot in his "Chronicle," when the Archivist, in a burst of gin-fueled eloquence, surmised,

> As any student of the Scripture is aware, there must be Contrition and Humiliation before the Lord takes possession of the pilgrim's Soul, a journey through pain exemplified by the passage of the Children of Israel toward the Promised Land. With our pastor unaccounted for, few would have argued with the assertion that God had led us into a wilderness of sorts, though it may have been rife with fast-food restaurants and paved with macadam. Surely, we were lost. But the fact remained that God, in His wisdom, had led us into the wilderness not because

He hated us, but because He loved us. Just as the ways of the Parent are mysterious to the Child, who knoweth but that He sent his Spirit to move us in the direction that He required?

"Where did the pastor go, Mom?"

"There's no need to yell, Jessie. As you can see, I'm sitting right here."

"But where *is* he?"

"No one knows, really."

"How come no one knows?"

"Because he disappeared, Jessie."

"*Why* did he disappear?"

"No one knows that, either."

"But, Mommy—"

"Can we change the subject, please?"

The Caruso family had gathered for supper in the dining room, joined that Friday night by Ulla, whose Volkswagen had been repaired by a suitor in the engineering department, allowing her the freedom to spend the night in W——— (at Jessie's special request) and give her roommate and her visiting boyfriend some privacy. Ulla's jeans were still torn softly at the knee, and her serenity seemed undisturbed by the news about the pastor, as well as by the family's latest bombshell: earlier that afternoon Devon had been sent home from his field trip to the Freedom Trail for possession of a "blunt," or, as the vice-principal defined it for Bobby over the phone, "a cheap cigar emptied of tobacco and filled with marijuana." A week's suspension was mandatory under his school's drug policy, though a decision was still pending, and the vice-principal, claiming that his hands were tied by a new "zero tolerance" policy, had mentioned the possibility of *expulsion*. Devon had tearfully claimed to his parents that the blunt belonged to someone else, that he was only "holding" as a favor, and he'd sworn that a "real" joint had never touched his lips, only "fake" ones that he'd rolled out of oregano with his friend Raji and tried to sell after school to raise some money for new sneakers.

"But you have *ten* pairs of sneakers," Bobby had protested during the 6:45 family conference in Devon's bedroom, delayed until Bethany could make it home from her yearly evaluation (yet another disaster, but she didn't want to think about it). "They're spread all over the house! Nike, Converse, Fila, Reebok, Adidas! I trip over your sneakers *constantly!*"

"But they aren't *new*, Dad," Devon claimed. "Some of them don't fit me anymore, and the coolest ones cost, like, a hundred twenty-five dollars a pair."

"That's criminal," Bethany added, "and you should know better than to cave in to fashion. Who needs all these sneakers anyway? They're a plague on every family in America! How can Michael Jordan sleep at night? I mean, who's worried about the *implications* of all these sneakers?"

"When have you gone without?" Bobby asked, trying his best to tower over his son's bed. "*When?*"

"Never."

"That's right! Never! We've always bought you everything you needed!"

"I *know*, okay?"

Now Devon was in his ashamed post-crying state, still able to shovel in the food, but sullen in a way that promised days of silence ahead and unusually quiet on the subject of Ulla's cooking (turkey meat loaf, wheat pilaf, broccoli spears). Every now and then the nanny flashed him an indifferent look; otherwise she left the disciplining to his parents, making her rounds from kitchen to dining room with an efficiency that, in Bethany's mind, evoked the phrase pinned to Anita's cubicle wall: DON'T BLAME ME, I ONLY WORK HERE. The girl was practically serving Bobby on her knees, sympathetic, no doubt, to his plight as the separated husband, and wistful for her own father back in Sweden, who was apparently a widower and some kind of geologist too.

"Piotr said something about a love note?" Ulla mentioned casually while clearing the table. "Was the pastor having an affair?"

"That's new," Bobby remarked, looking up from the newspaper. "That's something you never told me."

"Well," Bethany began, but the answer stumped her for a moment.

Devon mumbled, "Can I be excused?"

"I've never paid much attention to the rumors," she continued, dropping her eyes to the table, "and I don't trust the source, that vindictive Margaret Howard. It's a hall of mirrors over there."

"You're excused," Bobby told his son, "but head *straight to your room*. No video games, no TV, no phone calls to your friends. Our discussion about your field trip today is *far* from over, got it?" Devon left in a huff, passing Ulla without so much as a glance, and releasing most of the tension in the dining room.

"What's an affair, Mommy?" Jessie asked, breaking a family rule by standing on her seat.

"Jesus," Bobby muttered.

"Another time," Bethany told her, "okay? Right now I need you to sit down and stop asking so many questions. Why don't you give Ulla a hand loading the dishwasher. The adults here need a little chance to breathe."

"Can you tell me what the hell is happening here?" Bobby

asked once the girl had run off to the kitchen. "My wife won't sleep with me, my son's a purse snatcher and a budding dope fiend, and my six-year-old daughter wants to know what an *affair is, Mommy*? Can you enlighten me, Beth?"

*You forgot about Thomas*, she wanted to remind him, but instead substituted the more appropriate lie: "I have no idea."

"That's it? You have *no idea*, and that's it?"

"Obviously," she said, unable to stop herself from sounding lame, "we're going through a rough patch."

"I'll say," Bobby agreed. "Let me repeat myself. *Jesus.*" Then Ulla asked from the kitchen if anyone wanted ice cream, sending Jessie into a state of hysteria, and Bobby returned to the box scores in the paper, which reassured him with their columns and neat percentages, while Bethany excused herself to go upstairs and cry her eyes out behind the bedroom door, one dark thought away from going back on the Zoloft, craving the *release* of a joint but feeling far too guilty to roll one with Devon being punished down the hall. For the first time she wondered if the child might have figured out that she *indulged*, if perhaps Devon had been snooping around in her bedroom and come across her "stash," tiny as it was . . . Once her tears had stopped she opened the bottom drawer of her bedside cabinet and reached in back to find her quarter ounce, holding the Ziploc bag up to the light and detecting no change in the contents, short of counting the buds out one by one. She took a long, deep whiff of the herb's sweet fragrance (so calming in itself!) before tossing the bag in the back of the drawer and resolving never to indulge again. She felt no better, of course, but recovery was a painstaking process (at least that's what she gathered from the brochures Mike Flynn was always pressing on her). *Mommy*, Jessie called from the end of the hallway, *can you come here a sec?* Bethany checked her eyes once in the bathroom mirror to make sure they weren't too visibly swollen from her crying jag, then she followed Jessie's orders with an *On my way*, grateful for all second chances, and for the opportunity to be her daughter's most favorite slave of all.

Later that night Bobby's "package" began whirring with the signal, leading him to abandon the plastic comfort of his water bed, switch off the soft-core women's prison film with the remote, cross the nubby carpeting in his bare feet, and peer down from the apartment's only window, hoping that his body was not deceiving him again and that Bethany, with time running out, had decided to save their marriage with a visit in his favorite negligee in order to christen the "fornicatorium" with her first orgasm (and his first with a partner who wasn't on late-night cable TV). At the window Bobby thought he saw a shadow traverse the driveway—a *female* shadow—and pass shyly underneath the branches of the maple tree that the builders had transplanted roots and all to provide shade in the summer, leaves to rake in the fall, and a picturesque tableau in winter. *Man!* was the signal growing strong, and unless Bobby was mistaken, he heard footsteps on the staircase, soft, apologetic footsteps climbing in his direction, one step higher, one step closer, drawing nearer to him with each passing second, *his scrotum knew it*, and here he was in his *skivvies*, as his mother had always called them, now *what* in the world had he done with those Velcro straps for "safe" sadomasochism? And *where* had he stored that case of lubricating jelly? In his panic Bobby managed only to slip into his bathrobe (he believed the vertical stripes slimmed his figure), rushing out to the landing in order to meet Bethany with open arms and show his utter gratitude for her visit, his willingness to accept any and all concessions (especially if her apology took, well, a *certain* form that he hadn't enjoyed since the first night of their honeymoon in Sicily) and let their troubles remain in the past, while the future of their marriage looked *bright* for the first time in many lonely months, *things were looking up* with every footstep in the dark, and when she reached the landing, partially out of breath, a moistness rising on her upper lip, Bobby would part his bathrobe and welcome her back into the fold, letting her step from the shadows of their separation and reveal herself in negligeed glory—just one more step, now turn the corner, my sweet Bethany, and you're mine—

"Ulla!"

"Christ, Bobby, you scared me."

"Just let me tie my robe, here."

"Should I turn around?"

"Not necessary. Okay. There we go."

"You weren't expecting me?"

"I can't say that I was, Ulla."

"Am I invited in?"

"Are those *muffins?*"

"Yes, an assortment. I baked them for you."

"What are you, psychic?"

"Well, I try . . ."

Inside, the air seemed more flatulent than Bobby had remembered, and the water bed, ever temperamental, must have sprung a new leak, because Ulla found a wet spot in the carpet and advised him to clean it up before it left a water stain. She surveyed his apartment with a faint distaste and pronounced, "My place in Somerville is nicer."

He tried to explain to her that the project was unfinished, and he'd done everything but the wiring himself, on weekends and during his short vacation every summer; he watched in disbelief as Ulla balanced on the edge of the substandard bed frame, peeled off her German sandals, wiggled all ten toes at once, and threw herself backward onto the water bed with the precision of a scuba diver.

"What a blast," she said without enthusiasm, lying still while the mattress's heaving settled to a jiggle. "If I had a water bed, I'd never leave the house."

What torture was this? What cruel force of nature would devise a visit from Ulla the Remarkable when his resistance had reached a new low point? Blueberry, cranberry, corn, oat bran and raisin . . . Bobby held her plate of muffins gingerly and placed it on top of the VCR.

"Does Jessie know you're here?" he asked, traumatized to the point where he believed his six-year-old was only *faking* her childish qualities and had engineered this surprise visit from her nanny to test his fortitude.

"Jessie? Last I checked she was fast asleep."

"Bethany?"

"Sleeping."

"And Devon?"

"Same," she said, having spread her arms and legs out wide. "Don't worry, we're all alone."

Bobby's pulse was off the charts. "Is that so?"

"*Wow*," she said, "this is very relaxing."

Ulla proceeded to lecture him, while lying flat on her back, on the corrosive effects of television, movies, and mass-produced toys on his two children, arguing that, instead of buying the latest computer games and brand-name clothing, he and Bethany should invest in educational material and well-made Scandinavian products—and make an effort to cut down on *both* of their work schedules, leaving more time to spend in conversation with their kids about the environment, the arts and sciences, spiritual beliefs, and collective values. Hearing about his shortcomings as a parent actually made Bobby feel less anxious, and he settled into his treasured easy chair to listen—one of the few remnants left of his first years with Bethany, when they had rented that little house on a dead-end street in Needham. They had fought bitterly about that chair in Jordan's Furniture (their first public fight of many), Bethany complaining, at first sight on the showroom floor, that it reminded her of liver, while Bobby had appreciated the quality of the Naugahyde, and had claimed that, after a beer or two, it would look exactly like the real McCoy. Since Bobby was paying, he had won the fight, and on delivery day he remembered cutting off the price tag with an enormous sense of pride. He also remembered a particular night in October '84 when they had sex *with the footrest extended*, for what, in retrospect, seemed like hours, taking frequent time-outs to laugh at themselves for having so little self-control . . . With Ulla still lecturing him on the emptiness of American life, and his body newly insensate, cradled by the first piece of furniture that he had ever bought outright, the passage of time, to Bobby, seemed indescribably sad—and Ulla's strident voice, her pale white knees, and her angular, boyish body, struck him as having originated in a different world from the one he knew, a foreign country, a younger world that would outlive his aspirations and keep growing beyond anything that he could imagine, and that, indeed, had already begun to force him out . . . Here was a girl who, when he was a boy, would have ignored him, or, even worse, insisted on a platonic friendship, and now, for reasons that he couldn't quite fathom, she seemed open to the idea that he might hit on her, indeed she was counting on it! Listen to her speak! A voice from across the oceanic divide! And those muffins! Those home-baked muffins! So round on top and perfect in their cups . . .

Ulla lifted her head. "Are you coming over here or not?"

Where did he start with that question? Simple to ask and so complicated to answer with her muffins as *mute jury*, a question that would haunt him long after he had refused her invitation with *great misgivings* and handled her disappointment as best he could, eased himself up from the comforts of the old recliner, and walked her outside to the landing for an uncomfortable good night.

*Are you coming over here or not?*

Sigh. "Well, I wish I could."

"I'll keep my mouth shut, you know."

"I know."

"You don't have to worry, Bobby. It's just sex. People have it all the time."

"Please don't say that—"

"It's true!"

"All I can tell you is, when you're older, things in that area get more complicated."

Silence.

"So are you turning me down?"

"Yes."

"Wow."

"I can't believe it myself . . . Ulla, if you hadn't brought those muffins, I—"

"I knew it was a mistake!"

"I'm grateful, though."

Sigh. "Bethany's a very lucky woman."

"Right."

"I never lie, Bobby."

"*That's* a rare quality."

"Maybe so, but she's lucky all the same."

"Thank you, Ulla."

"You're the sweetest."

"Hardly."


God is an infinite sphere. The center is everywhere, the circumference nowhere, and in the empty space inside—the mysterious workings of the Holy Spirit. Or wait. Doesn't Christ fill the infinite sky above the earth? And what does it mean that the earth is also a sphere (though not infinite, exactly)? How can we even conceive of the infinite when our minds are so efficient at reduction? At underestimation? At mismeasurement and hasty correction? (Wasn't the soul in here someplace?) And God the sphere—is He merely our best invention? Or perhaps an eternal boundary (that phrase she remembered clearly) invested with significance enough to *desire* instead of fear? Can it rightly be said that we in the Pilgrims' Church are fearful of God? An *actual* God? If His commandments are only a metaphysical . . . no, a *metaphor* for self-improvement and better living, should we abide by them? And what does this infinite sphere thing have to do with me?

These questions were the extent of what Bethany could recall from the pastor's final Sunday sermon, reconstructed during the early hours of Sunday morning, the house silent and her children sleeping soundly, one week to the day since the last time she had seen Thomas alive. In darkness now she thought of him as *dead*, the victim of a useless suicide, while in daylight she clung to the idea that Thomas would come back to her, as unlikely as it seemed during the lonely final hour before sunrise. The "infinite sphere" sermon had confused her a week ago, competing for her attention with Jessie's fidgeting and fussing (she'd been a horror that morning), and Bethany was still struggling to understand what he was getting at—and what, if any, connection there might have been between his obscure reference to this *sphere* and the fact that he was missing. But she'd been forced to leave the sermon early that morning, dragging Jessie down the aisle by one arm, and they had waited in the parking lot for the service to end, her daughter's tantrum reduced to a whined *Do we have to go to Fellowship, Mommy? Yes,* she had answered, *we absolutely do,* and when pressed for details ("But *why*, Mommy?"), she had resorted to the arbitrary *Because I said so, all right?* Never a satisfying answer for Jessie, who had thrown herself into her tantrum's Second Act and cried steadily until the possibility of chocolate-chip cookies had overwhelmed her sense of injustice. *When does Fellowship start?* she began asking like a little schizophrenic, prompting Bethany to check her watch and mutter, *Not soon enough.*

She rose from bed at dawn, entering a trance of guilty motherhood that brought her to the kitchen, where, still in her nightgown, she made pancakes from scratch by the light of the oven vent, following a recipe that had somehow lodged itself in her unconscious, measuring, sifting, mixing, pouring, and frying in butter with traditional abandon, plating the perfectly round flapjacks in an appealing pattern, wrapping the platter with aluminum foil, and sliding her family's breakfast in the oven at a not-too-hot 175° (to prevent drying), followed by a thorough washing—by hand—of every dirty dish that had accumulated since Ulla had left the house on Saturday morning. That much accomplished by the unbelievable hour of seven, Bethany added to her itinerary a quick trip to Jessie's room (still sleeping, mound of stuffed animals scattered), placed her favorite bear beside her head on the pillow, and crept out again for a selfless shower, lingering only as long as necessary to wash her essential parts and apply a deep conditioner to her hair, paying special attention to her split ends. She stepped into her terry bathrobe with just a fraction of her usual self-loathing—the a.m. variety, as opposed to the p.m., more shallow and promising than her post-work *chasm*. Jessie was awake by the time Bethany had dressed, saying "good morning" to her stuffed animals one by precious one; downstairs Bobby had begun to take apart the kitchen in his quest for coffee, no doubt shocked to discover her thoughtful gesture warming in the oven.

"Isn't it early for church, hon?" he asked when she came downstairs, hovering by the coffee machine in his bathrobe and matching slippers.

"I'm never going back there again," she told him, surprised by the conviction of her own answer. "Don't worry about making breakfast. There's pancakes in the warmer."

"I saw."

She jingled her car keys. "I'll be back around one o'clock."

"Am I allowed to ask where you're going?"

"For a drive . . ."

Bethany's trance lifted for a moment when she reached Old Town and pulled her car to a stop across the street from the parsonage one more time. She wasn't sure what she would accomplish by visiting the place, but here she was, looking up at the darkened windows on the second floor and thinking of everything important that she'd ever lost: beginning with her father, a remote man who'd grown more distant with every passing year once her parents had divorced, remarrying an unseemly *six months* after the papers had been signed to an unbearable woman named Nanette. *Only second wives are named Nanette,* her mother used to say, *or dairy cows. You watch, they'll multiply and prosper.* And in fact they had, joining the exodus to the West and relocating to the outskirts of Denver, Colorado, which might as well have been, for a twelve-year-old girl who had never traveled west of Route 495, *the end of the earth*, and now her father, at seventy, was an avid golfer who sent his grandchildren "love" in the form of yearly Christmas cards with a portrait of his second family, all red-eyed from the flashbulb, uniformly chubby and freckled like their mother—plus a bonus for the children ($10 for Devon and $5 for Jessie), a salary discrepancy that Bethany would have addressed with her father if they actually had a relationship, but seeing as they were *estranged*, she just sent him a "thank you" card and quietly made up the difference. And her poor, sainted mother! Whose decline had been swifter, and steeper, than anyone had been able to predict: one moment she was an active and eccentric grandmother with an academic pension, two elegant Siamese cats (they were littermates), and one ailing German shepherd on kidney dialysis, the next her treasured dog Sieglinde had passed away, the cats—who could tell what powers of reason their tiny minds possessed?—had left through the pet door one afternoon and never returned, and Bethany's mother couldn't dress herself in the morning, remember who she was, or recognize her children. *Are you my mother?* she had asked Bethany once during the period when she was still being cared for at home. *I'm your daughter*, Bethany had answered patiently, *your only daughter, the youngest of your four children*, and then she had run through her older brothers' names, their wives' names, the various professions represented, and the relative ages of the eight grandchildren; meanwhile her mother had nodded her head politely, looking very thoughtful, in her usual way, but clearly retaining nothing. And now, this agile woman who had represented, for a time, everything that Bethany would aspire to, was *insensible* in mind and body and would end her life as someone else. Her third loss was more ambiguous, perhaps, but still entirely in keeping with the trend of being *orphaned*: Yes, she had lost Thomas when he vanished from the parsonage, and though his whereabouts—the pastor's actual location—was still a source of mystery and great concern, she could see now that answering his absence with facts was *entirely secondary*, the reality that he was *gone, simply gone*, seemed more important to Bethany—this and her realization that the congregation which had called him north to lead them with his melancholy ways and soothing voice had done so for their own salvation, while in truth they didn't understand the first thing about their pastor, and didn't deserve the wise and tolerant example of his leadership. All three lost: father, mother, and the love of her life, leaving only an imperfect woman (Bethany), married to an imperfect man (Bobby) with two imperfect children (Devon, Jessie), living together in a household touched by love, sadness, longing, fear, dishonesty, and rampant misunderstanding; the abuse of alcohol and psychotropic drugs; industry, religion, and human sexuality; and the unfulfilled promise of redemption from above, enacted on the cross at Golgotha.

The sun was out when Bethany arrived at her mother's nursing home and the attendants had wheeled some of the "guests" outside to bask on the front lawn, their skin impossibly pale and painted with age spots or tinctured bruises, failing bodies dressed up in T-shirts, warm up suits, and bright white sneakers the uniform of the active Senior Citizen. From a distance it looked as though they had gathered for a chat on the lawn, but as Bethany approached from across the parking lot she heard no conversation; one "guest" was sleeping in the sunlight, another stared into the middle distance, a third companion, the liveliest of the group, smiled at Bethany and enunciated her "Good morning" so perfectly that her voice seemed to have time-traveled forward from 1932.

"How are you?" Bethany asked, stopping for a moment in the shade beneath the entryway. A cat was dozing on a bench nearby, and the flower beds along the walk showed signs of recent work: bright red geraniums, purple marigolds, a single yellow tulip.

"Good morning." With the same friendly smile too.

"I said, *How are you?*"

"Good morning."

Bethany smiled uneasily and left the women to their silent communion, heading through the entrance (she set off an electronic beep) and noticing, as she stepped inside, a framed Picasso reproduction that had come to the nursing home with her mother: a simple flower-in-the-hand poster that she had always kept in her bedroom, hanging, now, in the entryway to greet visitors with its fragile optimism. The smell that met her inside wasn't putrid, exactly, but it did seem to build as she passed through the sitting room with its hotel-style furniture and bubbling aquarium, the air redolent of urine, bedsores, medicine, and starchy meals; the carpeted hallway and its alcoves were lined with immobilized patients, and Bethany felt relieved, on her way to the front desk, that none of the living shadows in her path turned out to be her mother. A sign on the courtesy desk informed her that KATHY was the senior nurse on duty, and a timid nurse's aide, upon asking Bethany if she needed any help, called KATHY's name over the loudspeaker. *Kathy to the desk, please. Kathy to the desk.* Aides and orderlies in pastel uniforms (red for women, blue for men) ambled by on obscure errands, seemingly oblivious to the "guests" on every chair, propped in every corner, pulling themselves along the corridors with the help of wheelchairs and aluminum walkers, hollowed of what made them recognizably human but unwilling to die . . . And this was the expensive long-term health care option! The state-of-the-art facility that had bled her mother's savings dry *in six months*, forcing Bethany and her brothers to pool their resources and share the cost above what Medicaid allowed—a not inconsiderable amount of money to be shelling out every month. The admissions process had all happened so fast, and since her brother Nate was a doctor they had deferred to him in all the major decisions, forgetting, somehow, that Nate's relationship to their mother had always been troubled, and failing to deal squarely with her veiled references to *euthanasia* between the initial diagnosis and her own vanishing act, the short and heartbreaking period of lucidity before the disease had stolen her entire substance. The mythical KATHY appeared just in time, looking harried, which seemed appropriate, and the two of them went off in search of Bethany's mother, walking shoulder to shoulder down the corridor and speaking intimately about her physical condition, bodily functions, diet, activities, and tendency to wander from the grounds—a common problem for which she had been fitted with an ankle bracelet that triggered multiple alarms.

"How often do my brothers visit?" Bethany asked, adding as an explanation, "We're a dysfunctional family. They never tell me anything."

"Every week or so," Kathy answered, "usually on Saturday or Sunday. Lewis brings his family quite often, and the other one, the doctor—"

"Nate."

"He usually visits on his own. You'll see how the place fills up once church lets out. Your mother just had breakfast, so I expect she's in the activities room."

"Which is . . ."

"Where we're going, right down the hall."

"Of course, yes."

"Those brothers of yours are tough to get a handle on," Kathy told her. "Aloof, you might say."

"They have their problems, I guess."

"I won't ask!"

"Not that I'm so stellar . . ."

"Let he who is without sin, right?"

"Exactly."

Along the way Kathy stopped to check on a few "guests," compare notes with a Jamaican nurse, and move an empty wheelchair from the hallway to a storage room. She was clearly the heart and soul of the operation, and Bethany, in her presence, felt inadequate as a caregiver and more than a little awestruck by her energy. Instead of asking how she managed it all and kept her sanity, Bethany lingered a few steps behind and watched her in action, hoping that some of Kathy's patience might rub off on her. At the door to the activities room Kathy took her shoulder for a moment and wished her a good visit.

"If you need me," she said, "just holler, okay?"

"Thank you, really."

"Anytime."

"Kathy, you're my hero."

The sunlit room was empty save for her mother, or rather, the body that had held her mother so completely for so long, dressed in a purple blouse, corduroy jumper, and threadbare cardigan sweater, all of which must have belonged to another patient, and seated at a round Formica table, one hand clutching an unbreakable coffee mug. A television nearby, playing a wobbly videotape, leaked light and a steady murmur of sound. Bethany took the chair beside her and said, "Mother." No response. Her sneakers were also from an unknown donor, and the ankle bracelet made her look as though she were under House Arrest for drug possession. Bethany leaned closer. "Mother, it's me." She turned this time and their eyes met, but her expression remained empty. "Look at the way they've dressed you," she said, "it's like you're a thrift-store shopper. I don't think I've ever seen you in a jumper and tennis shoes be-

fore, Mother. A caftan and sandals, maybe, but this getup?"
Her mother's eyes seemed to be following the movements of her
lips, so she continued in the same vein. "I'm going to talk to the
nurses about getting your own clothing back. And your hair! It
looks like they've given you some kind of *perm* . . . You never
would have stood for that, Mother, back when you were still
yourself, I mean. When you were *you* and not . . . in a nursing
home. Anyway, I hope you won't mind if I'm candid with you
this morning. You were always so blunt with me, and I've really
needed someone to talk to lately . . . So I'm going to talk. I
mean, who better to talk to than your mother, right?

"You were such a tyrant! Always! Railing against the
garbage that we wanted for Christmas every year, correcting
our English at the dinner table, complaining about the friends
we dared bring home from school, like Zoë Schwartz—poor
Zoë with her chronic overbite and headgear, do you remember
the way you used to scream at her, *Zoë! Stop being such a bore!*
Or how about the time when Lewis used his allowance to buy
himself that chocolate-covered cereal and made the mistake of
trying to hide it in the pantry? You were really at your best,
sniffing out his Count Chocula and calling all of us into the
downstairs bathroom for a ceremonial flush of his *contraband,*
I remember you called it *contraband,* that's how I learned the
vocabulary word at school . . . You were so solemn about the
whole thing, do you remember? Delivering a treatise on the importance of obeying rules before you emptied Lewis's cereal in
the toilet, but the little nuggets refused to sink, they *floated!* After flushing again and again you stormed out of the bathroom,
and I remember Lewis asking, *Hey, Mom, do you mind grabbing me a spoon?* Even you had to laugh! Because you were a
model tyrant, the sweetest, most benevolent dictator in the entire world." Bethany leaned over and released the coffee mug

from her mother's grasp, then gathered her two hands and pressed them inside her own, trying to warm her cold and shiny skin. "Lewis, do you know I hardly ever see him? I spend time with Nate and his family every Christmas, but that's about it for us, and with Jonathan in Brussels or wherever, I haven't seen him for at least five years, maybe longer. I miss them all, Mother, but mostly I've been missing you." Bethany tightened her grip on her mother's hands and looked straight into her eyes, trying, perhaps in vain, to reach whatever substance lay behind them. "You never told me life would be this hard, Mother, and I don't blame you for it, I really don't. I just wish that we'd had more time to know each other as adults, you know, sort of one woman to another, because I think we have a lot in common. We could have been more friendly to one another, don't you think? We should have tried harder to be friends instead of always bickering and fighting about, well, nothing that matters now . . ."

She let her tears fall without wiping them, clutching her mother's unresponsive hands as tightly as she could. "Mother, I've done a terrible thing, and I wish you could give me some advice. For the past year I've been having an affair with the minister of my church, a single man, and while I can't say how he feels about *me* anymore, I've definitely fallen in love with him. Do you remember how that is? Thinking about someone at every spare moment? Trying to be strong and stable but absolutely melting when you see him? It's funny, but I couldn't tell at first. I thought my medication was screwy, or I'd developed some new disorder that made me fixate on this poor man, except it turned out that he was suffering from the same fixation too. We were in love! At my age! To be in love! I love him always, Mother, all day long, and at night I seem to love him even more. It's the first time I've ever felt this way about someone, and probably the last time too.

"Because he's gone, Mother. I mean, how can you explain it

when someone *disappears*? One day he was here, loving me, and the next day he's just . . . *gone*, leaving me with the emptiest feeling, a sickness that may never, ever go away, and all this love for him that I don't know what to do with . . . Anything could have happened to him, Mother, anything, from driving his car into a ditch to being carried off by a tornado, to an assumption into Heaven straight from his driveway, or maybe something much, much uglier . . . I do know that he's kind and gentle by nature, and if he was forced to do something cruel to me, there must have been a good reason, because he's *wise*, Mother, so wise and knowing about the ways of the world, and I have to believe that he's alive and well and hurting just like I am . . . In my heart I can feel his pain, I really can, I know he's out there, and I know he's lost without me, just like I'm lost without you.

"There, you made me say it! *I'm lost without you!* It seems strange to say it while we're sitting together, while you're still *alive* and all, but it seems like forever since we've had a decent conversation, or even since you made a nasty little comment about Bobby, or tried instructing me on how to live my life . . . Maybe there's a part of you deep inside that can still understand me, Mother, maybe there still is, and that's the part of you I'm trying to reach, some neglected portion of your brain that remembers your daughter, or a muscle in your heart that might still beat for me a little . . . I love you, Mother, and I miss you, and that's what I came here to say this morning. I've tried and tried again, but there's just no replacing the love of a mother. There's just no replacing you."


"Why can't they find the pastor, Mommy?"

"That I don't know, Jessie. Everyone's looking for him as hard as they can. Right now they're trying to trace his car, but apparently they haven't found it yet."

"Does the pastor have a mother?"

"Of course, honey. Don't you remember when she visited the church? On Christmas last year?"

"No!"

"She's very handsome, just like him . . ."

"Does the pastor's mother know where he is?"

"No, honey, and that's part of the problem."

"Do you think she's sad?"

"Yes, I imagine she's very upset right now."

"Is the pastor's mother African-American too?"

"Yes, she is. That's usually how it works—"

"We have African-American kids at my school!"

"I know that, Jessie."

"There's Tonya, and Millicent, and Steven . . . And there's a new boy from *England*."

(Yawn.)

(Yawn.)

"How about calling it a night?"

"No! Don't make me go to sleep!"

"You have one minute maximum, okay?"

"Two!"

"One and counting, and that's it."

"I have another question!"

"Oh, God."

"Don't say that, Mommy!"

"Just be gentle, please."

"When is Daddy moving out of the garage?"

"I should have seen *that* one coming . . ."

"When can he come back inside and live with us?"

"Well, that depends on what your father and I decide about our separation—"

"WHEN?"

". . . Soon, how's that for an answer."

"How soon, Mommy?"

"*Soon.*"

"That's all I wanted to know, Mommy. You can leave me alone now."

"Sweet dreams, then."

"Don't forget to leave the door open!"

"Oh, right. I'm leaving it open as we speak."

"Sweet dreams, Mommy!"

"Thanks, dear."

"Jesus loves you!"


"I know where you scored your dope, Devon, and I want to know how long this has been going on. You're awfully young to be dealing with the likes of Bradley Howard and you should trust me when I say that he'll only take advantage of you."

"I was only holding like I said—"

"Don't even try and bullshit me! This conversation is just between the two of us, and I expect you to tell me the truth—"

"I'm telling you the truth, yo!"

"Are you going to just lie there staring at the wall all night or turn and face me? If you're trying to be an effective liar, Devon, you need to know that your *posture* isn't very trustworthy . . ."

"There, happy?"

"*Happy?* How can I be *happy* when my son might be expelled from school! When he's dressing like a gang-banger and hanging out with a dope dealer? That's right! It doesn't sound so cool anymore when your mother spells it out for you! I'm perfectly capable of watching MTV too!"

"Maybe I stole it from you."

"What?"

"*Maybe I stole it from*—"

"I heard you the first time! I'm not going to ask whether you've been snooping in my private things *without permission* or if you're getting your information from that cretin on two wheels—"

"I haven't been snooping!"

"Well, that's good news . . . I have one thing to say to you, Devon, and I know it might sound like a cop-out, but it's *incredibly significant*. I'm an adult capable of making my own choices! And you're a *kid*! That means you have exactly as many rights and privileges as your father and I extend to you as long as you're living under *our* roof. When you're out of college and living on your own, you can go ahead and install a *hookah* in your living room for all I care. But until then, you're forbidden to smoke *dope, cigarettes, dental floss, or anything else*. And I hope that I've just made myself clear."

"But that's a double standard!"

"Of course it is!"

"That's not fair . . ."

"*Live with it.*"

(Sobs.)

"You're a good kid, Devon, and you always have been, that's why your father and I are having such a hard time with this. Everyone makes mistakes—God knows I've made my share—but you've got to understand that screwing up now might have *serious consequences* for your future."

"I *know*, okay?"

"And the Bradley Howards of the world don't care! They make promises but in the end they won't protect you! As a matter of fact, they'll do everything they can to drag you down to their level, and it's important to remember that, because unlike Bradley Howard, you have so much potential . . ."

(Sniffle.)

"Do you understand me, Devon?"

"Yes."

"And you know we're always here for you?"

"Right."

"And will you promise me that you'll stay away from Bradley Howard and his blunts?"

"Okay."

(Sigh.)

(Sniffle.)

"I'm glad we talked, Devon. Why don't we both try and get some sleep for a change."

"Night, yo."

"*Night, yo.*"

"Shut up, Mom!"

"Sweet dreams to you too."


Later still, Bethany stood at the foot of the staircase leading up to Bobby's apartment, looking up at his window and its depressing Technicolor glow, seriously contemplating, for the first time since their latest trial separation had begun, a trip upstairs to offer her terms for reconciliation—a prospect that filled her heart with a combination of relief and gloom. The truth was, she felt unbearably lonely. And her children had effectively convinced her that happiness, for all of them, depended on the nuclear family being reunited underneath a single roof: on two parents sleeping soundly in the master bedroom, one child, the youngest, dreaming of animals in the room next door, the other restless down the hall, dreaming of independence . . . on the possibility, should nightmares wake the youngest child, that she might leave the hostile confines of her room and climb into an expanse of bed that she can barely fathom, nestling into the cool uncharted region between *father* (oblivious, threatening to snore at any moment) and *mother* (annoyed, whispering a stern but by no means definitive *just this once*), giddy with parental love and still able somehow to catch sleep when it comes, drifting away with a deep sense of security and the child's skewed idea of accomplishment, never questioning the nature of the intimacy she's just fought for and won . . . The tyranny of children! Raised and praised and permanently damaged by their human makers! Such a capacity for love and havoc they could be the world itself! Who knows: They could be the very image of God! And who was Bethany to value her own happiness over that of her *babies*, smaller combinations of herself and Bobby without experience to chasten them, knowledge to guide them, a career to grind them down save the grunt work of growing up—which *never stops*, Bethany reflected, growth is an enslaving process to be avoided, if possible, at all costs, same with progress and its attendant dreams (equality, beauty, wealth) that tantalize but never quite arrive as originally promised—and looking up, still looking up at Bobby's apartment window, waiting, at the foot of her husband's wobbly staircase, for inspiration to strike, resolution came to Bethany in the shape of a thought: *I will be an unhappy wife.* The tree branches above her rustled in a breeze, the light in Bobby's window flickered blue-and-white, and she nearly laughed at the cruel simplicity of her formulation. *I will be an unhappy wife.* With the phrase sounding in her head, Bethany looked down again and found the railing in the dark, pulling herself up the staircase first one, and later two steps at a time, climbing at a rate designed to startle Bobby with the stealth of her approach,

and to outrun, as best she could, her ambivalence about returning to a man whose love for her, though sincere, had been sup-
planted by another, more complicated love that had accounted
for every part of her; the railing that Bobby had pieced together
from scraps at the lumberyard could barely support her weight,
but she kept climbing, two steps at a time.

**10** Many thought it apt that spring's remarkable burst should turn fallow in the space of a month due to an extended period of sweltering weather, threatening even the better-tended lawns, the sweetbrier rose in the meadows overlooking the dying Mill Pond, the phlox carpeting the wood's edge at the nature preserve, and the sorrel growing in the shade of the deciduous forest, and supporting the prediction of drought first raised in the Old Farmer's Almanac that year, although the winter's heavy snowfall, for the moment, had kept the town's water supply at an acceptable level, and would postpone any discussion of conservation measures until the true Dog Days of mid-August. To the membership of the Pilgrims' Congregational Church the first weeks of summer, so often a time of *hope* and *rebirth* in the past, were haunted by their continuing uncertainty about the pastor's fate and an event of singular, even crushing, sadness: The Council, in preparation for the imminent return of the Reverend Harrison "Hal" Chambers, called back from retirement in Scottsdale to occupy the pulpit until the pastor's disappearance had, in some way, been resolved, issued an order for the removal of the Reverend Thomas Mosher's personal effects from the parsonage, lest the building, in their own words, become a "shrine to an unexplained defection" rather than a dwelling place for a living, breathing spiritual leader of an active congregation gathered in the name of Christ. (One reliable source would later reveal that the Council, not to be taken for fools in the matter, had wasted no time in ordering a full review of the corporation's assets, and the results of the audit, though never made public, had fully exonerated the pastor from the suspicion of embezzlement; indeed, according to a persistent rumor, later confirmed in the papers by a police investigator, the pastor had, for some reason, *failed to deposit* a number of his paychecks, resulting in a surplus in the payroll account of roughly eleven thousand dollars, no small amount by any reasonable standard of judgment.) A group of volunteers, under the co-coordination of the Reverend Jane Groom and the lay leader Mrs. Safarian, accepted the thankless task of loading the pastor's belongings into cardboard boxes, performed, on three successive evenings between six o'clock and nine, in *reverent silence* and with guilt in all their hearts—tears were not uncommon on those muggy nights, even for those not given to outward displays of emotion; the revolving fan in the study kept falling from the windowsill in eerie repetition; the mosquitoes, they agreed, were insufferable; and the "crew," as Jane insisted on calling the volunteers, hardly touched the sheet pizza that she had bought on the first night and kept reheating as their packing wore on, served, on white paper plates, with generic soft drinks in plastic two-liter bottles . . . During the third night of their ordeal, with the majority of the boxes sealed and stacked in the front hallway of the parsonage, awaiting the professional movers who would whisk all evidence of their pastor away and deliver his belongings back to his stoical mother (two weeks after the pastor's disappearance the usher Silva had driven to Annisquam at dawn and transported Mrs. Mosher to that morning's church service, *such remarkable composure*, the choirmaster Flynn had observed at a particularly somber Fellowship, echoing the consensus among the members of the church, who formed a line to express their sorrow and admiration for her son, *the great Faith of the woman is palpable*), a voice called out from the second floor, *I've found something! It's a note! I've found something!* Alone in the master bedroom, making one last sweep with the Electrolux before she closed the door behind her and began vacuuming the hallway, Mrs. Safarian's power brush had caught the corner of a sheet of paper that had evidently fallen from the pastor's desk—a false alarm, as it turned out, the page merely containing notes for the "infinite sphere" sermon that had left so many of them bored and/or puzzled, complete with a complicated diagram drawn in pencil, clearly erased and redrawn numerous times by the pastor's careful hand, reproducing the *sphere* as an indecipherable collection of dotted lines, rays, angles, and theoretical measurements, yet another obscurity to compound the mystery of his sudden departure. It seemed an *insult*, that inscrutable sheet of paper, a willful subversion of the congregation's right to know, and rather than include the diagram in the box marked MISC. PAPERS, the volunteers, upon reflection, tossed their discovery in the recycling pile and returned to the significant task of readying the parsonage for the Reverend Chambers's return from Scottsdale. Once the boxes had been packed and labeled, the carpets vacuumed, and the bookshelves dusted, once the closets had been emptied, the mattresses beaten and aired, the refrigerator cleaned with a solution of vinegar and water, and the freezer, for the first time in years (judging by the icy buildup), defrosted, the "crew" gathered in the front hallway and formed a circle around the pastor's stacked belongings, clasping hands and closing their eyes for a recitation of an appropriate Psalm, whispered (for her voice was no longer in her power) by the Reverend Groom:

*I cried unto God with my voice, even unto God with my voice; and he gave ear unto me.*

*In the day of my trouble I sought the Lord: my sore ran in the night, and ceased not: my soul refused to be comforted.*

*I remembered God, and was troubled: I complained, and my spirit was overwhelmed.*

*Thou holdest mine eyes waking: I am so troubled that I cannot speak . . .*

and when the prayer was done, they wiped their tears and exchanged hugs of consolation, remarking on the awful aspect of their sorrow; soon Mrs. Safarian checked her Rolex watch and announced that it was nearly ten o'clock, so they gathered their things and waited in the hallway while the usher turned out the lights, coming back with a flashlight to lead them all outside to the front walk, where the volunteers, after three long nights together, said their warm and reluctant goodbyes . . . As they returned to their separate cars, only Jane would notice that the peepers, after thrumming all night long, had fallen quiet, and she made a note of the impression for future reference, listening in the driveway while her fellow parishioners slammed their doors shut and pulled away, one by one, eventually leaving the driveway as empty as on the day they had first discovered that the Reverend Thomas Mosher was missing from the parsonage.


Sixty-three days. Not God's six to make the world, but an equally astounding *sixty-three days* of gestation. And by counting backward from the day her rectal temperature dropped below 100° Fahrenheit, Jane had derived a most likely conception date of Thursday, April 4—Maundy Thursday, a time when Molly's hindquarters had most definitely been wrapped in her protective undergarments. True, Jane had left her unsupervised for the duration of the evening's service, but the chlorophyll tablets had been working so effectively! And she had felt so *guilty* about always locking the poor creature away! Jane had resisted the first warning signs of pregnancy at four weeks (slightly enlarged abdomen, swollen mammary glands), attributing these changes to the onset of sexual maturity and the animal's ever-increasing appetite for treats . . . and then Thomas, dear Thomas, had *vanished* from the parsonage, leading to the second-hardest period that Jane had ever lived through (the first, of course, being the loss of her parents), between presiding over the chaotic church meeting when the roof had collapsed, trying to cooperate with the police while they bungled their way through a cursory investigation, and mediating the various disputes between the factions in the congregation supportive of the Council and the radical fringe, led by Piotr Swenson, who had demanded, among other things, the *immediate resignation* of all twelve board members and the formation of a committee to amend the charter for the first time since the turn of the century . . . So if her schnauzer's pregnancy had gone unnoticed for a little while, who could blame her? Not the vet, who, upon hearing Molly's symptoms over the telephone, had congratulated Jane on the impending additions to her family.

"But that can't be!" Jane had cried in her kitchen. "I mean, she's a purebred with all her papers! You're not telling me that any old dog from the neighborhood just—" She had stopped her inquiry there, feeling the room begin to spin while the vet had a good, long laugh at her expense.

"Genetic diversity is a good thing," he had claimed, stifling his last chuckle. "All you can do now is hope for the best."

*Hoping for the best.* How strange, she had thought in the weeks leading up to Molly's successful delivery, that a knocked-up schnauzer and a wise veterinarian would provide the material for a series of sermons that would begin the congregation's healing process and meet with high praise from all the warring factions alike. "An Immaculate Conception?" Jane called her sermon cycle, drawing a comic parallel between the Virgin Mother and the schnauzer Molly Bloom that struck the more conservative members of the church as utterly charming and Swenson's radical fringe as slyly subversive. Her mother had always claimed that *God has a sense of humor*, and Jane took great pleasure in testing—and proving, she believed—this maxim by telling the story of Molly's pregnancy in allegorical terms. She was especially pleased to deliver the final sermon in her "Immaculate Conception?" series with the Reverend Chambers in the audience, just returned from Scottsdale and looking tanned and physically fit, his head virtually shaved to enhance the *spiritual qualities* of his bearing, his beard grown whiter and shorn closer to his face, a characteristic sparkle in his eye that promised *harmony in the universe*, and his laughter so contagious—how long since the congregation had laughed together? Shared a smile? Prayed together without resentment?—when Jane described her first impressions of Molly's litter thusly:

Let me just say it this way, folks. As I stood outside the walk-in closet and gazed into the whelping box at those little mismatched puppies, it became quite clear to me that we weren't talking about a virgin birth here. Not unless the Holy Spirit assumed the shape of a hopeless mongrel with shades of terrier, poodle, rottweiler, and dalmatian . . .

How the Reverend Chambers had laughed! Freeing the members of the Council in the front row to let down their guarded expressions and laugh along with her sermon too, and from there the *joy* had reverberated throughout the meetinghouse, surely rising to the Heavens to meet God's ear and demonstrate how far they'd come in banishing *sadness* and *mischief* from the Pilgrims' Church and returning their thoughts to Christ, the mysterious workings of the Holy Spirit, and God the Father of all things, *a mighty Fortess, a Bulwark never failing, our Helper He amid the flood of mortal ills prevailing* . . .

The outpouring of affection at the morning's well-attended Fellowship had pleased Jane to no end, as had the sight of Molly Bloom nursing her new litter on a blanket underneath the apple tree, which had finally blossomed, surrounded by a group of children in their Sunday best, eager to witness the miracle of life up close: the panting, prostrate mother lying on her side; the squirming infants hungry for their milk, climbing over one another in a blind competition for the nearest nipple, the strong outracing the dreamy, the dreamy displacing the weak, and last of all in the feeding line, the runt of the litter, forced to await salvation on the blanket's periphery.

Margaret Howard left her bronze Cadillac running in the loading zone outside Hardy's Nursery, intending to make a quick trip inside and have one of the Ecuadoran workers load her trunk with a selection of annuals for the church grounds—some alyssum, or, if they looked hearty enough, a flat of impatiens, and perhaps some ornamental foliage to help fill the shady spots and line the outside borders of the flower beds. The bursitis in Margaret's shoulder had been flaring up again, her internist was lobbying for elective surgery on her gallbladder, and ever since Artemesia had resigned from the Grounds Committee, in an unfortunate piece of timing, she had been forced to do most of the weeding and planting on her own. Silva took care of the watering, of course, but the man was overworked and forgetful, and the weather had been cruel to everything but her lupines, which, though thriving in general, had gone to seed even earlier than usual that summer. The nursery looked to be doing a brisk business, especially in light of the heat wave, and Margaret, after wandering the aisles in a vain search for dusty miller, had a hard time tracking down her friend Anne Hardy, who believed, along with her partner and husband Thatch, in a hands-on style of business ownership. Finally an employee in a navy jumper had directed Margaret to the checkout counter near the stacks of peat, and there she fell into a conversation with Anne, a handsome woman in ancient green wellies, while Thatch, whose temper was legendary, busied himself outside in the topiary section by yelling directions at his employees.

"I've been following the trouble at your church," Anne told her with a serious shake of her head, "and it sounds like a damn shame to me. Imagine leaving so many good people in the lurch like that! Our rector has his own ideas about what happened, of course, and I'll grant you they had a *friendship*, but running from your problems doesn't seem that Christian to me. Around here people don't just disappear without a trace, not unless they want to."

"Don't I know it," Margaret said, leaning closer to avoid being heard by the other customers. "Between you and me, there's been talk of hiring an investigator to track him down. Anything to make him face the music, right?"

"Good idea," Anne said, "*good idea.*" She directed one of the Ecuadorans outdoors with a rolling pallet, waving her arms and repeating, *Abajo, abajo. El patrón. Abajo el patrón.* "Excuse me, Margaret, but you know how it is with today's workforce."

"I wish I didn't!"

"Wasn't that Bradley I saw in front of your building with a hedge clipper? Is he working beside his father now?"

Margaret felt a twinge in her shoulder and swung her handbag up to the counter, trying not to wince. "I'd rather not get started on those two incompetents, dear. Let's just say they're a *burden* on my heart and they deserve each other's company. How's little Thatch doing?"

"Oh, still trying to make his grandfather proud," she answered, reaching back to tighten the scarf around her head. "We told Thatch Jr. that Law Review was good enough for us, but he *insisted* on spending the summer in Washington again. The Supreme Court, you know. I must say that Chief Justice Rehnquist has really taken an interest, and Thatch just loves the responsibility . . ."

Margaret smiled through her shoulder pain. "He was always marked for success, that boy. Going way back you could see it in the way he carried himself. Such *confidence.*"

"He could call more," Anne said, "but we're both very proud of him, that's for certain. Now let's get down to business, Margaret. What can we send you home with?"

They spoke for a while about Margaret's soil quality, the weather conditions, her watering schedule, and what the nursery had in stock; then Anne filled out an order slip and sent Margaret outside to her car, promising that Thatch Sr. would bring her seedlings out to the loading zone personally. Margaret did admire the Hardys' work ethic and commitment to customer service, and made sure to tell Anne as much before she slipped her gold card back inside her wallet and took her leave, only slightly annoyed by the exorbitant total for a few flats of flora. Eleven minutes later (she timed him for the sake of curiosity), Thatch appeared with her plants, loading them in her car while she nursed her aching shoulder in the driver's seat.

"Shame about your minister," he said after closing the trunk and coming around to her window for a friendly chat. "Couldn't believe it when I heard. That's a real shame, all right."

"The Reverend Chambers is back with us now," she answered, "so I've decided the best thing is not to dwell on it. Hal's a good man and a stabilizing force. The other one . . . he just wasn't our kind of *people*, you know what I mean? He wasn't one of *us*."

"I know what you mean," Thatch told her, nodding, "and I'm pleased to hear you say it. Loud and clear. Hal's a man of character, always has been, and I was pleased to hear that he's come back for a spell. The man's a *credit* to the community."

"Hear, hear!"

"Anything else I can do you for today?"

"Not that I can think of, dear."

"Sure now? I could have some of the boys wash your car real quick, they do Anne's station wagon twice a week . . ."

"Oh, Thatch, no, thanks. They should really quit it with the sheep of Scotland and clone the likes of you instead."

"I'll run that one by Anne."

"No you will *not*!"

A moment later, just as she was pulling away from the loading zone, Thatch came back to her car and motioned for her to roll the window down. "Say, Margaret, I have a proposition for you. I'm not sure if you're aware of it, but Anne and me have a group that meets on Monday nights to talk about the issues. Good people, I can vouch for every one, who care about *values* and the integrity of America's future."

"Yes," she said, "I was aware of that."

Thatch's face had turned an unappealing shade of red. "We have coffee and cake and generally share ideas, and I'd like you to join us if you can make the time. You're welcome to bring Jerry too."

"Can I think about it?"

"You betcha," Thatch said, backing away. "Bye, now."

"Thanks again," she said, adjusting her climate control with the press of a button. "And give my best to little Thatch."

"Monday night at eight o'clock!"

"I'll think about it."

"Our place! It's at our place this week!"


Back on the church grounds, with all but one flat of the annuals unloaded, her Stride-Rites feeling a bit snug and her left kneepad refusing to stay fastened, Margaret was surprised to hear a familiar-sounding car pull into the driveway beside her own, and even more surprised, a moment later, to look up from her gardening and see Artemesia Angelis carrying her alyssum across the lawn. The two women hadn't exchanged a word since the calamitous church meeting, and, despite the mostly successful Order of Corporate Reconciliation service presided over by Jane Groom, Margaret had assumed their friendship was a thing of the past.

"I can't say that I expected to see you here again," Margaret said, on her knees, with her back turned to Artemesia. "You can put that flat down anywhere is fine."

Artemesia laid the flowers down with a barely audible groan.

"Except there. They'll die before I get to them."

She moved the flat into a shady spot nearby and said, "I came here to apologize, Margaret."

"So go on."

"I'm sorry about what I did at the church meeting," Artemesia told her after a brief silence. "I tried to make you look foolish in front of the gathered church, and I regret my part in that."

"I suppose it's a good start . . ."

"I'm sorry for lying too . . . For lying to you and everyone else for my own selfish reasons. Of course I never had an affair with Thomas, or even contemplated the idea."

"No, dear. You didn't. Though I may, for a moment, have suspected it myself. Anyway, I'm not proud of my own conduct that night either. With Hal back for the foreseeable, I'm for putting the *entire thing* behind us."

A starling dropped from a nearby tree and seemed to watch them for a moment before walking away in the grass.

"I have the pastor's Book of Worship," Artemesia confided in her, "the pocket-sized edition? I got this call one night from the usher and he said that he might have something of interest, so I drove to meet him later at the church parking lot and he just rolled down his window and handed it over. At first I didn't know what the secrecy was all about. But then I brought the Book of Worship home and checked the inside cover, and I saw his name, 'Property of Thomas Mosher'—"

"I've heard enough of that story for now," she interrupted. "And I'm disappointed to hear that Silva's become a dealer in stolen relics. Not that what you've got is all that Holy . . ."

"How's your shoulder, Margaret?"

"All right," she answered, taking a break in the unnatural heat to wipe her brow. "Thank you for asking. It was touch and go for a while after all the controversy."

"You may have heard that I'm leaving?"

"Yes, I'd heard something to that effect."

"I'm going on a mission," she explained, "through the UCC's global ministries program? I've been looking into it for a while and decided that now is the right time. They're sending me to Bangkok, Thailand, to work with a pastor there who specializes . . . well, he tries to help women and children, especially young girls, who've been forced into working for the sex industry, often to support their families, or pay for things like an education. *The basics.* There's a real poverty problem."

"And how does your husband feel about your trip?"

"Not so good," she admitted. "He's decided to lay down the law with me, and it looks like there might be lawyers involved . . ."

"And the *children*? What about the *children*?"

"It's just six months, and they can visit for a short time if they like . . . The truth is I'm not so popular at home right now. They'll get along fine without me."

Margaret resumed her digging while Artemesia loomed behind her, saying, after a spell, "I seem to remember sitting in this very spot and remarking how things were really changing around here. I must say that, with the exception of Hal's return, and maybe Jane Groom coming into her own, all the surprises lately have been of the *unpleasant* variety. Still I wish you luck with your endeavor overseas."

"Thank you, Margaret. That means—"

"You won't mind if I stay here instead of walking with you back to the car? I'd like to finish the planting with enough time to make my family some dinner."

"Of course, Margaret."

"Goodbye, then."

"I'll be back soon enough."

"We'll see."

And late that afternoon, Margaret Howard, thoroughly exhausted from her day of gardening and rather stunned by her interaction with Artemesia on the church grounds, turned her Cadillac into the driveway of her home and was disturbed to find, taking up her favorite parking spot, Bradley's motorcycle in its usual state of disrepair, parts scattered here, expensive tools lying there, forcing her to stop short and risk a case of whiplash. In her own driveway! The inept mechanic was nowhere to be seen (there had been no such diagnostics in the old days, of course, but Margaret had begun to suspect that Bradley was suffering from Attention Deficit Disorder), and only the Good Lord knew where Jerry was hiding (though the hour did suggest the possibility that he was napping). Rather than let herself get all worked up, however, Margaret closed her eyes and took a deep breath, practicing the relaxation technique that her internist had recommended in order to control her temper, and exactly sixty seconds later—she had counted in her head—she climbed out of the driver's seat, locked the doors with a *chirp*, and walked inside through the gaping garage door (yet another forbidden practice).

The word was on the tip of her tongue: BRADLEY! And what would have followed: GET THAT RUSTING HUNK OF METAL OUT OF MY DRIVEWAY! NOW! But she walked in through the kitchen and saw him immediately, *her only son*, sprawled across the leather couch with his shirt off, fast asleep, clutching a pillow to his chest as if it were his favorite teddy

bear, as if he were a boy again and they could start all over . . .
And she stood there at the edge of the sunken living room,
watching him sleep and listening to him lightly wheeze, the
same wheeze that had frightened her when he was still a toddler and had led to so many fruitless appointments with pediatric specialists, none of whom—with all their years of training
and expensive equipment—could find anything wrong with the
boy, save the *tendency to wheeze while he slept* . . . and then
acting on a wife's intuition she climbed the staircase to the second floor, laboring a little with each step, and stood outside the
master bedroom, listening to Jerry's breathing (yes, he was napping too) and to the soft, familiar groan as he rolled over to her
side of the bed, as he always did . . . She loved her men, though
they sucked her various accounts dry, tried her patience, and
often disappointed her, *she loved her men*, and this fact, at that
moment, seemed a miracle. Margaret left her husband to his
nap and continued down the hallway to her study, leaving the
door open a crack so that, when Jerry woke, she would hear
him calling, *Mags?* A tirade might follow, sure, and perhaps it
would escalate into a screaming match with Bradley, but at
least they were—none of them—lonely, still a family, and not
alone in the world.


Just before daybreak on the morning of July 21, while her pri
vate nurse dreamed of mourning doves in the chintz of the
"yellow bedroom" down the hall, the eldest and wealthiest of
the elder widows, Mrs. Thomas P. Hartigan IV, the former
Grace Bailey Holmes, passed away quietly in her sleep at the
age of ninety-three. In his heartfelt and gripping eulogy before a
packed house, the Reverend Chambers ignored the heat and
spoke at length about her remarkable life span, how she had

witnessed the so-called American Century from beginning to end, reminding her family, friends, neighbors, and fellow members of the Pilgrims' Church that, as unlikely as it seemed from their own historical perspective, when Grace Bailey Holmes was born at home in 1904 (she had made no secret of her age in later years), a woman didn't yet have the right to vote; racial segregation was not only legal under the Jim Crow laws, it was also enforced by angry mobs and instruments of the state; movies were silent save for the accompaniment of a live piano player; and critics and intellectuals like Henry James were engaged in a fierce debate about the spread of skyscrapers in Manhattan, an architectural advance first made possible by the invention of the passenger elevator a few decades earlier, and derided by James, in the pages of *Harper's Weekly*, as "extravagant pins in a cushion already overplanted, and stuck in as in the dark, anywhere and anyhow . . ." She had shared the growing pains of her young century, the Reverend Chambers pronounced over the flutter of fanning programs, losing her older brother Charles, an aviator, to the Great War overseas, marrying during Prohibition to the gentleman banker Thomas Hartigan (a trusted colleague of her father's over twenty years her senior), and settling into the grandest home that Old Town had ever seen, which she proceeded to decorate with an outrageous flair that scandalized the neighbors, as did her insistence on wearing trousers on the golf course, her sometimes bawdy language, and her refusal to take part in the afternoon teas organized by the matrons of the Ladies' Circle, who, as a group, ruled local society with a conspiracy of whispers, nods, and other secret "feminine" signals. *Unfit for motherhood*, judged the Circle's elite. *She'll bring infamy to her husband's good name.* Not so: Motherhood would fit her as snugly as a satin glove (here many in the church had sighed and tilted their heads) and her family would grow quickly, seven children in ten years, all healthy but the third, Maximilian Pierce, who had died in his mother's arms just a few hours after his delivery. Grace never forgot her infant son, not for a minute, and her considerable grief would ebb and flow through the decades, a reminder that life, however bountiful, has limits here on earth; it was the memory of Maximilian that first brought Grace to accept Christ at the altar of the Pilgrims' Church in 1942, and many of her charitable contributions, including a historic bequest to the congregation that the heirs have just made known, were given in his honor. (A murmur had circulated through the crowd, then, and the heirs, sharing the matriarch's sense of decorum, had kept their chins raised proudly toward the minister, young and old alike betraying *nothing*.) Imagine a world without the threat of nuclear weapons! Without the AIDS virus! Without the systematized brutality of the Holocaust! During the final decade of her life Grace had found it impossible to read the newspaper, confiding to those closest to her, and even, on occasion, to her minister (here even the heirs allowed themselves a fleeting smile), that the world seemed to have grown more cruel as time wore on, that a senseless rush for fame and money ruled the younger generations, and everything that she had trusted—the people, the places, the ideals—had either *passed on* or been corrupted by time, *changed utterly*, to quote the long-lived poet William Butler Yeats, and she was *heartsick* over all the *pain* and *suffering* that God, in His remoteness, seemed to allow among His children . . . And though she had for years been well acquainted with the Gospels of Jesus Christ, and had been dutiful in worship both at the Pilgrims' Church and, during her summers on the coast of Maine, at the First Church in Somesville, Grace turned back to the Scripture for guidance and discovered Christ's teachings *as if for the first time*, finding solace in His sacrifice and resurrection for the Glory of God and the good of man, to redeem us on earth and in Heaven, *as it was in the beginning, is now, and ever shall be, world without end.* And a remarkable change came over Grace, plain to the family members who came to visit her, the nurses and attendants who cared for her at home, and the members of this congregation who worshipped with her every Sunday—she was, in the parlance of the Evangelical movement, *saved. Mrs. Grace Holmes Hartigan, as she entered the tenth decade of her life, was saved by Jesus Christ.*

But the Reverend Chambers's poetic eulogy (which had continued at a similar pitch for over an hour, coaxing tears from nearly everyone present and smiles of love and gratitude from the family) would only be a prelude to his announcement, on the following Sunday morning, of the congregation's windfall: the elder widow Hartigan had willed to the Pilgrims' Church the equivalent of more than two million dollars in cash, blue-chip stocks, and Treasury bonds, a figure that had astonished even the most optimistic members of the Council and far surpassed the estimates that had been circulating in the days since the memorial service, bringing a reverent hush to the meetinghouse on that auspicious morning, *more than two million dollars, talk about Gloria Patri!* Fellowship that noon had been a real celebration of His sovereignty, the banquet table laden, thanks to a last-minute decision by the Council, with all manner of soft drinks, chips and other salty snacks, soft-baked cookies and frosted cakes; toasts were raised to Mrs. Hartigan's generosity with plastic cups of sparkling cider; and the Reverend Chambers, in his informal remarks, vowed to stay with the congregation until the Search Committee had extended the call to the perfect candidate (over the objections of Hal, who thought that she was ready for her own pastorate, Jane had pulled herself out of the running again), and promised that Mrs. Hartigan's bequest would usher in a new era of compassionate outreach to the underserved of society. Meanwhile, the children present had grown so excited from an abundance of sugar at midday that one of the Brooks twins—either Eddie or Freddie, no one could tell them apart—stormed the banquet table and toppled the coffee urn, creating a dangerous situation with the piping hot liquid, and narrowly avoiding the kind of accident that would have darkened an otherwise joyous day.

In August, Bethany drove to the Mill Pond at dusk to say goodbye to Thomas, parking her minivan at the gate (the Selectmen ordered it locked every summer to discourage teenage drinking) and climbing the access road in her work clothes, quietly hating her newest pair of open-toed shoes and trying to ignore the growing stink as she approached the crown of the hill and emerged at the edge of a clearing, greeted by an overflowing trash barrel, the natting cries of a lost seagull, and the tail end of a raccoon as it abandoned its search for edible garbage and scurried back into the woods for cover. That ruined piece of wilderness seemed as good a place as any to remember Thomas, and besides, if Bernie Swenson could be relied on as a witness, the Mill Pond just might have been the last place the pastor had visited before he disappeared (at first the authorities had claimed that the fact that his car was nowhere to be found had been a *good sign*, but as time wore on without a single lead, first privately, and then publicly, they had been forced to change their tune), and the team of divers had searched the bottom for him lovingly, scouring the trash-strewn depths with their brightest spotlights just to surface again, like everyone who sought an explanation for his disappearance, with the same fool *questions* that Bethany had been wrestling with since her first premonition that the pastor didn't love her anymore: Where had Thomas gone? Was he in trouble? Or in pain? How could he just disappear? What did his disappearance *mean*? The surface of the pond was deathly still at that hour, and Bethany steered a wide berth around the trash can on her way to the water's edge, afraid of running into more raccoons, fighting the urge to hold a scarf or something over her nose and mouth and keep from *puking*. Soon, however, she had grown accustomed to the smell of the pond, and wandered the shoreline with her eyes cast to the other side, watching the insects buzz across the water, slapping at a mosquito that had found her neck, and beginning to feel intuitively that Thomas *had never been there*, that coming to the Mill Pond to say goodbye to him was an absurd idea, and she had been *wrong* to believe the testimony of a fifteen-year-old boy on his skateboard, even if he was the child of her neighbors and a Swede. If her life thus far had been a litany of bad choices, punctuated by moments of accidental grace, then her presence at the Mill Pond that evening could be explained as a routine miscalculation, nothing to adjust her prescription about (yes, she was back on the Zoloft), but nothing, either, to prove the limits of her clumsiness, or to suggest that her human imperfections had exhausted themselves with exercise, and her days of embarrassing herself and causing pain to others, especially her family, were over . . . Jesus, did that sick pond *stink*! And she heard voices approaching from the woods, the unmistakable laughter of teenagers: ignorant, cruel, and innocent, still untouched, for the most part, by the notion of consequences, and she turned around to watch a foursome of delinquents stumble from the woods, first the wanna-be skinhead in a leather jacket, followed by his gangly friend with problem skin, carrying a twelve-pack of beer, and then, both at once, the pale girlfriends in tank tops with flannel shirts tied around the waist, staring out behind their thick eyeliner like *lost souls*, keeping mute as the skinhead said loud enough for Bethany to hear, *Hey, check that lady out*. Bethany, though she understood that it was in her best interest to look away, couldn't take her eyes off the girls with the eyeliner, wondering if they knew, secretly, that these boys they'd chosen to follow through the woods were undeserving of their bodies, their adoration, and their loyalty . . . The standoff lasted a few seconds before the teenagers shrugged and continued on their way, the girlfriends glancing back, every now and then, to monitor this adult apparition in a business suit, while Bethany gave up on her failed *goodbye* and made for the access road as quickly as she could in the growing darkness, still missing Thomas, and wishing, at the same time, that she could just forget him and continue with her old life, without being reminded of the way his love had recognized her in totality, and had allowed her, in return, to accept the possibility that God was watching from His dwelling place in Heaven, and something other than a lottery of competing self-interests ruled the outcome of her days and nights on earth.

A few months later, during a particularly depressing morning rush hour, Bethany thought she saw the pastor driving northbound on Route 128—the opposite direction from her commute—and she froze (later Bethany would remember the exact words of the announcer on NPR: *In Washington yesterday President Clinton announced an initiative to provide tax relief and other incentives for new home buyers*, a banality that neatly summed up his leadership, she thought, and the tenor of the journalists who covered him), overcoming her shock just in time to avoid rear-ending the pickup truck in front of her. She swiveled around in her seat to get another look, but the pastor's shadow had already gone. With nothing else to lose she tried to catch him, fighting her way across three lanes of bumper-to-bumper traffic, gesturing wildly, resorting to her hazard lights and leaning on her horn until she reached the nearest exit ramp and turned off the highway. From there, with time running short, she followed all signs for the northbound lanes, running a red light that would have lost her precious minutes and speeding around the on-ramp's curve to find herself in another traffic jam, this time lasting until the exit for Route 93—but as fast as Bethany drove in her underpowered minivan, and as hard as she wished for another sighting, she never caught up to the speeding Ford Probe (it hadn't been much of a car chase) and found out for sure if she had really seen her Thomas, or if she had wasted over an hour of her life trying to follow some look-alike with the nerve to drive the same ugly sedan: a stranger on the highway, oblivious to the fact that he resembled an awkward minister who had loved her well and truly and then *vanished* from her village. From time to time in the coming months, either during her commute to work or, less frequently, while running Saturday errands, Bethany would pass a car that resembled the pastor's and feel her heart begin to race, but the drivers behind the wheel were always so unlike him, and she felt *ashamed*, in the end, to still be looking for Thomas when his disappearance had been such a violation of their intimacy, and her marriage to Bobby, through hard work and the help of their Tuesday Couples' Group, seemed to be on the mend.

Yet she was still haunted by so many questions! Regular people didn't just disappear, after all, they simply *went somewhere else!* And *where* depended on their nature, didn't it? Here the pastor's melancholy seemed to indicate a bitter ending, yet she couldn't believe it herself—that Thomas, who was incapable of violence (this she knew instinctively), could lift a hand against himself, and nullify a lifetime of, well, *everything*: from language to love, labor to his calling, sex, faith, and the weather patterns in the atmosphere . . . his beloved Doppler radar, newspaper recycling, Bethany's hands lifting his Geneva gown and unfastening his belt buckle . . . So many questions! And they would only grow more insistent with the passage of time, leading Bethany, in the first cold days of December, to summon all her courage and place a phone call to Mrs. Safarian at the Pilgrims' Church, asking for her help in finding Thomas's mother (according to the operator, the only MOSHER in Annisquam was an unlisted number). She was relieved to get the clumsy answering machine, and left a brief, specific message with her request, using her number at work (so what if this amounted to *deception*? Wouldn't Bobby want her questions settled for his own sake?), and waited nervously for a response. And waited. Finally, three days later, Bethany emerged from a tedious briefing and, absent Anita, checked the message log on her desk and discovered, in her assistant's perfect script, a street address in Annisquam, no phone numbers at all, and the added wish GOOD LUCK, underlined for emphasis in ballpoint ink.

She dressed for work as usual on a sparkling morning and drove to the North Shore instead, her stomach empty, a travel mug of coffee steaming untouched in its rightful place beside the automatic gearshift, the landscape along Route 128 looking ancient again, as it did every winter, reverting back, it seemed, to that indifferent state of Nature faced with awe and hatred by the Puritans of old New England. Now a lonely plow cleared the parking lot of the Bali Hai in Saugus, while the salt-and-sand trucks, big yellow tanks advancing slowly, and impossibly, against the ill effects of the weather, clogged the morning traffic with their flashing arrows—move left, please—scattering minerals and rock salt that bounced against her coated undercarriage and threatened to pock her windshield. It was cold outside. The clear skies promised warmth and instead delivered icy winds, and the snowfall, so soft and picturesque, would presently melt, and then freeze, into an immovable dirty ground-mass lasting well into the spring.

Bethany found the right house, a modest split-level with cedar shingles on a quiet side street, with the help of a man at a nearby gas station and restaurant, the Willow Rest. She parked outside and zipped her warmest parka to the top (*please*, she thought, *let the Zoloft give me strength*), walking through the gate with no real expectations, just the feeling that she had no choice in the matter, coming to see the pastor's mother was the only option left to her, and if her presence was an imposition, her questions about Thomas too painful to answer, then she would apologize profusely to the woman, hold back all her secret knowledge of her son, and more or less flee . . . The car in the driveway seemed right for an elderly woman, and curtains, she noticed while climbing the front steps, were drawn tightly as if against the winter. Wasn't she from the South originally? And hadn't Thomas been tormented by chills? She banished all second thoughts and rang the doorbell, surprised to hear, at that moment, what sounded like the footsteps, and voices, of children, and she stepped back while the front door opened to reveal a woman near her age—a white woman, no less—with a toddler on her hip, another clinging to her leg, and still another, it seemed, emitting tantrum-like noises from the interior.

"I'm sorry," Bethany said immediately, "maybe I've come to the wrong address. I'm looking for Mrs. Mosher, she's an older woman? With a grown son who's a minister? Do they sound familiar to you?" The woman reacted slowly, as if bewildered by her questions, and to ease their exchange along Bethany produced from the pocket of her coat the street address she'd written down. "I'm sorry, but is this you?"

"That's our address," the woman answered, shifting the child on her hip with obvious practice. "We've only been here a few months, you see. My husband and I—well, he's at work—we're renting with an option to buy."

"So you've met Mrs. Mosher, then—"

"No, I haven't."

"You aren't renting the house from her?"

"A Realtor showed us the property," she said, refusing, despite the cold, to invite Bethany inside the house. She looked warily outside, as if expecting to discover a team of co-conspirators. "My husband knows more about real estate than I do, so maybe you should talk to him. We're renting with an option to buy, like I said."

"She's an, ummm, African-American woman," Bethany tried, "always neatly dressed? Near seventy? Are you sure you've never met her?"

"Yes, I'm sure," the woman insisted, her eyes becoming more unfriendly. "I've never met anyone by that description." The children were beginning to squirm, and the chill from outside had spread, it seemed, into her very heart. "I'm sorry, but right now I have my hands full—"

"Please!" Bethany blurted out, aware, almost immediately, that she was making a mistake. "I have a serious problem here, and I'm desperate for your help. *Please*. I'm trying to reach Mrs. Mosher, and if you have any idea how I might go about doing that—"

"I'm sorry," the woman repeated, taking the protective measure of removing the toddler from her hip and directing it, together with the other child, away from this stranger at the door, "but I've never met anyone named Mrs. Mosher. We do get a piece of mail from time to time, and that's all I can tell you. As you can see, I have my hands full with the children."

"What Realtor? What's the name of the Realtor?"

"I'm terribly sorry," the woman said, "really."

"Can I leave my phone number with you?"

"I don't think so," she answered, and shut the door.


Bethany thought she saw the pastor one more time, nearly four years after she had first laid eyes on him at the pulpit, three since they had begun their affair, two full years after she had dragged her squalling daughter from his final Sunday sermon, and almost eighteen months since her visit to Annisquam . . . To the everlasting joy of the children, especially Jessie, whose reaction had driven Bethany to consider sedatives, Bobby managed to win the Grand Prize of his division's "official" football pool: a weekend getaway for the whole family in the Big Apple that spring, complete with four tickets to see *The Lion King* on Broadway, a $50 gift certificate from FAO Schwarz, and two nights of "luxury" accommodations at the Marriott Marquis in Times Square. *Daddy, will you marry me?* Jessie had asked when he first announced the news at the dinner table (Bethany was still recovering from his "Super Bowl Party," which had included, sadly, an elongated sub from a catering service), and Bobby had gently explained to her, when the excitement had died down a little, that bigamy, or being married to two people at once, was a crime in every state including Utah. *Can I marry Ulla, then?* she had asked, raising another thorny problem that her parents had thought it best to avoid discussing until she was old enough to understand the issues.

Their "getaway" weekend, when it finally arrived, was

marred by a persistent downpour, making for interminable lines at the Marquis's taxi stand, and by lies, arrogance, and ineptitude at the front desk—situated, for some inconvenient reason, on the eighth floor of the hotel. The uniformed clerks kept insisting, with unconvincing haste, that rollaway beds for the children would appear at any moment, but as of Saturday afternoon they were still forced to double up (who knew that Jessie farted in her sleep even more than her father did!), prompting Bobby to "raise some Cain" with the manager on duty while his family waited in the bustling lobby. Both the hotel staff and the tourist clientele seemed unimpressed by his command performance and unmoved by his threats of litigation. Devon sought to ease his sense of embarrassment by watching the glass elevators rise and fall, while Jessie kept pulling on her mother's arm and asking, "Can I have an overstuffed sandwich?"

Everyone in the hotel seemed attached to either a child or a piece of luggage, often both at once, making the reason behind the hotel's error, to Bethany, quite plain. "Not now, Jessie, okay?"

"But I'm hungry!"

"We just ate!"

"I'm *starving* over here!"

"You are not, shorty," Devon muttered.

"Yes I am!"

"After we go to FAO Schwarz," Bethany told her, finally losing her patience. "And if you don't quiet down *right now*, I'm giving the entire gift certificate to your brother."

At a stoplight two blocks from the hotel Bethany could have sworn that she saw the pastor, crossing the street in his abstracted way, wearing a shabby raincoat (good but overworn), and holding an umbrella, at home on the crowded sidewalk, on the one hand nondescript, but separated, on the other, by his loneliness, which appeared to have deepened with their time apart, and she knew at once—or at least she *thought* she did—that she had found him, chanced across his exile the same way that she first had stumbled into his church that Sunday morning, and she wiped off the fogging window of her taxi to try to follow his path, but the light had already changed, the intersection was clear, and the cabdriver, an African, busy exchanging gossip about Internet IPOs with Bobby, sped away from the stoplight faster than she had thought possible, and just after laying eyes on Thomas, her love, for the first time since Fellowship two years past, Bethany lost him again.

"I hate Scar!" Jessie yelled in anticipation of the next day's matinee performance of *The Lion King*. "He's ugly and evil!"

"Mom, can you make her stop *sounding off?*"

"Simba's the best!"

"Shut up, already."

"*I will not!*"

By the time she made it back to the same corner from her hotel room the rain had stopped, and the million-plus lights of the new Times Square filled the air with a saccharine glow, making everything, even her own reflection in the plate-glass doors of the Virgin Megastore, seem vague and artificial. She averted her eyes from that shadow of herself as she passed by, ignoring the uniformed security guard who murmured *Yeah, baby* and stepped aside to get a better look at her figure. *Where do people come from? And where do they go? Who makes a world this unbearable?* she thought, walking through the center of an unfamiliar city, and she wondered, once again, how Thomas could have left her alone to survive, well, *this* . . . Bethany walked the confines of Times Square in a kind of circle, searching every face she passed for evidence of human kindness, and encountering more varieties of skin tone, age, expression, style, and character than she could quantify—and looking for Thomas in every one. *All those people*, she thought, standing outside the soulless Marquis on Broadway and trying, without much luck, to block out the ranting minister from the 12 Tribes of the Nation of Israel, *all those people*, she thought, looking up at the painted sign for the Heavenly Coffee, and down at the smiling image of Tiger Woods, *all those people*, she thought, turning back to the crowded sidewalk, *and not one of them is him.*